The Execution

A Breakbattle Academy Novel

Ruby Vincent

Published by Ruby Vincent, 2019.

Chapter One

"We are still investigating these incidents, but you should know, the evidence points to him."

"Don't be ridiculous. You have no evidence."

My eyes flicked down. The rug had been replaced—no doubt because of me.

"This symbol first appeared the day Mr. Manning and his organization protested at the basketball game."

"His organization? He did not form it, nor does he lead it," my mother replied. "There are almost thirty other students in that club. They all knew about the protest and any one of them could have done it."

"We are looking into them as well."

"Are you?"

I like the new rug, I thought. *The brown goes nicely with the red wallpaper.*

"We are, Ms. Manning, but there is the question of motive," Whittaker replied. "Your son suffered a series of battle defeats at the hands of the Elites. I'm told he also went out of his way to get close to the students who battled him and then they were attacked."

"You're suggesting there is something sinister about my child's willingness to forgive and make friendships with those who beat him," Mom shot back. "Is that concept so foreign? Do you not want students to brush off their defeats? Are grudges and rivalries what you hope to cultivate through your battle system?"

He's got new photos, I mused. *The guy he's with looks kind of familiar.*

"Absolutely not, Ms. Manning," Argyle cried.

"Then I don't understand why you are using these friendships as *evidence.*"

"He was able to get close to them and learn their routines," Whittaker stated. I wasn't looking at his face, but I imagine it was the usual mask of polite blankness.

"Are their routines top secret? No one could have known when they got up to run, or where they kept their gym bags?"

"Yes... others may have known."

"And we've established that others also had access to the mattress pad to plant these stickers."

There was a pause while I tilted my head back and contemplated the crown molding. The intricacy was exquisite. The E dorms were nothing to sneeze at, but this was by far the most gorgeous room in the academy.

"Yes, the pad was out of his possession for a few weeks," Whittaker said. "It was won by Cole Reed, but as he was one of the victims of the prankster, we don't believe he was involved."

"Did he not allow anyone else into the room during the time he had it? Were his eyes on it every minute of the day? Was he not the student who had a harmless uniform switch instead of being drugged or almost blinded? So it could be feasible that he was involved but was smart about covering his tracks?"

I always marveled at Mom's ability to silence people with questions they knew the answer to. Her talent was no less effective today.

I dropped my head and took in Argyle's and Whittaker's stony faces. Neither one made a move to answer her.

Mom didn't slow her roll. "I believe the only thing we have evidence of is that you have no grounds to expel my child."

A vein jumped in Whittaker's forehead as he nodded. "We have taken expulsion off the table."

"You will also take suspension, detention, and further meetings such as these off the table. Zeke has done nothing wrong. You will not treat him otherwise." She got to her feet. "We're done here. Let's go, Zeke."

I stood and followed her without a word or backward glance.

The sun was setting on Breakbattle Academy when we walked out onto the expansive lawn. A muggy heat blanketed the campus and no cool breeze blew to provide relief. Not that anyone but us needed it. The grounds were completely empty.

My first year of Breakbattle Academy ended hours ago. It was a surprise when Argyle knocked on the door in the middle of my packing and said we were needed in the principal's office to discuss there being a second.

We approached the car and spotted Jordan's head bobbing to the music. I could sing along to every line, she had the noise so loud. She lowered it when she spotted us through the window.

"How did it go?" she asked.

I slid into the backseat and slammed the door. "Mom handled it."

"I knew she would." Jordan twisted around in her seat. "What's the punishment going to be for those bastards? Your principal better have expelled them."

I cut eyes to my mom as she rounded the hood for the driver's seat. "We can't talk about this now."

"What do you mean?" She noticed where I was looking. "You did tell her they attacked you, right?"

I pressed my lips together.

Her eyes widened. "Zee! You have to—"

"I'm going to handle it myself," I got out in a rush. I snapped my mouth shut just as Mom opened the door.

The ride home wasn't quiet. Mom went on a tirade about pompous, mediocre men that let the tiniest bit of power go to their heads. Jordan didn't help the situation by hyping her up and going on about making anyone who messes with me pay.

Mom parked the car in our drive and stormed into the house. I had a feeling today's conversation would find its way into the book. It was Jordan who came around to help me with the bags. By help, I mean she planted herself next to the trunk and leveled me with a look I didn't need to see to feel.

"Why, Zee?"

I stuck my head inside, reaching for my duffel. "No one else knows what they did," I said simply. "I told Derek and Adam not to say anything."

"Why would you do that?"

"My bruises have healed, so Mom won't know either."

"Tell me why, Zee."

I grabbed the duffel and lifted. I hitched it onto my shoulder and it was promptly pulled out of my grasp and tossed back into the trunk.

"They assaulted you, Zela." Jordan tugged on my arm and pulled me around. I let her gather me in her arms. "They beat you up and stripped you. They can't get away with that."

My hands hung by my side, not returning her embrace. She squeezed me tight, as if trying to push her comfort deeper into my skin.

"Don't worry," I said softly. "They won't."

THERE WAS NO SUCH THING as a typical summer for me. For other kids, freedom from school meant water parks, family visits, and slipping into near-vegetative states in front of the television, but for me, there was always a new place, a new town, a new life to adjust to, so there was no such thing as typical—until now.

I woke minutes before my alarm clock and shut it off before it could blare. A quick trip to the bathroom to brush my teeth and tie up my hair and then I was ready.

My yoga mat unfurled and softly fell to the carpet. My limbs gave into the stretch, singing out as the kinks and knots formed in the night loosened. Three weeks into summer and I had my routine down. Morning yoga to relax my body, and then push-ups, planks, and lunges to strengthen it.

"Hold it there," said the woman in the workout video who had become my daily companion. "Don't forget to breathe."

I finished the video, then started another one. My muscles ached under the strain, but not as badly as the start of this summer, and nowhere near where I was before I came to Breakbattle. The workout routine ended and I was out the door before the man said goodbye.

"Where are you going, Zela?" Mom called from the kitchen.

"For a run, Mom."

"Excellent, my only one." I picked up the pride in her tone. The use of her pet name for me was a giveaway. My only one. The only child she would ever have. "Mind and body, Zela. You are embracing and building the sources of your power. Today, I made quinoa fruit salad and avocado toast for breakfast. We will continue this healthy track together."

"Sounds delicious. See you in a bit." I slipped out the door before she could heap any more praise on me. I was building the sources of my power, but not for reasons she would ever approve of.

The sun beat on the pavement, giving rise to a thick, sweltering heat that made the air hazy. I was warm from my morning workout, and as I picked up speed, beads of sweat collected on my forehead. I pushed myself harder than usual today. For the first time since the start of summer, there was going to be a change in the routine.

A familiar car was parked in my driveway when I returned. Jordan looked up from a bowl of breakfast that was most likely mine.

"Hey, Zee. Ready to go?"

I shook my head. "I have to eat and change. What are you doing here? I told you I was leaving today."

"That is why I'm here. I'm coming too."

I blinked. "I'm sorry. What?"

"My mom called Adam's mom and she said I could stay. Not for the full two weeks, but I'm coming up with you now."

"Again. Why?"

She ripped a bite off my avocado toast and swallowed before answering. "You've been super weird since you got back, and I'm worried about you."

"Jordan!" I hissed. I ducked out of the kitchen to make sure Mom wasn't nearby, and then returned to the island. "I haven't been weird," I said softly.

"Yes, you have. Worse, you aren't talking to me about it and you tell me everything. From now on, I'm going to be all over you until you tell me what's going on."

Sighing, I tilted my head back to the ceiling and asked for strength. I forgot how persistent my cousin could be.

"Can you at least leave me some breakfast?" I finally asked. "I have to shower real quick and then I'll be back down."

I hoofed it upstairs and washed the morning from my skin. The heat on my achy muscles was soothing, but not enough to slow my mind.

What do I do? Should I tell her the truth?

You tell her everything and she's always backed you up, another voice reminded me. *She won't stop now.*

By the time Zeke returned to the kitchen, Zela had made up her mind. Jordan moved on to my smoothie. She froze with her mouth hovering over the straw when she saw me.

"You're dressed as Zeke? Why? I thought Adam knew who you were."

"He does." I took my seat and rescued my food from her. "But his mom doesn't. I honestly don't know what she'd do if she found out, and I can't be kicked over to the girls' side. Not now."

She snagged my hand as I reached for the fork. "Zee, why would you want to go back to that place?"

"Nothing has changed. Derek and I left things in a weird place. He didn't seem angry with me for lying. He was actually nicer than he had ever been to me those last couple weeks of school, but that could just be because he felt sorry for me. Since then, I haven't heard a word from him and I can't lose the progress we've made. He saw me as a friend. I can't let that change."

"I get the stuff with Derek, I really do, but what about those other guys? The Elites have it out for you, and worse, they know your secret."

"They won't tell anyone."

"How can you be sure of that?"

"They just won't."

Her eyes narrowed on me. She must have picked up something in my tone. "Zee, what is going on with you?"

"They're not going to say anything," I repeated. "They're not going to get away with what they did to me. They're not going to sleep a fucking wink without my face slipping into their nightmares."

She slipped her hand out of mine, eyes widening as she drew away.

"The single most important thing after getting closer to Derek... is making every one of them pay."

Jordan stared at me as I picked up the fork and stabbed a piece of strawberry.

"That's the truth," I said. "But it doesn't look like it's what you wanted to hear."

She was quiet for a long time, studying me as I calmly ate my breakfast.

"Zee," she began. "That is... exactly what I wanted to hear."

I paused mid-chew.

She hopped out of her seat and ran around the island. I squeaked when she seized my shoulders. "You better not let those bastards get away with what they did. I want you to give them hell. Every. Single. Day! I want them naked on the fucking floor crying their eyes out!" She shook me. "And don't let up until they beg, *beg,* for forgiveness! You understand me?"

I didn't have to nod my head as her shaking was rattling it for me.

"You just tell me how I can help."

Despite everything, I smiled. I was lucky to have her. Even if she was the only one who could know the truth. At least someone did.

ADAM STOOD ON THE TOP of the stairs, waving as the car approached. He didn't come along to pick us up, choosing instead to let his driver come and get us. It still boggled my mind that I had friends with drivers and—

"Shit," Jordan breathed. "Look at this place! It's unreal."

Esme ran out of the manor as the driver parked the car. Adam grabbed the giggling girl and draped her over his shoulder.

"Hey, Jordan. I heard you were coming."

"I have to thank your mom a million times for letting me stay over. Mine won't let me stay the whole time though. She doesn't want me to impose."

I climbed out of the car and walked around the trunk.

"It's not an imposition," I heard him say. "It's pretty chill over here with a new baby in the house. You're going to help us polish off the food our chef stuffs us with, and see if you can keep up with me in the pool."

Esme was wrapped around Adam's shoulders like a feather boa. Her face hung upside down, hair almost brushing the stone steps, and that did not stop her from sticking her tongue out at me.

"Hey, Adam. Thanks for inviting us."

"Of course, Zel— Zek— Zel—"

I decided to save him. "Let the wig be your guide," I said as I gestured at my get-up. "Call me Zeke."

"Zeke, I'm glad you're here." He flashed me a smile—that sweet Adam smile that said more than words needed to. "Come in. I'll show you your rooms."

"Rooms plural?" Squealing, Jordan raced after him. "There's a good chance I'm never leaving."

I followed at a slower pace. Adam dropped Esme off in the living room and let Jordan into her temporary room. The last thing I saw was her flinging herself on the bed before we moved on to mine.

"You'll have your old room next to mine," he said. "Like I said, we're keeping it pretty chill. I'm going for a swim later if you guys want to join." He peered at me over his shoulder. "You can chill by the pool."

"Sounds good."

"Want to hold Jessie?"

My face lit up. "Can I? I'd love to. Where is she?"

He laughed. "Dang. That finally made you smile. If you're not careful, I'm going to start thinking you only like me for my baby sister."

I giggled. The sound was foreign for how long it had been, but still, it felt good. "I liked you before the baby, remember? I just like you more now."

We cracked up and I felt something loosen inside of me. Coming here had been the right choice.

An hour later, Jordan and Adam were splashing in the pool while baby Jessie chilled in my arms. The six-month-old relaxed in one arm while I read with the other. We found her awake in her crib, nibbling on her toes, so we snuck her out for some sun. Jessie was so ridiculously cute not even Adam could call her a wet sponge anymore. Every five seconds, I bent and nuzzled her chubby cheek.

In the pool, Adam reared up and whacked the ball over the net. Jordan leaped and sent it back before disappearing under the water. He and Jordan had gotten into a rather intense game of pool volleyball.

"Gonna have to do better than that, Moon!" she crowed. "Volleyball's my game. You Breakbattle kids don't know nothing about that."

He laughed. "I'm taking that challenge. Loser washes the dishes!"

I rolled my eyes at their antics. I did love that they were heading toward friends though. Adam was quickly becoming an important person in my life; he should be friends with the other one.

I heard the sound of the sliding glass door behind me.

"There she is. I see you boys liberated Jessie from her crib."

I grinned as Val stepped around the lawn chair. Her figure cast a blessed shadow over us. "We couldn't help it. She's only gotten more adorable since I last saw her."

"That she has." Her face was the picture of love and gentleness as she bent to stroke her daughter's cheek. "I'm going to take her and give her lunch, but I wanted you guys to know you had a visitor." She raised her voice so Adam could hear. "You might want to come out of the pool now, baby."

"It's cool, Miss Val."

I froze.

"I came here to talk to Zeke."

"Okay." She lifted Jessie out of my hold. "We're also having lunch in half an hour, if you want to join us."

"Thank you."

Another shadow fell over me and my breath caught in my throat.

"Hey, Zeke," said Derek.

What was he doing here? How did he know I would be here?

"What are you reading?"

The question knocked me out of my shock. "It's... the fourth Pendergast book. You got me hooked."

"Glad you like it."

Derek looked good. Derek always looked good, so that wasn't saying much, but out of the stuffy Breakbattle uniform, he opted for a leather jacket, dark shades, and a loose pair of jeans. The look was simple, but it lent a distinct bad-boy vibe that I'm sure he was happy to cultivate.

"Whoo!" Jordan cried. "I said you didn't want none of this!"

Derek jerked his head toward the manor. "Is it cool if we go somewhere and talk?"

Talk about what? Was the other shoe going to drop? Are you going to dump me for lying to you? Are the taunts about creepy stalker pervert freaks going to come back with a vengeance now that you don't feel sorry for me anymore?

I worked myself up into a proper tizzy as I led Derek back to my room. My hand shook as I reached for the knob and let us inside.

Derek didn't need an invitation to stroll into the middle of the space and look around. I eyed him as I closed and locked the door.

"How did you know I was here?" I asked.

"Moon said you were going to come over this summer. I told him to text me when you did."

"Why didn't you text me?"

"I thought you might need some space."

"Oh."

He doesn't look mad, I thought. *And the insults aren't flying. Does that mean we're okay?*

"I was worried you were pissed at me," I finally said. "Because I didn't tell you the truth."

His face crumpled into a frown. "Mad at you? Why would I be mad? If you're a boy, then you're a boy."

And then it broke. The hard, tight knot in my throat that had been strangling me as I fought not to cry, broke apart as I raced across the room and threw myself in his arms.

"Whoa."

I ignored him and squeezed him tighter, burrowing my face in his neck. I had no time for his tough guy, don't-need-no-one-else routine.

"Thank you," I whispered.

"For what?" Derek's arms hung by his side, making no attempt to hug me back.

"I forgot for a second that you were a good guy."

He snorted. "Happy to remind you," he said, but after a minute, he lifted his arms and wrapped them around me.

"Thank you," I repeated, "but I am a girl. Zeke is nothing but a costume."

His grip on me loosened. "What? But then..."

I pulled away and trudged over to my bed.

"Why?" Derek sat down on my other side. He still looked more curious than mad. "I don't get it."

"Believe it or not, it was the only way my mom would let me go to the academy," I said, opting for a version of the truth. "She doesn't approve of them separating the genders, but she changed her tune at the idea of me going in as a boy and experiencing firsthand how different women have it."

"Still that seems a bit... extra."

"I really wanted to go to school there. I did what I had to do."

He nodded. "'Cause of your math stuff. Breakbattle has the best teachers."

I didn't bother to correct his assumption. It worked for me to let him think it.

"Were you going to hide the whole time?" he asked. "All four years and never let anyone know the truth?"

I took a minute and considered that. "No," I finally said. "I would have told people. Friends." My eyes drifted up and met his. "People I knew I could trust. I trust you. That's why I'm not worried about going back to school. You'll keep my secret."

Derek looked away. His golden locks fell across his face, shielding his eyes in the same way mine would. "If you trust me... would you let me see the real you?"

I blinked. "You mean... you want me to...?"

"If Zeke is just a costume, take it off."

I touched the strands of my wig. It was a simple request, and on the face, there was nothing wrong with it, and yet, it felt strangely intimate.

"Okay," I whispered.

Slowly, I stood and reached for my buttons.

Derek's eyes bugged. "You don't have to strip!"

I laughed. "Relax. I'm wearing a tank top under all of this." I undid my shirt and shrugged it off, revealing the tan bindings that had become my constant accessory over the last year. Derek didn't take his eyes off me as I unwrapped them. Next, was my wig. Every time I took it off was a relief that caused a sigh of pleasure. This time was no different.

I ripped it off and threw it on the bed. My silk cap went after it. I shook and let my blondish-brown tresses fall around my shoulders.

"This is the real me. Zela Rae Manning."

"Wow," he breathed.

Biting my lip, I peeked at Derek through my hair, awaiting his verdict.

"How can such a pretty girl... turn into such an ugly guy?"

I made a strangled noise. "Derek!"

He tipped over onto the sheets, laughing. "It's almost a crime to let you put that wig back on."

I smacked his flailing legs. "Only you could compliment and insult me at the same time."

"It's my gift." He propped himself up on his elbows, grinning at me. "Just focus on the compliment part."

"That part feels weirder than the insult. Are you going to be nice to me now that you know I'm a girl?" I gave him a lopsided smile. "I've seen you with your breakfast buddies, snuggling up in the corner and feeding each other grapes. You can treat me the same way you did before."

He chuckled. "Breakfast buddies? I like that. It's true I'm nice to the ladies, but I'm a gentleman. It's the only way to behave. But you"—he bumped my knee with his—"I'll be nice to you because we're friends."

"That works for me," I said, fighting a smile.

"And as your friend, I will fuck Zach, Landon, Michael, and Cole up."

My smile melted away.

"I'm serious, Zela." Derek easily slipped into my proper name. "It doesn't matter that they thought you were a boy. They went too far and they're not getting away with it."

I traced the lines around his eyes, the wrinkles in his forehead, and the sharp twist of his mouth. This was the anger I was expecting to see, but it wasn't directed at me. It was *for* me.

"Tell me what you want me to do, and I will. I'll back you up with Whittaker. I'll beat their skulls in. I'll get them kicked out of the Network."

"Wait." I jerked up. "You can do that?"

"My dad is as high up as it goes. If I tell him I want them gone, they'll be out." He pulled his phone out of his pocket. "Say the word."

I gazed at the cell. I was so tempted it hurt. It would kill them to be kicked out after everything they've done. "No." I pushed his hand down. "Not yet, anyway. I want to deal with them first."

"Okay. Tell me when you change your mind."

I noticed his use of when, not if.

"Can we change the subject?" I asked.

"Sure. You can tell me what else I don't know about you."

I turned and crawled toward the pillows, getting comfortable. "There's nothing else to tell. Zeke and Zela share the same backstory."

"You really lived in twenty-six countries, paraglided, jumped off mountains, and wielded machetes?"

I giggled. "Were you holding out hope I wasn't that cool?"

"Yeah, I was." He came up and claimed the spot next to me. "You make my life look incredibly boring and I'm the kid of a movie star."

Grinning, I went for my phone. "I can show you pictures now. You can see the ones from Switzerland."

Derek leaned in until our shoulders brushed. I don't know how long we sat there, laughing over my pictures and the stories to go with them, but the knock on the door was like snapping out of a dream.

"Zeke? It's time for lunch."

"Coming," I called.

"I should go."

"What? No." I turned to him as he slid off the bed. "Val said you could stay for lunch."

"I've got my own house and my own chefs making me lunch."

"When will you come back?"

He shrugged.

"I'll be in Evergreen for two weeks," I continued. "Maybe I could come by your place sometime. I could meet your parents and—"

"No." It was his tone that silenced me. His shoulders were taut under the leather jacket, back stiff. "You can't come to my house."

"Oh. Okay."

Maybe he picked up something in my voice, because his shoulders loosened. "It's just my parents are renovating and the place is a mess. I'll swing by again sometime before you leave."

"Promise?"

He gave me a look over his shoulder. "How did I not notice before that you were a girl?"

I nudged him with my foot. "Promise me, Grayson."

He heaved a sigh. "I promise."

"Good." I got up too and started my transformation back into Zeke. Derek watched me until I buttoned up my shirt. "Want me to walk you out?"

"I'm good. See you next week."

Derek and I left the room and parted at the end of the stairs. I walked into a full dining room and went straight for Jessie. Jaxson handed her over easily and I snuggled the baby as I sat down to a delicious taco spread. It was the right choice to break the routine and come here. I got to see Jessie, hang with Adam, set things right with Derek... and I found out I held their future in the Elite Network in the palm of my hands.

I hid a smile in the baby's curls. There was so much I could do with that power.

Chapter Two

"You can ease up. You've been pushing yourself hard."

"One more mile," I huffed. My lungs burned. Sweat trickled down my spine and soaked the waistband of my pants. I ignored it and kept breathing the way Michael taught me. In. Out. In. Out. And hating that it reminded me of him.

Adam had no trouble keeping up with me. He was in peak physical condition as Jordan had taken to telling me in more graphic terms. He was on the level I needed to be. The level of the Elite.

We finished the last lap and slowed up in front of the gates of the Promenade.

"Want to go in and get something to drink?"

My eyes swept over the sprawling shopping center. "Isn't this where you all hang out over the summer? What if we run into one of them? I can't handle that right now."

Adam didn't ask who them was or argue further. "Stay here. I'll get us chocolate milk. It's the best post-run drink."

"I don't know if that's true, but I want it to be, so I'll say yes."

Chuckling, he jogged off. I walked up to the wall and pressed against it as I stretched and worked out the kinks.

"Zeke?"

I stiffened. Why was I so ridiculously unlucky? All I wanted was to fly under the radar.

"Zeke, is that you?"

I frowned. *Wait. I know that voice.*

"Melody?"

It was her. She stepped out of a slick black convertible and waved to the red-haired man inside. He drove off with a beep.

"Hey, Zeke. What are you doing here?"

"I'm visiting Adam for the summer."

"Adam." Melody's hand flew to her bun and smoothed it down. "Is he here?" she asked, peeking over my shoulder.

"He went to get us drinks. He should be back soon. Want to wait with me?"

"My friends are waiting for me, but... I could... just to say hi."

I hoped she couldn't pick up my amusement. These two were so cute and made cuter by their cluelessness.

"There is something I wanted to tell you, so I'm glad I caught you."

"What's up?" I asked.

"Things were rough with the club last year and Whittaker threatening to shut us down if there was another protest. People were scared and a lot of the girls didn't want to risk being involved and getting lumped in with For All."

"For All?"

Melody came to my side and leaned against the wall. "That's what I've been calling him ever since you told us what the symbol meant. Calling him a prankster wasn't right since what he did to Landon and Michael was no prank. We'll never go as far as hurting people, but I am going to get the administration's attention this year. What do you say? Still a part of the group?"

"I was never out of the group," I replied. "Just tell me what to do and where to be. No one wants this busted system taken down more than me."

She squeezed my arm. "You're the best, Zeke. Keep your phone close when school starts." Her eyes drifted over my shoulder, and I was blessed by seeing her face light up. "Adam, hi."

"Melody? Hey." Adam walked up to us and held out my chocolate milk. "Glad I got to see you this summer. Waiting for September was too long."

If possible, Melody's smile got wider, and I silently applauded Adam. The boy was smoother than I gave him credit for.

"Thanks." I relieved him of the milk and backed away. "I'm going to run back, but you two should stay and catch up."

"But—"

"Wait—"

I cut them both off. "Adam, Melody's going to meet up with her friends. Why don't you walk with her while she tells you the plans for Stand Up this year?"

"That's a good idea." Melody reached out and brushed a speck of dust off his shoulder that was most likely nonexistent. "Do you have time?"

"Um, yeah. Let's..."

I jogged off, leaving them to it. That was a good deed. Surely it helped to make up for the ones to come.

"I CAN'T BELIEVE SUMMER is over," Jordan moaned. "It went way too fast."

I sat on my bed, neatly folding my Zeke clothes and packing them away. My time in Evergreen had come to an end. Returning home meant resettling into my routine, and the days passed quickly in a haze of yoga, push-ups, and avocado toast. Now the only thing that stood between me and my arrival at Breakbattle were twelve hours.

"The best part was staying at Adam's place." Jordan threw herself on my bed and tugged the jeans from my fingers. "Tell me. Is Adam seeing anyone?"

I paused in reaching for another T-shirt. "What? Why do you want to know that?"

Jordan bit her lip. Her feet kicked in the air as she grinned at me. "He is so cute, Zee, and sweet, and funny, and cute, if I didn't mention that already. We were totally flirting."

My eyes bugged. "F-flirting?! When were you doing that?"

"Pretty much my entire stay. He kept sitting next to me when we ate."

"To get to know you."

"To accidentally brush against me," she corrected. "He kept challenging me to volleyball rematches."

"To get a shot at winning."

She gave me a look. "To see me in my bikini."

"Jordan," I cried. "Adam was *not* flirting. He likes someone else."

"Are they dating?"

"No, but—"

"Then he's keeping his options open. We've been texting a little, but he hasn't made any moves. See if you can get me an invitation the next time you stay at his place."

I gaped at her. "Did you hear the part where I said he likes someone else?"

"I couldn't hear it over the part where you said they're not dating." She threw the jeans at me and they fell over my face. "He's different, Zee. I don't know any guys like him."

"Adam is special for sure," I said through the legs of my pants. "But it will be tough between Melody and going to different schools. Forgive me if I stay out of this one."

She laughed. "Do what you gotta do. So, how's it going with Derek? Have you been texting all summer too?"

I shook my head. "I send him texts. Sometimes he replies and sometimes he doesn't. He came back to see me before I left like he promised, but he's a hard guy to pin down. I never really know where I stand with him."

"Are you any closer to getting an invitation to his place?"

"No, and now that you mention it, he got tense the first time I brought it up." I pulled the jeans off my head and went back to folding. "I don't know what that's about, but I know there is a lot more he hasn't told me." My shoulders slumped as I let the fabric slip from my fingers. "I don't know anything about him when I think about it. He likes to read, play basketball, and sleep with movie extras. That's all I know."

"Well... what does he know about you?"

I lifted my head. "What? What do you mean?"

Jordan met my eyes steadily. "I know you, Zee. You don't tell people very much about yourself, and it makes sense. You moved around so much, there was no point baring your soul to people you'd never see or speak to again. If you want Derek to open up to you, then you have to be willing to do the same. You might even have to do it first. That's how it works."

"Oh." That soft sound was all I could manage. It never occurred to me that Derek was giving back to me as much as I was giving him.

But where do I go from here? How do I open up to him when there are still so many things I can't say?

My mind twisted and chewed on that all night, but I had no answer by the time Mom slammed her door and started the engine.

I didn't say much on the drive to school, but that did not mean it was quiet. Mom kept up a steady stream of instructions as we went.

"Do not let that principal intimidate you."

"I won't."

"You've done nothing wrong, and he needs to do a better job of policing his school," she continued. "Be careful around your classmates, but pay attention too."

"Yes, Mom."

"Also, when will you be participating in this tournament I heard about?"

"Yes, M—" My automatic response died on my lips. I turned away from the window to stare at her. "What?"

"You being in the F Class is a travesty that should have never been allowed to happen, let alone go on for as long as it has. Mrs. Argyle informed me the only way for you to move up is for you to do a tournament, so when will that be happening?"

"It's not that simple, Mom. I'd have to wait till the end of the year and whoever I beat would have to take my place in the F Class."

She looked away from the road. "That is unfortunate, Zela, but I will not stand for you to receive a subpar education. If you do not get into the proper classes, I will transfer you to another school and this experiment will be at an end."

What? My lips trembled as I tried to make sense of what she was saying to me. *She would pull me out after everything I've done, and what I still have left to do? She can't!*

"You can't!"

Mom's mouth pursed into a thin line and I quickly amended my tone.

"I mean… I don't want to leave, Mom. I've made friends here, and I've been doing a lot of self-study. I'd never let myself fall behind."

She nodded sharply. "That is because I raised a proactive young woman who isn't afraid to take on challenges, but in this case, that should not be necessary. I did not send you to school for you to teach yourself. I'm proud of the fact that being Zeke has opened your mind and set you on a path of self-improvement, but I expect you to advance, Zela, and I am immovable on this. Am I understood?"

I bit hard on my lip to contain another outburst. When I trusted myself, I said what I always did.

"Yes, Mom."

Twenty minutes later, our car pulled into the academy parking lot. Mom helped me bring my bags to my old dorm and kissed me goodbye on the front steps. I waited until I saw the tiny blue spot that was her car disappear before going inside. I set my course for the dorm building, but my destination wasn't my room.

It was early. Not many people had arrived, not even Adam, but if this year was like the last, they would be here.

Derek opened his door on the second knock. A wave of steam and citrusy sweetness wafted out of his room, signaling he was fresh from a shower.

"Zee? What are you doing up here?"

"I need a room number," I said. "The Elite move in early for dinners and parties and basking in their greatness, so I know he's here. I need to speak to Cameron."

He gave me a crazy look. "Cameron? What for?"

"There is something that I need to say to him and it's going to be face to face." Jordan's words tugged at my mind until the rest was pulled free. "Afterward, there is something I need to say to you."

Derek crooked a brow. "Damn. Am I in trouble?"

I laughed. "Often, I suspect, but this time, not with me."

A smile tugged at his lips. "In that case, Cameron's room is 623. Want backup?"

"No. He won't do anything. I've realized by now that he lets others handle his dirty work."

"If you say so."

I nodded and moved away, heading for Cameron's room. It loomed in front of me, beckoning me forward as every scenario of how this could play out went through my mind. I said he wouldn't do anything, but I didn't know that. Just because Cameron had to go through others before, didn't mean he wouldn't happily come at me directly if I gave him the chance.

By the time I lifted my hand and knocked, anxiety chased away the last shreds of my confidence. I'd be lying if I said it didn't make me feel better to see Derek leaning against the doorframe, watching me.

"Who is it?"

"It's me."

I didn't say more, and the person on the other side of the door did not ask me to clarify.

I jumped when the door swung open. Cameron looked me up and down like he was making sure I was real. I gave him the same scrutiny.

He wasn't in uniform yet. Cameron wore a tight, but expensive sweater, a pair of dark jeans that hugged his body, and simple white socks on his bare feet. His hair hung in soft waves around his ears, the result of a recent change to growing it long. He was gorgeous, immaculate, perfect—until his pink lips twisted into a snarl.

"What the fuck are you doing here?"

My expression remained neutral. "Do you mean outside your door, or in this school?"

"Both!"

"Are you mad your plan to get me expelled didn't work?" I smiled, but it held no trace of mirth. "That was smart planting those stickers on me. The whole thing was a long game and I didn't see it until it was almost too late."

Cameron's expression gave away nothing but his dislike.

"The battles," I continued. "The changes to the system, winning, losing, and the posters. I should have seen you were the common denominator when everything started going down with the pranks and attacks, but I was stuck on one thing... the fact that you have no good reason to be mad at me and should have grown up and moved on a long time ago."

His grimace disappeared. "What did you just say?"

"It was my fault for believing that you did," I plowed on. "What did I do to you that you didn't bring on yourself? A measly two months' detention for your twisted trick with Derek was nothing compared to what it cost me and Adam. You *never* had a right to be mad at me, Cameron. Never!"

My heart picked up speed to match the rise in my voice. My chest rose and fell, straining against my bindings as anger boiled my blood.

Cameron stepped back. "Get in here."

"What? Why?"

"You want to do this? Let's do it. But I'm not talking to you in the fucking hallway. Get in."

I wasn't a fan of his tone, or his sneer. Neither made me feel like walking into an empty room alone with him was a smart move, but with one last look at Derek, I stepped over the threshold and went inside. He closed and locked the door behind me with an audible click.

Hot breath ghosted over my ear. "You think you have it all figured out."

"I know you orchestrated getting your hands on my things so you could—"

Hands grabbed me from behind.

"Hey!"

"Relax." Cameron yanked my phone out of my pocket. "I'm just making sure."

Satisfied there was no recording, he gave it up without a fight when I snatched it back. I watched through narrowed eyes as he moved around and planted himself in front of me.

"No recorder," I said. "That means there's nothing stopping you from telling the truth."

"You want to hear it? Yes." He adopted the same stance, arms folded, eyes slits. "I made sure you kept losing your stuff until I got my hands on something I could use. Did you like my use of the math symbol? I thought it fit you well."

"Why, Cameron?" The question burned on my tongue. "Why do all of that? You hurt Landon? Drugged Michael? What kind of sick person does that?"

"I finished what you all started!"

I reeled back. "What we started? What are you talking about?"

"You don't get it," he hissed. He leaned in, putting his face in mine until I was forced to back away. The door pressed against my back, halting my retreat, and penning me in with Cameron. "You think it's as simple as you running to Argyle and getting me detention? It didn't *stop* at detention, you idiot. Coach put me on probation. My dad went apeshit and dropped my summer internship at the company."

I folded shaky arms and looked him dead in the eye. "You deserved it for what you did."

"But it didn't stop there," he hissed. His brown eyes appeared almost black with the glittering rage that shone within its depths. "It's not just me, Manning. There are people above me. People I answer to. It was decided that you and Moon needed to be taught a lesson so you'd never get it into your head to go blabbing about the Network.

"I was fine with getting back at Moon. I never liked that fake, nice-guy, let's-all-be-friends bullshit when he was hustling just as hard as the rest of us to get what we were owed. Melody was a hot piece of ass and I was happy to play with her for a bit."

My stomach churned. How could anyone be this vile? "She isn't a hot piece of ass. She's a person. A good one. And she was never a part of this."

"Moon made her a part of it." Not a flicker of remorse appeared in his eyes. "I came up with something for him and something for you, and I was happy to let it end after the bleachers collapsed. Moon loses his girl. You get shown up for the stupid homeschooled loser you are and then get caught as the prankster and end up with two months' detention of your own. It was supposed to stop there. I wanted to go back to my life and forget you were ever in it."

My fingers dug painfully into my forearms. It was everything I could do to keep my tone even as I replied, "Then why didn't you?"

"Because *you* didn't let it end there!" Spittle fell on my cheek. "You challenged me to that fucking battle and humiliated me in front of the entire school. Coach knocked me down to co-captain and the Network came after me for losing to an underclassman *F*. I lost my position as a leader."

A flare of anger surged through me. "Because I won fair and square to a battle *you* agreed to. You went after Landon,

Cole, Michael, and the entire Elite Class just so you could turn them against me?! What is wrong with you?!"

"I went after them because they turned on me!" Air whizzed against my cheek as Cameron punched the door. "I went to confront you the day after the battle and found you wrestling with Landon. He was training you, *coaching* you, and I realized you fuckers had been plotting against me the whole time!"

"It wasn't like that," I cried. "I asked them to help me get better at sports so I could *stop* the battles and fights. Not to humiliate you."

The harsh lines of his face deepened as he scowled. "Like I believe that. They're brothers and they turned on me to help you." He peered around. "But where are they now? I bet they'll think twice next time before betraying the Network, and as for you, they've left you in F Class where you belong."

They did so much more than that.

Visions flooded my mind. Screaming for help as the Elite boys pummeled me. Trying to crawl away and Zach catching me and ripping off my wetsuit. That punishment did not fit the crime of embarrassing him and losing a stupid position.

"You went too far, Cameron." My grip on my arms was becoming painful, yet I ignored the piercing sting of my nails. "You really hurt Landon and Michael, and by now, the administration knows I was set up."

He laughed. It was a sharp, humorless sound. "You think they're going to find out it was me and I'll be expelled? You can't be stupid enough to believe I put my hands anywhere near the solution or the water bottle."

"I'm not stupid. I told Whittaker it was you from day one—"

His grin twitched.

"—but if he hasn't expelled you already, then he hasn't found anything or he isn't looking. Either way, I'd need proof to go to him and I have none."

"That's right. This little conversation won't help you either because I'll deny everything."

I picked myself off the door. "I know you will. I didn't come here to get something to take to Whittaker. I came because I needed to make a decision and you helped make it."

His brows snapped together. "What does that mean?"

"It means I'm leaving." I took a step, pushing him back, and reached for the doorknob. "Remember one thing—it didn't have to be this way. You brought it all on yourself."

Cameron's face smoothed out until the furrowed brow, twisted lips, and narrowed eyes were gone. He was the picture of serene perfection once more. "No, Manning. You did."

I said no more as I walked out the door. Derek was standing exactly where I left him.

"What happened?" he asked.

"Can we go inside?"

He stepped aside to let me in and I went straight for his desk chair. I pushed it to the side of the bed and plopped down as had become my habit. "He admitted he was behind it all. He pushed it that far because I beat him in the battle and cost him a position in the Network. Did you know about that?"

"Yes." Derek stretched himself out on the bed. "He was already in deep for letting two recruits get to Argyle and almost spill our secret. You guys kept your mouth shut, but it would have been bad if you came clean and she believed you. Losing a battle to you on top of that showed he wasn't fit to lead the new brothers and now he's been replaced."

"By who?"

He shifted away, looking up at the ceiling. "I'm not telling you that."

"Why not?"

"Why would I?"

I sighed. "Fine. I'm not here to talk about that anyway."

"Then why are you here?"

I reached out and closed my hand over his arm. He shifted around and looked at me curiously. "You offered to get back at them for what they did to me, but I said no because I'm going to do that myself." My grip on him tightened. "I'm going after them with everything I've got and nothing will stop me. If some kind of brother/loyalty crap is going to be a problem for you, let me know now."

He shook me off as he sat up. "No brother crap. I keep Network business to myself, but if you want my loyalty, you have to earn it, and none of them have. I'm not going to stop you, Zela."

The use of my name struck me. It was such an odd feeling hearing him say it.

"But why are you telling me this?" he continued.

I leaned back in the chair, feeling the cool leather against my neck. I was coming down after my faceoff with Cameron.

"Because if I want you to be honest with me, I have to be honest with you."

He frowned. "What do you want me to be honest about?"

I shrugged. "Nothing. I'm just saying."

"Okay," he said, but he didn't stop studying me as he leaned back onto the sheets.

I shifted and pointed at the pile of books on his nightstand. "You've got the next book in the series. Wanna read?"

He was quiet for a moment, then he nodded. I took that as permission to climb up next to him and settle on the sheets. We passed the night in silence except for when Derek finished his book and asked me to give him the other. It was the perfect way to spend my last night before school began. The calm before the storm.

"I UNDERSTAND NOW WHY you wake up early."

I blinked at Adam as I dropped my shower stuff on the bed. "What?"

Groaning, he pushed himself up and the covers fell to his waist, exposing his chest. Finding out I'm a girl hadn't made him feel any less comfortable going around without a shirt on. "You're trying to make sure you're in and out before the boys come in," he said. "I'll have your back if you need me. I'll be lookout. Chase people away saying the toilets exploded or something."

I giggled. "Even the thought of that is horrific, but thanks. I appreciate it."

Adam left to get ready. I waited for him like I always did, and we headed for breakfast together, but as we neared the dining room, I slowed down.

"Go in without me," I said when the doors loomed in front of us. "There's something I need to do."

Adam didn't argue with me and went on ahead. I stepped out of the path and found a spot further down the hall to stand and wait.

I scanned the faces of the boys and girls as they streamed inside, looking for one in particular.

Where is he? I couldn't be so lucky that he would have transferred to another school—

I stood up straight. There he is.

Zachary Fields rounded the corner. I looked him up and down as he strode through the hall, buttoned-up in his pressed uniform with a bold, embroidered E on the chest. I stepped out as he neared the cafeteria doors, and as though he felt my eyes on him, he turned and our gaze connected.

I didn't speak or close the distance between us. One move. I lifted my hand and crooked a finger. Zach peeled away from the pack without breaking his stride.

I traced the lines of his face as he approached me. I couldn't tell what he was thinking. But then, I never could. That was how he was able to surprise me with his cruelty again and again.

Zach planted himself two feet in front of me. "What?"

Taking a slow, imperceptible breath, I hooked my fingers behind my back. I didn't want him to see they were shaking.

"You," I said clearly. "You're not going to tell anyone about me."

His brows shot up his forehead. "Excuse me?"

"You heard me." I took a step, then two, closing the distance between us. "You're not going to tell anyone what you found out in the locker room, Fields, and if you already have, you're going to tell them you made it up."

Zach's backpack hung on his finger over his shoulder. It fell with a crash as he folded his arms. My eyes followed the movement, recalling those filthy hands grabbing and tearing at me, his fingers digging into my thigh as he exposed my body for everyone to see.

My stomach heaved.

"What makes you think that, Zekina, or whatever the hell your name is?" He advanced on me. "I can't believe you were stupid enough to come back. You don't belong here and none of that shit would have happened if you hadn't come for us first. You're out of your mind if you think I'm not talking to Argyle and getting you kicked out."

I stayed silent as he made his speech. "You done?" I asked. "Good. Now, I can tell you what is actually going to happen. You're going to keep your mouth shut so that *you're* not the one who gets kicked out of school. You assaulted a girl in the locker room. You beat me up and ripped off my clothes and if you think that just because I didn't report you, I don't have pictures and a promise from Derek to back me up, then you're the one who is out of your mind. No one is going to care that you thought I was a guy. All they will hear is that you beat on innocent women."

Zach's smirk slipped. "You don't have pictures."

I said nothing as I slipped my phone out of my pocket and held it up to his face. He paled as my thumb swiped across the screen, revealing everything he and his friends did to me. This time, my hand was steady.

"I'm assuming we understand each other," I said as I put my phone away. "You're going to keep my secret and you'll make sure the others do so as well."

Zach's response was to shoot me a poisonous glare, spin on his leather shoes, and storm off. I didn't let that worry me. He would keep quiet. I knew it.

At a slower pace, I entered the cafeteria and joined the line for breakfast. My gaze followed Zach as he reached them, and when my eyes landed on Landon, my stomach twisted even tighter. I walked off the line. There was no way I would be able to swallow a bite.

It wasn't right for him to look so perfect. His hair had grown out and thick, jet-black strands fell in waves around his eyes, begging to be pushed back. I couldn't tell what color his eyes were today, but his natural warm browns were seared in my memory.

On his other side, sat Cole and Michael. Michael's handsome, angular face was smooth and unblemished. Gone was the white bandage and the pink, healing scrapes along his face. He was perfect once more. Much like Cole who had always bore the face of an angel, even if his snappish, prickly insides did not match. The three of them leisurely ate their breakfast. It seemed the days of those three having nothing to do with one another was over. I could only think of one thing that bonded them together.

Zach pulled out a chair and sat in front of them. I dropped my gaze before either one could look my way.

"Hey, Zeke!"

The cheerful greeting was so at odds with how I felt, it took me a second to register. Owen and Justin waved from their spots at our table. I slowed down when I noticed there were more people than usual. Adam, Melody, Justin, Owen, Nico, Tanner, and Derek I expected, but the two new faces I wasn't. A girl with short hair and a red scarf sat between Adam and Melody, while a brown-haired boy with a dusting of freckles on his cheeks took what should have been my place next to Derek.

I eyed him as I walked around and pulled out a chair next to Justin. "Hi, I'm Zeke. Are you guys new?"

Melody nodded. "Freshmen," she said. "And our littles."

"Your whats?"

Derek leaned back in his seat as he folded his hands behind his head. "Our littles. Whittaker decided to start an Elite mentorship program this year and we get to be the guinea pigs." He jerked a thumb at the boy. "This is Hunter."

Hunter waved as he sank lower in his seat. I waved back, feeling a touch of sympathy for the new kid. If he was as nervous as he looked, Whittaker had just delivered him into the hands of a wolf. I wondered how long it would be before Hunter ran away from his new mentor.

"And this is Serena," Melody spoke up. Serena acknowledged me with a jerk of the chin. "You know they make us move in early. Argyle and Whittaker held a special assembly and told us trust was beginning to break down among the classes, and we needed to foster better relationships as we moved forward and strove to bring our class to new heights."

Derek scoffed. "Whatever the fuck that means."

"What do you have to do?" I asked Melody. "Are all the Elites doing it?"

She shook her head. "Just the sophomores taking on the freshmen. We show them around, answer their questions, help them form battle strategies, give them advice, and stuff like that. And my first tip"—she turned to Serena—"you can't wear that scarf. We're not allowed to accessorize the uniforms outside of the exceptions in the handbook."

Serena's face crumpled into a scowl. "You're kidding. I'll get in trouble for wearing a scarf?"

"You'll get detention for wearing a scarf."

She folded her arms. "But I'm Elite. Don't we get to do what we want, or what's the point?"

Owen and I shared a look.

"Elite get more privileges," Melody replied, "but we follow the same rules as everyone else."

Serena rolled her eyes so hard I feared she'd hurt herself. "Ugh. Whatever. We don't have to sit together, do we?" She pushed her chair back. "I'm going to find my friends."

"Bye," Melody called as she waved her off. She did not sound sad to see the back of her. The minute she was gone, Melody claimed the seat next to Adam. "So how was the rest of your summer?" I heard her ask.

I turned to Derek. "What are—"

"I have to go too." Derek pushed away his untouched plate and got to his feet. "Coach wants to see me. You," he said to Hunter. "Let's go."

The younger boy snatched up his breakfast taco and scurried after him. With nothing left to distract me, my eyes wandered and drifted toward them. I felt their pull like magnets, like bees to the hive, like moths to light.

I looked at Zach, Cole, Michael, and Landon, and each one of them was looking back at me.

Chapter Three

"Hello, sophomores, and welcome to your second year at Breakbattle Academy. I will be your teacher this year. You may call me Dr. O'Quinn."

The woman who stood before us was imposing. That was the only word for her. Heavy brows cast shadows over her eerily light-colored eyes. Her gray and brown hair was pulled back into a severe bun and her pantsuit repelled wrinkles. She had only to give us a look for the class to fall silent.

"This semester, you will take English II, Critical Writing, Geometry, and Networking. Next semester, World History, Spanish II, Debate, and Chemistry. Any questions about that?"

My hand shot into the air, drawing those brightly colored eyes to me. "Yes, Mr. Manning."

She knows my name?

"Dr. O'Quinn," I began, getting over my surprise. "What is networking? I read the course description, but I didn't understand it."

"Good question, Mr. Manning. Networking is one of the courses unique to this academy. Despite its name, it is actually vocational education where you spend focused time planning for your future careers." She walked up and down along her desk as she spoke. "This will look different as you move through the years. Gathering information, making a plan, interviews, job shadowing people in the community, career fairs, filling out applications, writing college essays, the list goes on.

"This course may present as an elective on your transcript but it is mandatory. Participating in the battle system seems too much of a hassle until you know what you're building toward and why hard work is such a necessity." She pierced me with her look. "Does that answer your question?"

"Yes, Dr. O'Quinn."

She nodded sharply, then continued with her introduction. Part of me missed Mr. Dawson by the end of it. I got the impression she would be a good teacher, but a strict one. The feeling seemed spot on when she caught Tanner chewing gum and promptly sent him out of the room.

"Now," she said as she closed the door behind him. "We have much to accomplish this semester, so let's begin. Open your English textbooks to page twelve and read the passage silently to yourself."

The sound of books smacking the desk and backpacks being unzipped filled the room. We worked in near silence throughout the morning. Dr. O'Quinn did not allow any one of us to talk unless called on. We broke for lunch and met up with Tanner outside.

"Can you believe that—?"

"Shh!" I hissed. "Wait until we're out of the wing."

I peered over my shoulder just as O'Quinn stepped into the doorway. Lines crinkled around her eyes as she narrowed them on us. The woman must read minds.

We escaped into the main hall and Tanner let loose. "She made me stand outside all morning! Dawson didn't give a shit if we chewed gum. What's her problem?"

"She is going to be nothing like Dawson," Adam spoke up. "I met her a couple of times when Mom invited the faculty to our Christmas parties. She hardcore believes in the Breakbattle method and thinks every F is an A waiting to happen; they just haven't taken on enough battles yet. I overheard her by the eggnog telling Mom that the school should set battle quotas. If we're not in at least five a semester, we're put on probation."

My mouth fell open. "What? Tell me she didn't pass that on to Whittaker."

"He loves thinking of us as experiments," Nico added. "He'd snap that up."

"It was two years ago and it hasn't happened yet," said Adam. "Last year, he got in it with the parents for the changes he made to the system, so I think we're safe. I'm just saying O'Quinn doesn't play around. If someone challenges us to a battle, she'll approve it without asking why."

I wasn't certain what to make of that. It seemed she wanted us to improve, but the "by any means necessary" method could turn sour quickly.

She might come in handy this semester though. The thought crossed my mind. *For what I'm going to do, it's better that no one asks why.*

The four of us went into the lunchroom, got our food, and wandered over to Derek's table. He sat at one near the head table instead of our usual near the back, but there were no pretty breakfast buddies to distract him this time. I was sitting with him no matter what he said about it.

"Damn. Take the hint." Derek held up his book. "I'm reading. Go away."

"Nope." I set my tray down with a firm thump and pulled out the seat next to him. "But I won't bug you. You're falling behind. I'm already on book nine."

"Yeah? Did you like the eighth book?" Derek set his book down and, as bold as he pleased, reached over and took one of my chocolate chip cookies. He was chewing on it before I could open my mouth.

I shook my head as I passed him the other one. He said thanks before polishing off that cookie too. I wasn't bothered with him taking my dessert. I was starting to notice his fondness for chocolate and I was collecting every new thing I learned about him like a child picking up shells on the beach.

"It was different from the others in the series," I said, "but in a good way. They are showing us they can still surprise us."

"Excuse me?"

I twisted around and found a short boy with an E on his chest standing behind me.

"Can I sit with you guys, Derek?" asked Hunter.

"Yes," I said quickly, beating him to it. Lord knew what Derek was going to say and I wouldn't let him terrify the helpless young kid on his first day. Derek made me cry the first time I tried to sit with him, and there was no need for round two. "Sit next to me, Hunter."

Derek shrugged and took my milk.

"Hey," I cried. "That I did want."

"Too bad." He took a swig. "You can't have cookies without milk."

"Why didn't you get your own food?"

"The food tastes like rancid shit, but you get mad when I order in. The solution is I get the decent stuff on your plate."

"I— Wha— I don't get mad when you order food! I've never said anything about it."

"You didn't have to." Derek held up two fingers in front of my face, making my eyes cross. "It was all in that death glare you threw me whenever I had pizza and you were munching on their mystery meat. I thought you'd whip the machete out on me."

"That's not true!" I shrieked, giggling. "Although, I am thinking about it now. You're out of your mind if you believe you're taking my food all year."

His grin lit up his whole face, banishing the scowl lines that sometimes seemed a permanent part of him. "How are you going to stop me, Zee? I play ball with you. I know"—he moved and my apple was off my plate before I could blink—"that you're too slow."

I seriously considered popping him upside the head as he tore off a bite of my apple. His eyes danced as he chewed.

A noise to my left broke me out of my violent thoughts. Hunter struggled to smother his laugh.

"You guys are funny," he said when he caught me looking. "I hope I make friends like you."

"I wouldn't call him my friend at the moment." Derek barked a laugh. "But you will make friends, Hunter," I continued. "Did you grow up in Chesterfield or Evergreen?"

He shook his head. "Neither. I was born in Evergreen, but my parents moved out of state when I was little. I don't know anyone here."

"You're like me. I was born in Chesterfield, but traveled all my life. Breakbattle is a tough place, but you have all your privileges and Elites rarely get challenged by anyone other than As. You can focus on school and stay out of the drama. If you do get into drama, Derek will have your back. He doesn't bow down to the Elite bullshit, and once you get past his porcupine exterior, he's got marshmallow in his center."

"What kind of crap are you telling this kid?" Derek nudged my shoulder. "Why would I have his back? You're as close to a best friend as I got, and I barely like you."

I spun on him. "Eat my apple and hush."

He threw up his hands, smirking away, and I struggled not to reveal the thrill that went through me at hearing him say best friend.

"Don't listen to him," I said to Hunter. "You're going to be fine. I'm not going to see what happened to me happen to anyone else."

Hunter's brows drew together. "What do you mean? What happened?"

My gaze flicked away to Landon, Michael, and Cole's table. I noticed them come in when I was goofing around with Derek. I wondered if I would always sense their presence.

"I was targeted by bullies," I said simply.

"They challenged you to battles over and over again, didn't they?"

I tore my eyes away. "What? How did you know that?"

Hunter picked up his cookie and broke it into pieces. "I heard that happens. It's why you said I wouldn't have to worry about it being Elite. They come after people until they take everything they have. Just like that girl Rebecca Taylor. My teacher told us about her in class this morning."

"It's not a normal thing," Owen spoke up. "And Adam's mom is the school therapist. She's not like the others. She really has our back."

The two fell into conversation while my attention wandered back to their table. Miss Val was a nice person and she had helped me when the principal was prepared to write me off. I could not thank her enough for that, but there was only so much she could do. She could not punish the Elites for what they did to me, because she could never know what they discovered that day in the locker room. She could not punish them for me, so I would.

Now that I'm thinking about it, I should get started.

I pushed back my chair and stood.

"Zeke?" Adam asked. "What's up?"

"There's something I have to do," I replied, but I wasn't looking at him. My gaze was fixed on three boys in particular. "I'll be right back."

Michael raised his head as I neared their table. Our eyes met over the mess of noise, overcooked food, and groans about returning to school. Not for the first time, I wondered what was going on behind those eyes. I could never tell what Michael was thinking. Not even when he stood over me while his friends beat the crap out of me.

As I got within inches of their table, all three of them stopped eating and stared at me. I slid across their faces in turn, taking in their different expressions. Anger for Landon. Irritation for Cole. Blankness for Michael.

I looked at them, and then I veered away and crossed two tables to find the one I was searching for. I stood behind one of the boys and tapped him on the shoulder as I pulled something out of my pocket.

He stopped laughing at whatever his friend said and glanced up at me. "What do you want?"

"Hold on." I squinted at what I wrote on my paper. "Okay. Are you Brian Saxe?"

"Yeah." I spotted him glancing at my chest. "What do you want?"

I cleared my throat. "Brian Saxe, I challenge you to a battle in math."

His fork clattered to the table. "But you can't— Aren't you an—"

I pointed at the boy next to him. "Callum Mercia, I challenge you to a battle in math." Then the boy on his right. "Bo Clark, I challenge you to a battle in math."

"Mateo Acosta."

"Huxley Goodman."

"Kashton Turner."

I went down through my list, challenging every boy in front of me. When I was finished, the entire table—no, the entire cafeteria—had fallen silent.

I unhurriedly refolded my list and put it back in my pocket.

"I'll tell you the privileges I want when we get it approved," I said to their dumbfounded faces. "I will be on your floor first thing after school. See ya then."

I gave them my back but I didn't return to my table. I walked out of the cafeteria, head held high. The smile didn't grace my lips until the doors slammed shut.

"ARE YOU GOING TO TELL me what's going on?" Adam grabbed my arm and pulled me to the side. The trail of F boys heading out to the soccer field went on without us. "Why did you challenge *half* the B Class to battles on your first day?"

"I had to."

Adam waited, but I didn't offer more of an explanation.

"Why did you have to?" he finally asked.

I glanced around. "I just did. Okay? Adam, it will make sense later." I made to walk away. A hand flashed out, blocking my escape.

"This is about getting back at the Elites." Adam did not phrase that like a question. He didn't make it sound like one either. "Tell me and I'll help. Derek isn't the only one who has your back."

My head jerked up. "What? Adam, I can't. You don't want to be a part of this."

"Yes, I do."

"You're a nice guy, and I'm not planning to hold back."

He shrugged. "That's fine with me."

"Adam, this is serious."

"I know that."

I threw up my hands. "Why do you want to help me anyway?! This isn't your fight!"

"It is my fight." Adam removed his hand, but only to put it on my shoulder. He gently turned me to face him. "You're my best friend and I wasn't there when you needed me. That's never going to happen again."

Adam rested his palm against my cheek. A sweet, comforting gesture that I knew wasn't for Zeke. It was for Zela. My eyes stung with tears.

"Let me help you. I want to."

I ducked my head and his hand fell off. "Okay," I croaked. "I'll tell you and... you can help. Just don't make me cry."

He laughed softly and after a minute I did too. I quickly brushed a trail of wetness from my cheek. "Let's go, or we'll be late."

We made it to the field in time by the skin of our teeth and the glare from Coach let us know.

"Cutting it close, boys." He pointed at the bleachers. "Grab a seat." We climbed the stairs and sat next to Nico and Tanner.

"Alright," Coach began. He planted himself before us and gripped his clipboard behind his back. "You're not freshmen anymore. You trained every week for a year and I saw marked improvement in each one of you. This year, you're eligible for spots on the team and you'll get it by showing me something out there. The letter on your chest means nothing on the field. Your talent and hard work does. So if you want onto the team, earn it. Understood?"

"Yes, Coach."

"Is that understood?"

"Yes, Coach!"

He clapped by smacking his hand against the board. "That's what I want to hear! Now, up. Two teams. Start your drills."

Maybe it was just me, but it seemed my class descended on the field with renewed vigor. It wasn't often we heard that we could go for what we wanted without our letter defining us. I didn't care one way or the other about getting on the team, but Tanner blew through the drills like this was his try-out.

Coach switched up the teams again and kicked off the match. I played well, scoring three goals, but I might have done better if my mind wasn't elsewhere.

Am I really going to tell Adam what I'm planning to do? There is a reason I didn't want him or Derek to know. I became the enemy of the Elite unwillingly last year. This year, it will be on purpose.

"Zeke! Heads up!"

I snapped back into focus as something hurtled toward my face. "Wha— Ow!" Pain blossomed in my forehead and I staggered back to the roar of cheers. "What the hell?!"

"Nice job, Manning," Coach called. "Next time make the goal on purpose."

My team scooped me up before I could get a word out and hoisted me off the field. We won and all it took was bouncing a ball off my face. I eventually slipped out of their grasp and caught up with Adam. He was waiting for me steps from the main entrance.

"Let's hear it, Manning."

I sighed. Yes, I was really going to tell him. To be honest, the first part of this equation was tricky, so I could use all the help I could get. "Okay. First, we challenge the Bs and..."

DR. O'QUINN'S BROWS were in danger of disappearing into her hairline. "Excuse me? You need approval for..." She glanced over my shoulder at the army of boys behind me. "Approval for ten battles."

"Yes, please."

"For what, exactly?"

"I would like their library times."

"Their library times," she said slowly.

"Yes, ma'am. One a day for ten days. This year is important and I have to work harder than ever. I'm giving it my all this year, so of course, I need time in the library." I flapped a hand behind me. "I've challenged them all to maximize my chance of winning and spread the battles around. The staff haven't made a rule against targeting but I have."

If she heard the admonishment in my tone, she ignored it. "And why have you chosen students from the B Class, Mr. Manning. Cs and Ds also have library time."

"Bs get seven hours a day in the library. If I'm going to devote real time to studying, then time is what I need."

O'Quinn studied me, her face giving nothing away. The boys whispered and grumbled behind me as we remained locked in our staredown.

"Mr. Manning," she said after a solid minute had passed.

"Yes, ma'am."

A smile broke out on her face and the shock of it made me take a step back. "I absolutely agree with you, and let me say, I admire your initiative. This is what the battle system is for," she said as she came around her desk. "You have to set a goal and do what it takes to achieve it." O'Quinn put her hand over my head as though she strongly wanted to give me a pat but rules about touching students held her back. "Mr. Dawson told me you were his most impressive student and I'm beginning to see what he saw in you."

She gave up on patting the air and gestured toward the door. "Go on, Zeke. I will go up with these boys and get the battles approved. I know you have homework to do, and I don't want to keep you."

"Thank you, Dr. O'Quinn."

Adam picked himself off the wall when I stepped outside. "What happened?"

"She approved them all." I peered over my shoulder. "I also think she loves me now."

"Then she'll have no trouble with me coming up to her desk tomorrow with six more."

"Seven." I pulled out my list and handed it over. "These are the boys you need to challenge. When Michael and Landon were helping me train, they told me about the boys I would most likely be able to beat in a challenge. All their 'find the weaknesses' training with the Network, I bet."

"What does that mean?" He moved away and we took off for the dorm. "What did they tell you?"

"They explained how they sort the classes," I replied. "The Elite are the best of the best. Top percentile. Highest scores on the trials. The A Class are students that were close, but didn't make the top ten. After that is the B Class. Bs are on the level of As with their placement test scores, but were dragged down by their crappy performances in the trials. Cs are average at both. Ds are even worse than them and Fs... are everyone else."

He nodded along. "That makes sense. So, they told you to challenge the Bs because you've got the smarts, but they're not as hard to beat at sports."

"Exactly. We both know you can take on anyone in this school, but just take on these guys. You've got your own stuff with the swim team. You don't need to go hard on these battles."

He plucked the list from my fingers. "I'll go as hard as you need me to, Zee."

I glanced up at him. "I noticed you're calling me Zee now. Did Jordan tell you my nickname?"

"I heard her calling you that enough times. You don't mind, do you? It feels weird saying Zeke, and it's not like people would think twice about Zee."

"It's fine. Zee and Zeke are the most harmless names people will be calling me by the time this semester is over."

ALL EYES WERE ON ME this time last year. I was the F the Elites had set their sights on and everyone wanted to know why. This year, their eyes were on me again. That happens when you get ten battles on the first day. Well, I say ten, but it turned out to be eight. Two of the boys picked swimming as the physical test and I turned those down. Except for when the threat of failing forced me into Coach's class, I was not stepping foot in the natatorium.

My first battle kicked off the next day at four o'clock on the dot. Dr. O'Quinn looked proud as she rattled off instructions for the geometry test. She placed the paper on my desk, and to my surprise, she did pat my head.

"Good luck, Mr. Manning."

I nodded as she went back to her colleague. The expression Callum Mercia's teacher was throwing me was not pride. I put it closer to perplexed with a hint of annoyed. She must have thought I was wasting her students' time with battles I couldn't hope to win but I didn't care what she thought. As long as she kept approving them, I'd be able to accomplish what I set out to do.

"You have thirty minutes. Begin."

I flipped the test over and put pencil to paper without hesitation. Geometry wasn't my favorite and it showed throughout homeschooling. As a result, Mom drilled it into my head until I aced every practice problem to her satisfaction. When our thirty minutes were up, I knew I'd gotten a hundred.

I chanced a peek at Callum.

He looks pretty confident too. Like I thought, this is going to come down to the physical battle.

The four of us stepped out of the classroom and found two boys waiting. Adam and Ryler Mitchell had their battle directly after ours. They joined us as we tramped out to the wrestling gym.

Stepping inside, memories smacked me like cold air to the face. Landon and me grabbing and twisting on the mat.

The way he smiled when I did a move perfectly. The feel of his hands when he pulled me close only to flip me on my ass. The taste of his lips when he gave me my first kiss.

I dug my nails into my palm and the sharp sting dragged me harshly to the present. He took my first kiss, then he looked at me like *I* was the monster when he refused to believe me and ordered his buddies to beat me into the ground.

It's okay, I thought as Callum and I squared off. *I'm coming for him next.*

I'm coming for all of them... and it begins now.

Coach called it and I lunged.

EIGHT BATTLES IN FOUR days and I won six of them. Adam won all of his, proving once more he didn't belong anywhere near the F Class. Derek didn't ask me why I was doing this, but when I burst into his room the following Sunday night, I could sense his curiosity brimming beneath his standard unpleasantness.

"What do you want?"

"To hang out." I brushed past him into his room. I halted when I realized we weren't alone. "Oh. Hello, Hunter. What are you doing here?"

He grinned sheepishly from his seat in the desk chair I often claimed. He kicked his feet, legs so short his toes barely brushed the carpet from the height Derek set his chair. "It's mentor time. We have a lot of schoolwork during the week and Derek has basketball practice. This is the only time we can meet."

I lifted a brow at Derek as I addressed Hunter. "Has he been mentoring you?"

"He's... uh... reading."

"And I just got to the good part." Derek hopped on the bed, sending one of his pillows to the floor. "Both of you get out."

"No."

I walked around his bed and climbed onto the other side. I was getting bold and I knew it. Saying no to him, inserting myself into his space. It was dangerous. Derek was like a coiled serpent ready to strike at one wrong move but my days of fearing I would push him too far were over. We broke the barrier the day he found me naked on the floor and held me until my throat was too raw to sob. He was mine now. My friend. My Derek. We both accepted that even if he would never admit it.

"We'll give you all the mentoring you can stand, Hunter," I said. "Pull up your chair and ask any of the questions you have."

"Ask three questions," Derek cut in. He didn't lift his head from his book. "Make them good ones and then leave. Time is up in ten minutes. Then I want to talk to you."

I didn't need to ask if that last statement was for me. I knew it was. Hunter and I accepted our terms. The younger boy moved the chair closer. His expression swung from uncomfortable to eager.

"Can I ask you something first, Zeke? Why did you do all of those battles? Everyone was talking about it. They said Fs barely challenge anyone but you've been shaking things up since you got here. You even challenged an Elite upperclassman and won."

I cut eyes to Derek but his attention was glued to the pages. "It's simple and hard to explain at the same time. Something went down during my orientation and I missed the placement test. Things got out of hand last year, but now I'm working to make it right. Fs don't have a lot of resources to improve, so I have to battle. I'm gunning for top spot this year."

"Wow." Hunter swiveled the chair until I could only see half his face. "You must be really into the battle-and-come-out-on-top stuff."

My expression hardened. "Not even a little. This is how it has to be done, Hunter. If Fs want so much as to set foot in the library or go to the Christmas dance, they have to battle for it. There is no opting out for us."

"Like me, you mean." He lowered his head. "Sorry. It must be hard being forced into the lower classes when you never belonged there." Hunter turned back to face us. "So no one questions the system or fights back?"

"That's your second question," Derek warned.

I nudged his shoulder. "People do, but when we did, Whittaker came down on us hard."

"We?"

"Stand Up. It's the club Melody started with the main purpose of pushing back against the system. We held a protest last year and this year Melody has new plans for the club."

"Really?" Hunter shot forward in the seat. "Can I join too?"

"And that's three." Derek closed the book with a snap. "Yes, you can join the club. You can also consider mentor time over. I'll be at your door at six a.m. tomorrow morning for basketball practice."

Hunter didn't appear thrilled at the early morning wake-up call and who would be, except me.

"Let the kid sleep," I said. "I'll get up and practice with you. It's been a long time since we played."

He shrugged. "Fine."

I waited until the door snapped shut behind Hunter before rising on my knees and facing him head on. "What is it?"

Derek's eyes swept over me, piercing and probing like he was seeking through the layers for the real person beneath. "Why are you doing these battles? Is this a part of your revenge plan?"

"Yes."

His gaze turned even more assessing. "Are you going to tell me?"

"Maybe, but not today."

He inclined his head, accepting that easier than I anticipated. "Do you need help?"

"Yes, and you're already doing it. I have to keep improving my game and you're helping me get better at basketball."

"Huh. So I get the hardest task."

I laughed. "Shut up." I settled in next to him, getting comfortable. "Tell me what chapter you're on."

"Shit. They just got off the plane in Germany and..."

EVERYONE STARED AT me when I walked into the cafeteria the next morning. Or most of the students stared at me, some gave Adam a few looks, and the rest were honed in on the head table where most of the staff, Miss Val, and Vice Principal Argyle sat. Sitting in the middle of them, was Principal Whittaker.

"What's going on?" I whispered to Adam.

"Don't know. Mom doesn't tell me everything."

We grabbed our food and joined the rest of our table. Conversation was subdued. It was hard to focus when we kept sneaking glances at the head table, wondering when Whittaker was going to get it over with and tell us what he came to say.

Ten minutes later, he got to his feet to a room that had already fallen silent.

"Good morning, students."

"Good morning, Principal Whittaker," we chimed.

"I hope you've been settling into your new year because I have no doubt this will be our best." Whittaker's smile swept over us. It was a smile I knew well. It shone back at me in every photograph on his walls and every time last year when he approved a new method of battle torture.

What does this smile mean for us now?

"I've waited a long time to share this with you and the moment has finally come." Whittaker spread out his hands as if to embrace us. "Breakbattle Academy and our revolutionary teaching method will soon be adopted nationwide. We're expanding and opening four more academies within the next four years."

A tsunami of sound broke into his speech, but his smile did not dissipate. The room filled with a mix of cheers, applause, whispers, groans, and the shocked faces of my friends that spoke volumes.

Whittaker raised his voice over the noise. "This could not have happened without all of you working your hardest and proving every day that the battle system shapes young minds into powerhouses of excellence. You deserve the applause!"

Whittaker, Argyle, and most of the staff clapped as the students' cheers reached a crescendo. All except for one. Miss Val's head was bent over a blue notebook I had spotted one too many times in her office. Her face was unreadable as she scribbled something between the lines.

"Thank you. Thank you." Whittaker waved for silence. "Now, this expansion has been in the works for years, before my time, and it's an honor to see it achieved during my tenure. It is even more of an honor to have received the call this morning that members of the state board of education wish to observe us in hopes of integrating our system into the public schools."

Whittaker punctuated that with a thrust of his arms like he expected applause and he got it. The Elites, As, Bs, and even the Cs were stomping and banging the tables. The rest of us were not.

"Integrated into public schools?" I hissed. "Can that happen?"

"It can happen," Adam said. There was an edge to his voice I rarely heard. "I wish I was surprised."

I twisted around. "What do you mean? Did you think this was coming?"

He shook his head. "Not like this. I just thought once last year that it was a good thing Breakbattle was the only school like this, or else others might get it into their head to funnel their budget only to the geniuses and athletes. We have two gyms and a track field so spotless you can eat off them, but the F dorms are covered in stains we don't want to know about.

"Fs don't get anything but the bare basics as a constant reminder we're not good enough. That's a crappy way to treat a kid and now they're trying to spread it to other schools."

"It's not right."

My eyes slid off Adam and landed on Melody. With one look, I knew she heard everything we said. "It's not right and... I'm going to put a stop to it."

"How?" I glanced at Whittaker. He was still beaming so wide I could see all of his teeth. "We can't stop them building more schools."

"I'm going to figure something out." She rose from her seat and walked out as the celebration raged around us.

I didn't know what that meant. I didn't know what any of this meant, but I had that stomach-writhing feeling so like the one that plagued me before I redecorated Whittaker's carpet. That feeling like everything was about to go wrong.

Chapter Four

The pencil slipped past his pink lips, rolling between his teeth as he left little *dent, dent, dents* on the wood. There was a tiny wrinkle between his brows as Cole scrunched his forehead in concentration. Not like the one that came about from being annoyed. This was even cuter.

Michael sat on his other side, his face smooth although he had twice the amount of books in front of him. Landon sat with them, scribbling something in the margin of his notebook. Landon's tongue poked out as he squinted over the table and I felt the cinders of my crush reignite.

It turned my stomach. What was wrong with me? After everything they did to me, why couldn't I see them for the monsters they were. Landon didn't deserve the feelings that lingered. Cole had no right to the smile that fought its way to my lips the rare times he laughed. Michael should lay no claim to the comfort it stirred in me when I heard his voice in my ear telling me what to do during my nightly runs.

I ducked further behind the shelves, peering at them over spines of dusty tomes. This was the first time I had stepped foot in the library but it was a credit to the wealthy institution that housed it. Rows and rows of books, computer stations in the back, study tables along the stacks, and an ever-watchful librarian who squinted at me suspiciously when I handed her my battle-won day pass.

I hadn't been waiting long for them. These guys had been my friends. I knew their routines. Wrestling, swimming, and track practice directly after school. Back to their dorms for half an hour to shower and get their homework, then it was the library until dinner where they were promised peace and quiet to study instead of the racket of an all-male, teenage-boy dorm floor.

They walked in together right on schedule and I ducked behind the shelves as they found a table near a glazed window. They got down to studying right away, not bothering with chitchat.

I took a steadying breath. *This is it, Zela. Don't lose your nerve.*

The boys loomed closer as I emerged from the stacks. It was Michael who spotted me first. He elbowed Cole and the wrinkle became more pronounced as he frowned.

"Hi, guys." I flashed them a beaming smile. "Mind if I sit?"

"Yes," Cole snapped.

I sat my butt down anyway. "So what are you studying? Derek says the Elite teachers like to hit you with tests as soon as you come back. Have you gotten—"

"What are you doing here?" Landon interrupted. This close, I could see his eyes were gold today. They narrowed as I gazed at the contacts, as though he was reminded of why he had gone without for weeks.

"I'm guessing we're skipping the pleasantries," I said mildly, inside my heart was tapping a wild tune on my rib cage. "I just wanted to make sure Zach gave you my message and we're all on the same page. You're not going to tell anyone the truth about me."

A snort brought my attention to Cole. "You can't hold those pictures over us. We didn't lay a finger on you, remember?"

My fists balled under the desk. Anger tinged with something else curdled my blood at hearing how unaffected he sounded. I remembered every single fucking second of that day and it wasn't right for it not to tear him apart as much as it did me.

"But we were never going to say anything," he continued. "We tried to pull that psycho off you and got a cracked rib and black eye for the trouble. We never wanted to know what you've got going on in your pants, and as far as we're concerned, we never found out."

I wondered if he thought this would be the part where I thanked him. Instead, I rose from the seat. "I'm glad we understand each other. See you around, Cole. Michael." The taller boy remained silent. I turned to the eyes that had been burning a hole in me since I sat down. "I like the eye color today, Landon. It suits you." I touched a lock of his hair to push it back and he recoiled like my fingers burned.

Nostrils flaring, he bared his teeth. "Don't fucking touch me!"

I kept my face blank as I backed away. "Bye, boys. I'll see you tomorrow."

"No, you won't," Cole and Landon said at the same time.

I didn't reply as I walked away. It wasn't until I escaped out the doors that I released the breath I had been holding.

Was their agreement to keep my secret lifting the weight off my chest or was it the brief touch of Landon's silken strands?

It's the first one, I told myself firmly. *You do not like Landon Foster anymore.*

I repeated that to myself as I headed outside to watch the soccer tryouts. I didn't break free of my chorus until I sat down next to Adam and pulled out my notebook.

"Do you think Tanner will make it onto the team?" Nico piped up from the seat in front of us. "He said he played all summer with his brothers."

"He'll make it," I said. "He's quick to adjust the angle of his shots and account for the variables of the opposing team and their shifting goalie. He's discovered his best position is three feet to the left of the goal and a kick at a sixty-one- to seventy-degree angle in the upper corner of the net out of Maxwell's reach. He's good enough for junior varsity at least."

I felt their eyes on me without looking up, but I did so anyway. Both stared at me openmouthed.

"What?" I cried. "Derek says to stop with my sports math but it does help. Math is in everything, whether people know it or not. I'm telling you, Tanner is going to get on the team. I'd bet you my dessert but Derek will probably get to it first."

"I'll take that bet anyway," Nico said. "Your dessert. It's on."

Tanner got on the team.

He whooped as he read his name on the list the following morning. I let out a yelp when his arm was suddenly around my neck and his other dug into my hair. "Yes, Zeke! Nico said you straight up called it!"

I pulled out of his grasp before he could knock my wig off. "You're good, Tanner. You really improved over the summer. I'm glad Coach recognized it."

The smirk hung proudly on his lips. "I don't have fancy trainers like the Evergreen kids but my brothers don't mess around. Patrick is on his college's intramural soccer team and Benson's girlfriend taught him to play. They made sure I got on the team and now"—he grabbed me again but didn't go for my head—"we won the bet so we'll take those desserts."

Adam laughed. "What we? We only bet Zee our angel cupcakes."

"Don't be stingy, Moon. It's not a good look on you."

We chuckled. Tanner released me and spread his joy to his best friend. He and Nico pulled ahead while Adam and I followed at a slower pace.

"About the tryout," he began. "What was up with the notes? You were scribbling in that notebook from the game till I passed out in bed."

I reached behind me and patted my backpack. "I'm studying, Adam. Learning what the best players do right and what the bad players do wrong. Practices are closed but I can watch tryouts, solo practices, and unofficial games. So that's what I have to do."

"Why?"

"We can't challenge the Bs forever. After a while, it's too much like targeting, and besides, they don't have as many privileges as the As or Elites. I'll need to up my game eventually, which means I have to get better."

"Just tell me who you want me to challenge and I'll do it."

"I know you will but you can't transfer those privileges to me and there are a few that I need to get myself."

"Alright. Just tell me when." He bumped my shoulder. "Does this mean we're going to the basketball tryouts today?"

"Yep. I have to cheer Derek on if nothing else. On top of that, we all have something to learn watching him play."

"The real thing to watch is Cameron's head explode when Coach Singh puts him on the varsity team. He's going to go mad."

I had a feeling he was right about that.

Cameron Dupre sat front row and center on the newly made bleachers. By his side was his constant shadow, Santiago. Both boys glanced at us as Adam and I climbed the stairs for the F seats. I hadn't spoken to Cameron since that fateful day in his bedroom but his hauntingly beautiful eyes seemed to find me whenever I entered the same room. There was never anything but a smile on his lips these days but I knew what lurked beneath, simmering beneath the surface waiting for the right moment to be unleashed.

Cameron and Santiago did not take their eyes off me until Coach Singh blew his whistle. Goose bumps dotted my body and they did not fade until I was finally free of their gaze.

"Don't worry about them." Adam laid a hand over mine. "They're not going to mess with you again."

"I thought that before and the false sense of security almost got me expelled. I'm not underestimating Cameron Dupre this year."

"Listen up!" Singh's shout brought our conversation to a stop. "We're going to run through a few drills today and tomorrow you'll receive the results. We'll start with full-court dribbling, form shooting, passing, pass and cut layups, a speed drill, and then finally, a scrimmage game. Any questions?"

No one raised their hand. Unlike the soccer tryouts, this wasn't open to all classes which was why Tanner and Nico didn't bother to come. Only sophomore and freshmen As and Elites were allowed. Derek stood out from the pack.

Fweet!

The whistle cut through the silence once more and the players broke apart to take their positions. I knew more about basketball thanks to Derek, which made my calculations and note-taking much easier. It also made it clear that he was dominating every drill.

Derek passed and caught the ball with ease. He streaked across the court so fast my eyes ping-ponged in their sockets tracking him. He scored six points on the other team while they were still catching their breaths from the drills.

His team won. Singh almost cracked his face in half smiling as he gripped Derek's shoulder. I couldn't hear what he said to him but I could guess.

I went up to his floor that night and peered through the window. I was careful to make sure the coast was clear before I went inside. I had more enemies than a person should have up here.

Derek let me in, too proud about making the varsity team to go through his routine of telling me to go away. Coach didn't bother to make him wait for the results and told him straight out.

I said we should watch movies and sneak treats from his mini-fridge to celebrate and he jumped on it. That night, he passed out halfway through *Die Hard 3*, his blond hair splayed against the satin pillowcase as gentle snores escaped his lips. He looked so sweet and vulnerable like this that I moved the laptop and slipped beneath the covers, letting my eyes flutter shut even though I expected to wake up to his shouts. I didn't care.

I fell asleep that night feeling something I hadn't felt for a long time... that I belonged.

SOMETHING WAS POKING me. I wriggled, face scrunching up as I was dragged from sleep. It was hard and digging into the small of my back.

What is that?

I shifted again and it moved.

What is—

My eyes sprang open. *Oh my—*

I flipped over, gasping, and Derek retracted his finger with a smirk. "Finally. You know you snore, right?"

"You snore!" The comeback was lame but it was all my sleep-addled brain could come up with. Relief beat back the adrenaline as it came together that it was just his finger.

"I gave you a pass and now you think you can sleep here whenever?"

I stretched lazily, letting my bones shift and pop. "Your bed is a lot more comfortable than mine."

He grinned. I wasn't expecting it. It surprised me, then it made me smile too.

"Let's go, stalker perv. We have basketball practice before breakfast." He climbed out of bed and headed for the bathroom. "I'm on the team now. Gotta stay sharp."

"You couldn't be sharper if you channeled the spirits of the great basketballers before you and let them possess your body," I called through the door. "All you do is read and play basketball. When do you have time to study?"

"Don't need to study. I'm naturally brilliant."

I rolled my eyes and flopped down on the bed. He could drag me out when he was done with his shower. I was catching a few more minutes of sleep.

Forty-five minutes later, we were on the court and I was putting the stuff I learned at the tryouts to the test. Derek actually praised me after we finished.

"That didn't suck, Manning."

Yes, that was praise in Derek-speak.

I let my good mood carry me throughout the day. It buoyed my spirits as I crossed the expansive lawn for the gym. The air was filled with shouts and laughs as boys streamed out of the main building. The swimming tryouts were today and Coach Nelson was another one who picked by merit, not class. It was the only way he could have Adam on the team. And he wanted Adam on the team.

I veered off from the pack and went in a different direction. I wasn't watching the swimming tryouts. Adam was already on the team and I did not go into that place unless necessary. There was another person I assumed would be skipping it. I pushed through and there he was.

Landon lay spread eagle on the mat. Still and quiet, he gazed up at the ceiling like someone who had a million things on his mind but couldn't hold on to one thought long enough to do anything about it. So he would do nothing.

I closed the door soundlessly, not wanting to break the peaceful spell until I had no choice. As I approached, he put his hands behind his head and resumed his sit-ups.

"Looks like you need a partner." I hid a smile when he fell back in surprise. "I've got some time if you have a spare singlet."

Landon scrambled to his feet. His colored eyes burned hot enough to set the building ablaze. "Get out of here."

I continued strolling up, bouncing a little on the balls of my toes as I did. "You'll have to put more force in it than that. Derek throws me out of everything from his room to my chair. I'm immune now."

"Fuck off!" Landon advanced on me, fists balled. He didn't stop until he was so close I breathed in his hot pants as they burst from his lips.

"What are you going to do?" I whispered. I looked deep in his golden eyes. "Are you going to hit me, Landon? Finish what you and your friends started?"

His mouth peeled back in a snarl. "I don't have to hit you, *Zeke*. I wrestled with you. All I have to do is throw you over my shoulder and toss you out on your ass."

My skin tightened. I know he could. Not for the first time, I remembered I was messing with guys twice my size who had gotten me beaten. If I found myself trapped in a room with the Elites again, it would be them who decided if I got out.

"Don't do that," I said softly—soothingly. I lifted my hand like I was going to touch him but thought better of it. He hadn't reacted well the first time I did that. "I want to talk to you. Just talk."

"I'm not interested." He gave me his back and walked away.

Just like that, fury bloomed in my soul. "Why?!" I shouted. "Why are *you* mad at *me*?! What gives you the fucking right?! It was you who refused to trust me. You who didn't give me a chance to explain that I was framed. You who let them beat me and Zach violate me!" I lurched forward and shoved him. "You did that! But you think you can walk around acting like you were betrayed!"

I tried to shove him again but he spun around and caught my hands so fast I had no time to react. The look on his face made my shouts die in my throat. I had never seen this expression on him. I didn't know a face that handsome could contort like this.

"You don't think you betrayed me?!" he roared. Spittle fell on my cheek. "You fucking lied about everything including who you are! Is Zeke even your real name?! You played me the whole time and you expected me to trust you when Whittaker walked out with those stickers?!"

My eyes prickled. *Stop it. Stop it! I am not going to cry!*

"Yes, I did because it wasn't about you!" I took a step forward, but there was only a scant amount of distance between us to begin with. I pressed myself against his chest, feeling his fury like a living thing burrowing through my skin and pulling the words from me by force. "I wasn't trying to play you. I became Zeke because it was the only way my mother would let me enroll in the academy. I l-liked you." My voice cracked, but I didn't stop. "I liked you, but I had no idea you felt anything for me. No hope that you ever would since I was pretending to be Zeke."

He threw up his hands. "Fucking surprise! I'm bisexual!"

I staggered back, falling out of his space and losing my grip on anger. "You are?"

"Yeah, I am." He stalked back up to me. "You have a problem with that?"

I growled—yes, growled. This was always the trouble with Landon. His presence had an effect on me like something I only felt from two other assholes, but Landon had gotten there first, burrowed beneath my skin, and made me do things I never thought Zela or Zeke could do.

"No, I don't have a *problem* with that! Keep up, Landon. It's you who has a problem with me!"

"Because you lied to me!"

"You never gave me a chance to tell you the truth!" The scream ripped from my throat. The words would have bled if words could, but their ejection from me left a hole that did bleed. I was blindingly, scorchingly angry, and so much of it was for Landon. "I was going to tell you that night that my name is *Zela*! I was going to tell you everything because you deserved to know and I was willing to risk losing you if that was the price.

"I never hurt you, Landon. I sat beside your bed in the nurse's office and tried not to cry because it killed me that someone got to you and there was nothing I could do. That you would turn around and believe I was the bastard who attacked you—"

I broke off, trying to breathe, and Landon just stared at me.

"Make no mistake," I whispered. "It was you who betrayed me. I've known only cruelty from Zach since that day in the woods. I never got the chance to build a friendship strong enough with Cole and Michael that they would trust me, but you... you were my first crush and my first kiss and you hurt me when I would have never let anyone hurt you."

I jabbed his chest. I knew I wasn't strong enough to push him back, but he stumbled anyway. "You have a lot to make up for, Landon Foster, and you better fucking get to it before you lose me for good."

With that, I turned and stomped out. I slammed the door as hard as I could on his shocked face.

"YOU OKAY?"

"I'm fine!" I slammed my trunk a bit harder than necessary.

Adam tilted his head. He was spread out on his bed, homework on his lap. "Want to try that again? Maybe the next time will be more convincing."

I opened my trunk only to slam it again. "You know you boys are fucking infuriating!" I hated using the f-word, but one talk with Landon and I lost count of how many times I said that hated word.

"Mom tells me that at least once a week."

"Well, she's a bloody saint for dealing with four of you!"

He chuckled. "Going British now? You are pissed. You'll be cursing at me in Spanish next." Adam heaved himself off the bed and came around to my side. "Want to talk about it?"

I threw myself back against the trunk, struggling with my need to rage and my want to talk to my best friend. In the end, I went with the latter and decided to call Jordan later. She was the best person for a rant session about golden-eyed jackasses. She dealt with her fair share of jerks as well.

"Landon isn't just mad that he believed I was For All," I said after taking a steadying breath. "I think he's pissed he fell for me at all. Like Zeke was all some setup to trick him, but I truly had no clue he had feelings for me."

Sighing, Adam sank onto the floor. "You guys hooked up?"

I lowered my head. I never told Adam this part of the story. "We kissed. Once. But it was life-changing, Adam. I don't need to have kissed anyone else to know that. How can you kiss someone like that and then... do what he did?"

His fingers curled around mine. "This is not an excuse because there is none, but Landon's dealt with a lot of stuff because of his sexuality. Middle schoolers can be vicious as hell. Especially ones that don't think consequences apply to them."

"You knew he was bi?"

Adam nodded. "But it wasn't for me to tell."

"No, I know that." I dropped my head. "I just wish things had been different."

He squeezed my hand. "They can be different now. You haven't told me your plans for him. Are you going to give him a chance to apologize?"

"I expect him to apologize—repeatedly—but I don't know what I'll do with it. Not yet."

"That's okay. You don't have to decide right now."

Adam stood and went back to his homework. I watched him with an odd feeling stirring inside of me.

I decided what I was going to do. I knew before I walked into that gym and speaking to Landon only solidified it, but he would never know. Not until it was done.

Knock. Knock.

I waved Adam down. "I'll get it."

Tanner stood on the other side of our door. "Hey. You busy?"

"I'm about to start my homework. Want to join us?"

He shook his head. "Nico said you were spouting your math stuff at the tryouts, saying why I was doing so well. You've got this stuff figured and... I'll start practice tomorrow with the Elites... so if you could..." Tanner trailed off, flushing deeply.

I smiled at him, deciding to save him some misery. "If my math skills can help, I'm happy to share."

"Thanks, man. Let's go."

Darting back inside, I snagged my notebook and followed him out to the field. It wasn't empty this time of day, but we grabbed a spot toward the back. The grass swallowed the seat of my pants as I got comfortable.

"Run through your drills," I ordered. "Pretend our backpacks are the goal."

"Got it."

Tanner set our packs a few feet apart and began his drills. There was an intensity on his face that I wasn't used to seeing. He ran through a footwork drill that I didn't know how to critique—I wasn't a coach—but when he got down to kicking, I put pen to paper.

"So?" he said after getting a few kicks in. "What do you think?"

"T, you're really good." I cupped my hand over my eyes to peer at him. "You're only going to get better on the team."

"But..." Sweat dripped down his forehead. His jersey clung to his skin, sticking like the remnants of summer heat that had yet to be chased away by an autumn chill.

"But," I continued, "I did notice you're great at getting height but kicking at a low angle doesn't always work out."

He blew out a breath. "The straight shot. My brothers said I needed to work on that too."

"Try it out. I'll tell you if I pick up on anything."

Tanner practiced the shot over and over while my analytical mind whirled.

"You need to lock your ankle and kick with your foot at this degree." I lifted my leg to show him but he looked at me like I was crazy.

"Stop talking in geometry, man. Just tell me what to do."

"Hold on." I peeled myself off the ground and reached for his ankle. I adjusted it the way I wanted. "You want it like this. To remember, think of it like you need to hit the ball with your laces. Try it."

Tanner kicked and the ball shot through our backpacks like it had been wanting to do that the whole time.

I cheered and then made him do it again. We must have been talking, working, and calculating for a while before I finally noticed that we were attracting a crowd.

Tanner paused with his foot poised to strike when he realized I wasn't speaking. He twisted around to see our audience. "What?"

"What are you guys doing?" one of the boys asked.

"We're practicing."

"What was that you were saying about how to do a bending shot?"

"You have to kick the ball at an angle," I replied.

The boy looked around at his friends. "Do you guys want to practice with us?"

I recognized him. He was a C that Owen and Justin sometimes waved to when he passed by our table.

"Sure," Tanner said. "I need a real goal."

That was all it took for me to spend the rest of the afternoon talking angles and adjusting sweaty ankles. The boys were grateful and they clapped my back as they jogged off the field.

"Thanks, Zeke," one of them said. "See you tomorrow."

I blinked. Tomorrow? When did we make that plan?

Eventually, I dragged myself upstairs and started my homework. I had a lot on my plate, but soon, it would all come together.

TWO WEEKS PASSED IN a haze of schoolwork, studying, and training. I don't think I ever worked harder in my life, but it was paying off. Months of summer exercise and putting it to the test with battles had resulted in a body that was leaner. My grades had always been good, but now Dr. O'Quinn openly smiled when she handed back my test and papers. I don't know if she knew about the orientation disaster or if she thought my good grades were a reflection of her, but either way, I felt her pride.

"Excellent work as usual, Mr. Manning."

I put down my pencil to accept my essay. "Thank you, Dr. O'Quinn."

"I appreciated that you mapped out every step," she continued. "The college you want to go to, the courses you'll take, and the positions you'll apply for. You have given your future career the attention and planning it deserves and I have no doubt you'll go far."

My cheeks warmed as they always did when she took to heaping praise on me in front of the class. Our networking assignment was to write a detailed essay on what we wanted to do when we were older and how we would get there. I wasn't trying to be the teacher's pet—the movies I watched said that was a bad thing. Even so, getting less than an A was not an option.

Our teacher moved on. "Adam, I was similarly impressed with your plans for your father's company."

She handed out the final paper seconds before the bell signaled the end of the day. I was the first one up and headed for the door.

"Whoa. Where are you going?" Adam stopped me with a hand on my arm.

"I have to go upstairs and then I'm going to the library."

Nico pushed through us. "Again? But we can't go in there. Why don't we study together like we used to?"

I bit my lip. "I have one more library pass left. I battled for it. I have to use it."

His face fell.

"But we can study after dinner," I said quickly.

"Aren't you going for a run after dinner?" Adam asked.

"I can push it back." I inched toward the door. "After dinner?"

Nico nodded, his smile returning. "Cool."

I waved as I hurried out the door. The stairwell was packed with guys tramping off to their sports classes and I needed to pick up the pace if I was going to have enough time to change and make it to mine.

I topped the final landing and paused before the doors of the Elite Wing. I had been careful about avoiding them on their dorm floor but that was easy when they were locked up in their rooms. There was no avoiding them now.

Slipping through the double doors, my eyes fixed on her class and I made a beeline for it. My hand closed over the knob when I heard—

"Hey! What are you doing here?!"

I threw it open and darted inside. Mrs. Peterson jumped. Her pen went flying.

"Mr. Manning? What on earth are you doing?"

"I'm sorry, Mrs. Peterson," I said as Zach appeared in the window. "I didn't mean to scare you."

He narrowed his eyes when he met mine, but then they flicked up and noticed the teacher behind me. Just as quickly, he left.

"Do you need something?"

"I was hoping to see the sign-up sheet for the Archimedean Club."

"Oh, yes." Mrs. Peterson had nothing but a smile for me. She was such a kind woman, working with an arrogant bunch of jackholes. "Are you going to join again this year? You're eligible to join the team now."

She reached into her desk and pulled out a piece of paper. I read it before answering her. "Yes, I'm going to join," I replied as I honed in on one name. "I just need to know the spot I'll have to battle for."

She sighed. "I'm not a fan of academic clubs being a part of the battle system. As far as I see it, any student who wants to spend their free time furthering their education should be encouraged, but it's not up to me."

"It's alright, Mrs. Peterson. I'm willing to work hard for what I want."

"That is a great attitude." She put her arm around my shoulder and squeezed. She had no qualms about touching me. "I look forward to being your teacher once again, Zeke."

"Thank you." I handed the sheet back to her. "One more thing..."

She peered at me over her glasses as she returned to her desk. "Yes."

"What are the other clubs I can join? Fs are never eligible to put their names down, so they don't put the sign-up sheets in our wing."

"That's true. Oh, but there are so many you would be perfect for." She popped out of her seat. "Come with me. I'll show you."

Eyes latched on to me when I stepped outside. Some curious, one delighted, and one hostile. Zach stepped in front of me, blocking me in the doorway.

"What do you think—"

"Mr. Fields." I sensed Mrs. Peterson at my back. "Do you need something?"

His expression cleared so fast I thought I imagined his glare. "No, ma'am. Just saying hi to Zeke."

"I see. Well, you better get on to wrestling practice."

Zach inclined his head, the picture of respect. "Yes, ma'am."

He loped off, shooting me one last look, and Hunter ran up to take his place. "Hey, Zeke. What are you doing here?"

"Just checking out the clubs, but I can't talk right now. I have to get to basketball practice too."

"Okay," he said, but he stuck with us as Mrs. Peterson led me down the hall to a bulletin board. Almost every inch of the green butcher paper was covered by flyers, sheets, and decorations. The academy offered way more clubs than I knew about, all with different requirements to sign up, and none that mentioned Fs.

"What do you think of the Future Leaders Club?" Mrs. Peterson suggested. "Or Key Club? With your math skills, you could easily be an engineer..."

I let her words fade in the background as I pulled out my notebook. I wrote the names of three clubs in the margins of my basketball math research.

"Thank you, Mrs. Peterson," I said. "I have to get to class, but I'm going to look into all of this." I backed away.

"Of course, Zeke. I hope to see you soon."

I tossed Hunter a wave and then booked it to the gym. I slid onto the bleachers moments before Coach blew his whistle.

"Cutting it close, Zee," Adam whispered out of the corner of his mouth. "I know you're planning things with your insane mathematical efficiency, but you're taking on a lot. Let me help."

"Adam." I kept my voice low as Coach launched into the drills for today. "Planning is over. It's time to act and most of this I have to do myself, but trust me, you are helping."

"But, Z—"

"Moon! Manning!" We jerked at Coach's bark. "Is there something you want to share with the rest of us?"

"No, Coach," I said.

"Then shut it."

We shut it and basketball practice got underway. After our game, I went back to the dorm to freshen up, grab my homework, and my last library pass. Tucked within the folds of my binder was my notebook and the next steps I would have to take.

The library was quieter than libraries tended to be when I walked in. The low murmur of voices flowed through the space like a soft hum most days, but today the place was almost empty.

Mrs. Durham gave me her customary pinched-lip stare when I handed over my pass. She never spoke to me, but I got the feeling she would be happy when her world wasn't being disturbed by F intruders.

I took my things to a table near the computer stations and pulled out my homework. I was halfway through my

English assignment when the door flew open. Cole, Michael, and Landon breezed in on a wave of cologne. I knew because I parked myself directly in front of their usual table.

I looked up as they passed by and met Landon's gaze—for all of two milliseconds before his jaw stiffened and he looked away. Cole pretended not to see me at all and Michael gave me a look I couldn't decipher.

I dropped my eyes to my home screen as they took their seats, but every now and then, I'd glance up and look at Landon. The other boys had their backs to me, but him I could see clearly.

There was a fine stubble along his chin. Landon was always clean-shaven, hair perfectly styled, uniform clean and ironed, so the presence of those tiny black hairs was having a strange effect on me.

He must have been rushing this morning—hurrying into his singlet to roll around on the mat. His muscles bulging as he put his arms around someone else and brought them down. Pressing down on me—I mean, them—as he secured their wrists above their heads.

Landon absentmindedly rubbed his chin and I gulped. I couldn't help thinking what it would feel like to rub my hands against his cheek and feel the prickling sensation of his—

Suddenly, his eyes flicked up and he looked at me. I stiffened at being caught, but I fought the impulse to drop my gaze.

Landon's eyes were steel gray like the sky before a storm. It was the perfect color for him. His face conveyed so many raging emotions as he met my eyes. I could see the battle was raging, I just didn't know which side was winning.

I turned my head toward the stacks, and then looked back at him. Clearing my throat, I closed my textbook and rose from my seat.

I ran my fingers along the spines as I moved through the bookshelves. I did not stop until I reached the books at the very back. I did need a book that I couldn't remember at that moment.

Was it for English or networking? Did O'Quinn assign homework for networking? What section am I in anyway?

My vision cleared to the sight of history tomes.

Wouldn't hurt to check these out while I've still got a library pass. Maybe my next battles will be for that subject.

I reached for a comparative history book and a hand closed over my wrist.

"You should have told me."

I held still, not daring to turn around. "I wanted to. I would have."

"Your reasons for hiding it don't make any sense. Why would you need to pretend to be a boy for your mother to let you go to school here?"

I decided on the simple version. "My mom is writing a book on female empowerment and unequal treatment between the sexes. Mom thought she and I could learn something from entering a separated school as a boy."

"So this was a twisted experiment!" he hissed.

"It wasn't—"

Landon spun me around and I stumbled, falling onto his chest. My nose buried in the folds of his blazer and his heady scent of rosewood soap filled my nose and went straight to my head. My heart picked up speed. Landon must have felt the fluttering of my pulse in my wrist.

For fuck's sake, Zela! Focus!

"Am I in her book too?" Landon continued, seemingly unaware of the effect he was having on me. "Is there a chapter on playing guys like fools? Huh? Or maybe—"

A flash of anger surged through me. I tore my hand free. "Or maybe it had *nothing* to do with you," I hissed, holding back a shout. "There isn't a chapter about playing guys but there is one on the fact that you never listen!"

That probably wasn't true but it silenced him. He snapped his mouth shut and his stubble jaw ticced.

I took a deep breath. We couldn't keep fighting or we would attract the librarian. I'm sure she would love a reason to kick me out.

When I spoke, my tone was much softer. "I'm not going to do this with you anymore, Landon. I told you the truth."

He threw up his hands. "How am I supposed to believe you?" Landon's voice wasn't nearly as soft as mine. "I thought that you were— That you—"

He shoved away, turning his back on me. He didn't say anything for a while. So long, I lifted my hand and touched his back.

"You were the first guy I ever tried to be with," he whispered, "and you weren't even a guy. You have no idea what it took for me to kiss you."

My hand traveled across his back and gripped his arm. I made him face me. The battle raged within his eyes, and although I didn't know which side was winning, I knew it was tearing him apart.

"You know what makes you a great wrestler," I began.

He blinked. I could hear the "What is she talking about?" go through his mind like he said it out loud.

"You never give up." My eyes moved down and I didn't hold myself back anymore. I pressed my hand to his cheek, feeling the stubble press into my palm. Goose bumps popped all over my skin. I held my breath as I waited for him to pull away.

He didn't.

"No matter what's holding you down," I continued, "you keep fighting until you get to the top. Your stubbornness is one of the things I like about you." I stroked his cheek, heady on what he was letting me get away with. "But right now... it's making you act like a complete idiot."

Landon made a choked noise. "What?"

My gaze sharpened. "I told you I was framed, Landon, and that should have been easy for you to believe. You know exactly who would hate me enough to try to get me kicked out of school. You know who would be angry enough at *you* for training me when he was using you to bring me down."

Landon's jaw went slack beneath my palm. "C-Cameron?"

I nodded.

"But— But he— My contacts. Michael and Cole and the Elites. Why would he do that to—"

"Why would he take advantage of weaknesses to get what he wants? Who knows? It's just so unlike him." I loaded that with a heavy dose of sarcasm and he winced.

He said nothing for a moment. We gazed at each other as my hand continued to stroke his cheek, almost on autopilot. I broke out of my trance when he reached up and curled his fingers around mine.

His eyes weren't stormy now. They were clear—serious. "How am I supposed to know you're telling the truth?"

I tugged until my hand slipped free, then I backed away. "You don't, Landon. You can't fight me on this one. You can't keep pushing ahead until you win. You just have to let go... and trust me."

I reached behind me, pulled the book I wanted off the shelf, and walked away, leaving him standing among the tomes.

Cole's and Michael's eyes followed me out of the library, but this time I avoided them. I hurried out with five hours left on my pass. Someone grabbed my arm.

"Wow. Chill, man. It's only me." Tanner straightened me and then let go. "It's lucky you came out. We were about to risk detention busting in there looking for you."

"We?" I twisted around and got a good look at "we." Four guys from my class nodded at me. "What's up, guys?"

"Here's the thing," Tanner said. "I did what you taught me during practice and Coach went on about how I improved my straight shot and that the other guys needed to work as hard as me. They asked me how I did it and I said it was all you." He flashed me a chipped-tooth, but endearing smile. "So..."

I didn't need to ask where he was going with this. "So... you want me to practice with you again," I finished.

He pointed over my head. "With all of us. I told them you were a good guy and would be down to help. What do you think?"

I glanced at my watch. "When do you want to practice?"

"After dinner."

I shook my head. "I'm studying with Nico after dinner."

"Before dinner, then," he said quickly. "Or now. Or tomorrow morning. Please, dude. Coach barely talks up anyone other than the Elites. One practice with you and I impressed him. You're my secret weapon."

I smiled despite myself. He was laying it on plenty thick but I got it. It was rare for Fs to be acknowledged. This was his chance to be one of the best and that mattered a lot in a place like this.

I looked down at my watch again. *I could do an hour or two with Tanner and the guys. After I start my homework, have dinner, and then finish the rest with Nico. I can make this work.*

"Okay," I said, "but only for an—"

"Yes! Guys, he said yes." Tanner threw his arm around my shoulder and dragged me off to the field. Like always, it wasn't empty. A couple of boys from the Elite Class were kicking the ball around.

Sullivan was the first to spot me. He pulled up short and Rhys's kick went sailing over his head. Sullivan pointed me out and the next thing I knew Jose, Rhys, Wyatt, and Sullivan had stopped what they were doing to stare me down as we walked past for the other goal.

"Fuck them," Tanner said under his breath. "We all know you didn't do it."

My head snapped up. "Know I didn't do it? Do what?"

"There's no way you're For All."

My eyes flared. "You know about that?"

Tanner snorted. "Everyone knows about that, Zeke. All those Evergreen silver-spoon babies are friends with each other. They tell each other everything and eventually it spreads to us Chesterfield kids. They think you attacked them and got away with it, but that's not your style."

"It's not?"

"Nope. You face people head on." There wasn't a trace of uncertainty in his voice. "When you wanted that Cameron shit to back off, you challenged him to a battle even if it meant dropping out of school. You're not afraid to stand up for yourself. Sneaking around in the shadows isn't what you would do."

I wasn't sure what to say to that. I liked Tanner. We hung out, studied together, cursed being Fs together, but Nico was his best friend, not me. It wasn't until now that I sensed that he may be more perceptive than I gave him credit for.

"Thanks, T," I finally said.

"Uh-huh." He dropped his hand and jogged onto the field. Our bonding moment was over. "Come on, Zeke. I'm working on bicycle kicks today."

"I still need help with the straight kick," one of the other guys said.

"Coach says I have to practice my corner kick," said another one.

I held up my hands. "Okay, okay. One at a time." I set my things down on the grass and pulled out my notebook. "Let's run through the straight kick first."

What was supposed to be a one-hour practice turned into three before I knew it. The setting sun, and my grumbling stomach, eventually clued me in to the fact that I had gone way over time.

I stood and dusted the grass from my backside. "I'm starving, guys. Let's call it for today."

Tanner wiped his sweaty forehead on his sleeve. "Cool with me."

We packed it up and filed out once again to an audience. The Elites were still there, but at some point, they had moved from the field to the bleachers, silently watching us practice. I tried not to look at them as I headed for the cafeteria.

My timing was good. I reached the dining room just as Adam stepped into the line and pulled a tray.

"Hey, Adam."

He saw me and picked up another one, handing it to me. "Hey. It's your favorite today. Baked spaghetti."

"Finally. Good news."

He laughed. "How was studying?"

"There was precious little of that. I helped some of the boys in our class with their game."

"That was cool of you. We can finish our homework together after this."

I followed behind him, holding up my tray for goodies as we went. "I'll have to."

"I was much more productive than you," he said. "I doled out a few more challenges. I'll make them official tomorrow."

"Great." I attempted to reach for my notebook one-handed. "Who was it? I'll cross their names off and challenge the others to—"

My tray wobbled and a hand flashed out before I could yelp. Adam caught my food with a chuckle. "Put your plans for domination on hold for a minute, yeah?"

I giggled. "I guess it could keep until I get to the table."

"Want to get out of the way?" a voice snapped.

Jerking, I spun on Cole. His eyes narrowed into slits. "Move."

I bristled. "You—"

"You have to work on that attitude, Reed," Adam said in a voice that was almost friendly. "Isn't that what Coach Nelson said? Or you'll never be swim team captain."

Bright spots of color stained Cole's cheeks. "And you think you will, Moon? Coach will never pick your lazy ass. At the end of the day, it's the one who wants it the most that will win."

Adam said something back, but I didn't hear it as I glanced over his shoulder at Landon. I couldn't read his expression as he gazed at me. I had no way of knowing if the battle raged on.

Not unless he talks to me. Say something, Landon. Tell me you believe me.

A hand gripped my shoulder and dragged me away. Probably a good thing, Cole looked ready to blow. We got our dessert and stepped off the line. I turned to walk to our table and Landon caught my eye. I stopped dead when he stepped forward.

"Oh, Zee," someone said, but it wasn't him. Landon paused as Adam came to my side. "You have something. Let me get it."

"What?"

Adam's fingers tangled in my hair and pulled something free. He held the blade of grass up to me and I chuckled. "How did I get so messy and I wasn't even the one playing?" I looked down at my uniform. "I must be covered in grass and dirt."

"No, you're good. Here." He flicked my nose, making me giggle, and then gently brushed off my left cheek. "There. Perfect."

"Thanks," I called as he continued on. I turned back to Landon and my smile faded. The vein in his jaw was throbbing hardcore now. He looked from me to Adam's retreating back, and in that second, I realized he made a choice.

Landon stepped back in line. He, Michael, and Cole got their dinner without sparing me another glance.

Chapter Five

"Zeke? Zeke? Zeke!"

I shot up, eyes tearing open. The momentum knocked me off-balance and I fell off the bench and hit the pavement face-first.

"Ow."

Hands grabbed me under the arm and lifted. Nico and Tanner dusted me off. "Dude, you fell asleep."

"No, I didn't."

Tanner gave me a look. "There's a puddle of drool on that bench."

I flushed hot. "There is not," I snapped. Tanner's raised brow told me I did so with more force than was necessary. "Sorry," I said in a better tone.

I pressed the heel of my palms to my eyes and willed myself not to be tired. "I might have closed my eyes for a second, but I was up till three in the morning studying."

"Studying for what?" Nico asked. "We did all of our homework before dinner."

I shook my head. "I have two battles today for a spot in the Future Leaders Club and the Science Club. Tomorrow, it's the Archimedean Club. This is the final week to join, so if I get in, I'm in for good."

"Zeke, why are you doing this? I get the math club, but you've never said a thing about wanting to be in those other clubs before."

"I have to step up my game this year," I said simply.

Tanner shoved me. It wasn't hard, but I almost ended up on my face again. "You can't even stay upright," he deadpanned.

"I can when people aren't scaring and shoving me!"

The boys laughed. "Let's go, Zeke. They're serving pancakes today."

"Chocolate chip," Nico added.

I perked up. I was committed to my new healthy way of life to the point of opting for salads and fruit for my meals, but I hadn't kicked my love of pancakes yet and I didn't plan to.

"I'm coming," I called after them. I quickly peeled off my damp track shirt and put it in my gym bag. Going to bed at three meant I only got three hours of sleep. I had to wake up at six this morning to shower and get on the track after Michael's usual time, but three hours last night was better than the two I got the nights before.

It's embarrassing being found passed out on a bench but it will all be worth it. These last few weeks won't have been for nothing.

The first month of school was nearing its end and every day brought me closer to putting my plans into action.

Most of our friends were seated when the three of us sat down, except for Derek. I found him with his breakfast buddies giggling near the front table. On the plus side, I'd get to keep my chocolate chip pancakes, but on the other, it had been a while since we hung out. All my running, training, and studying didn't leave a lot of time for chilling in Derek's room reading books.

"Guys." Owen nudged me. "Check it out."

I followed his gaze to the door. Cameron and a girl I had seen around the cafeteria a few times grabbed the knobs and pulled open the double doors. A hush fell on the room as the principal, vice principal, Miss Val, and a couple of the teachers streamed in.

"Another announcement," Adam said.

Melody spoke up from his other side. "But we know what it's about."

No one denied it.

"Morning, students. Attention."

I cut my pancakes into two, four, eight pieces. The task didn't distract me enough to prevent me from hearing what he was saying.

"Tomorrow morning, members of the board of education will be arriving to tour the school," Whittaker announced. He pointed to the students on either side of him. "They will be escorted by members of staff and our two student representatives: Cameron Dupre and Macy Long."

I peeked at them through my lashes. Both students smiled pleasantly at the crowd, the image of intelligence, handsomeness, and perfection Whittaker wanted associated with this school. So far, Cameron had been just that. I hadn't dealt with him or his friends in weeks. None of them so much as looked in my direction.

"The board members will be our guests for the week," Whittaker went on. "They need time to sit in on the classes, speak with the staff, and get to know all of you. It goes without saying that you will be on your best behavior this week. If you're thinking of testing me on this, know that any infractions made during their stay will carry double the penalty.

"Tardiness will result in two detentions, not one. Disrespecting your teacher will grant you a punishment of two weeks of no privileges. Is that understood?"

"Yes, Principal Whittaker," we chorused.

He nodded sharply. "Although, I'm certain we will have no problems. You are good, talented, hardworking students and you strive for excellence in the Breakbattle way. Let's be sure the board sees that. We will revolutionize the education system in this state, and one day, the entire nation."

"Whoo!" The Elites kicked it off and cheers went up around the room. My table didn't join in.

"Now what?" Nico asked. "If the members are being stalked by the Elites, they'll make sure they only see and hear the good stuff."

"And rat us out if we try to tell them what this place is really like," Tanner added. "Not to mention O'Quinn would be more than happy to load us up with double the detention if we piss her off."

I thought as I chewed a piece of sweet, fluffy pancake. "Maybe we won't have to risk detention," I said. "If they're staying here and walking all over the place. They'll see the state of the F dorms, how stuffed our classes are, and that we're kept out of everything unless we battle for it. They'll see for themselves this system is too harsh."

"We can't risk that."

All eyes flew to Melody. She dabbed the corners of her mouth and neatly folded her napkin. "F students still get everything they require to pass and no more. The board members might see that as perfectly acceptable."

"So what do we do?" asked Owen.

"I know exactly what to do." She pushed back her chair. "But I can't say it here. I'm sending a text to everyone in the group tonight with instructions."

Melody walked over to another table, probably to tell them the same thing. I didn't bother to listen to the rest of Whittaker's speech after that.

The boys and I packed it up and headed to class. We arrived at the door the same time the teachers, staff, and principals were filing out. Miss Val paused to kiss Adam's cheek. Cameron stopped to throw me a wink.

"He's been more smug than usual," Adam said under his breath as he returned to my side.

"Who? Cameron?"

He nodded. "Something's up."

"I don't like the sound of that."

Dr. O'Quinn stood at attention in front of her desk as she did every morning. "Hello, boys. Take your seats and read silently to yourselves as we wait for the class to begin. Oh, and, Zeke?"

I stopped and let the others go on ahead of me. "Yes, Dr. O'Quinn."

She smiled. The wide-toothed grin looked out of place among her loose, gray pantsuit, tight bun, and piercing eyes, but it was a pleasant one nonetheless.

"There is something I need to speak with you about after class. Don't let me forget."

"Yes, ma'am."

I sat down and pulled out the book she assigned us for English homework. The class slowly filled up as I read and wrote notes.

"Alright, class," O'Quinn announced. "A few announcements to begin our day."

The boys quickly settled down.

"First, Career Day will be held next week." She clasped her hands in front of her. "People from the community will be coming in to speak with you. Their goal is to tell you more about their jobs and the paths they took to get to where you hope to be."

She reached behind her and picked up a stack of papers. "This is why I had you do those essays. I wanted you to truly think about where you're headed." She held up the papers. "This is a list of attendees. Make note of who is coming and write down a few questions to ask them."

O'Quinn stepped forward and began passing around the sheets. I took mine and scanned it with interest. My networking essay detailed how I wanted to major in mathematics and then go on to become a professor. I wanted to teach others to love math the way Mom did with me, but also have the support and funding to do my own research.

The list was broken down by name, field, and which company or organization the attendee worked for. I immediately circled the three working in mathematics.

My pencil froze over a name.

Ryder Shea (Construction) – CEO of Shea Industries

Adam's dad is coming too. I wonder if his other dads...

I found their names right away.

Ezra Lennox (Media) – News Reporter

Jaxson Van Zandt (Music Industry) – Owner/Producer of Interstellar Records

Maverick Beaumont (Technology) – CEO of Maverick Technology

All of Adam's dads were coming. I would have to stop by and say hi.

My eyes drifted down to another name three below Maverick Beaumont.

Dominic Dupre (Finance) – CEO of Dupre Financial Holdings

Cameron's father.

I hesitated for one more second and then circled his name.

"Okay, class." O'Quinn's voice dragged my attention away. "As you've heard, members of the state board of education will be staying with us this week. What you may not know is the F Wing will be their first port of call."

Whispers broke out until a look from her quieted the room.

"They will spend part of their time tomorrow observing us," she continued. "We'll carry on with class as normal, but the last ten minutes of the block will be spent answering any questions they may have. Understood?"

"Yes, Dr. O'Quinn."

"Final announcement," she went on. "There will be a fall dance next month held in the wrestling gym. It will be coed."

A brave soul whistled.

O'Quinn's head snapped around. "Gary Marsh! Outside now!"

Marsh trudged out, mumbling inaudibly under his breath.

O'Quinn sniffed. "As I was saying, the dance is for both campuses, but unfortunately, not open to every student. Ds and Fs who wish to attend must battle for the privilege."

"Sounds about right," Nico mumbled behind me.

"That's it for now." Our teacher peeled herself off the desk and moved around to the chalkboard. "Let's see if you did the reading."

CLASS PASSED IN A BLUR of textbooks, chalk dust, and stern looks from Dr. O'Quinn. I went up to her desk after the bell sounded for lunch.

"You wanted to speak to me, Dr. O'Quinn?"

"Ah, yes." She put down the eraser and turned to me with a smile. "It's about Career Day."

"Yes?"

"What we do every year is allow a few students to volunteer with the set up and break down of the event. Students enjoy this because it's five volunteer hours toward graduation and they tend to snag some one-on-one time with the attendees. There are spots for two F students and I would like you to be one of them. What do you say?"

"I would love that," I replied. I didn't have to think about it. "Thank you, ma'am."

"Perfect. I'll let Vice Principal Argyle know."

I waved goodbye and then ran to catch up with Adam and the guys.

The end of the school day saw me back in front of O'Quinn's desk waiting for Will Strup and his teacher to arrive. Will was a C and member of the Science Club. I watched him in other battles, and even though he always picked wrestling and tended to win, he favored the same moves. My research also included speaking to Justin and he told me Spanish was Will's weakest class. It felt a tad wrong to challenge him in a language I was fluent in, but after Will, I had my first battle with an A and I needed this to be easy.

Only Elites and As could sign up for the Future Leaders Club and I *needed* into that club. As may not be on the same level as the Elites I battled, but they were still plenty tough to beat.

Wincing, I pressed my fingers to my temples. A dull, persistent ache pounded behind my eyes. If I was honest, the headache cropped up days ago and never really went away.

It's because of all the late nights, I thought. *I just have to get through the week, get into the clubs, then I'll go home on Friday and pass out for two days.*

"Zeke? Are you alright?"

I dropped my hand. "I'm fine, ma'am. It's only a headache."

She tutted as she pressed her palm to my forehead. "You're not warm, but if you're not feeling well after the battles, I want you to see the nurse. You've been looking quite pale lately."

"Okay, I will."

The door swung open. Will and his teacher walked in. I took my seat and he claimed the one next to me, shooting me a poisonous glare on the way. My battle sprees had the whole school talking. My wins against the upper classes had their jaws on the floor. My choosing Will as my next opponent had him in a mood. He demanded I take the challenge back four times before I told him to either accept or take his ten points off.

He threw himself down as O'Quinn rattled off the instructions.

The academic test was as easy as I knew it would be. We were given a set of sentences to translate from English to Spanish, then another set to translate from Spanish to English. I was done with twenty minutes to spare. Will took the whole time.

O'Quinn collected the tests and the four of us headed out. My wrestling clothes were beneath my uniform, so I was in and out of the bathroom in minutes, ready to go. Will came out and gave me a baleful look as he stepped onto the mat.

I didn't understand his attitude. Battles were a part of our life. What made a challenge from me any worse than one from a D?

"You boys know the rules," Coach Franklin began. His muscles rippled beneath his skintight shirt, making him look more intimidating than he already was. "I want a clean match. Step up. Shake hands."

Will gripped my hand tighter than necessary. "I know what you're doing," he hissed.

I scrunched up my face. "What?"

"It's not going to work, F," he went on like I hadn't spoken. "Your fucking crusade ends today. I'm not losing to you."

My jaw slackened. *Crusade? How did he know?*

Coach blew his whistle and we got into position. Will came at me fast at the first opportunity, but I dove out of the way. This was his game plan. He went in hard, coming at his opponent from every angle until they eventually tripped up.

Will lunged at me again and I twisted in a near imitation of a pirouette. It was fitting. Wrestling was like dancing. I got behind him and wrapped my arms around Will's middle in an embrace and pulled him close. He let out a soft grunt as I swiftly brought him to his knees and laid him out flat on the mat. Coach awarded the first points of the game to me.

Thirty minutes later, I walked out of the gym the winner and Will walked out with his middle fingers in the air. "Fuck you, F!"

"Nice guy," I muttered.

O'Quinn shook hands with Coach Franklin and then came over to me. "Well done, Zeke. You've earned your place in the Science Club. One more battle, and then you'll get some rest." She leveled me with the steely-eyed stare she reserved for the rest of my class. "I mean it. You have class and another battle tomorrow. I want you fresh and ready to go."

"I will be very fresh, ma'am."

She led the way to the classroom. Mason Prescott and his teacher were waiting outside the door when we arrived. There was no glare when he met my eyes. His gaze slid away as though I was wholly uninteresting.

We went inside and sat down to another Spanish test. This time we had to read a short passage and answer questions.

"On hot days the temperatures could skyrocket as high as one hundred and... three degrees... on hot days..."

The sentence blurred. I squeezed my eyes shut and rubbed them with the tips of my fingers.

Focus, Zela. We're almost done.

I shook myself and opened my eyes. I wrote the final sentence seconds before the teachers called time.

Back outside I went, but my destination was the basketball courts. Mason loped next to me, hands in his pockets, expression relaxed.

"You look confident."

I glanced around. "Who? Me?"

The corner of his mouth crooked in a smile. "You think you have this sewn up."

Mason was an attractive guy. In a normal school, he might have been the best looking, but stacked against unnaturally beautiful beings like Cole, Michael, Landon, Derek, and Adam, he bordered on average. Everything except for the soft, sweet-smelling mop of curls on his head. It was his best feature, and it was clear he took good care of it.

"I think I could curl up in your hair and take a nap right now," I replied, "but that's about it."

He barked a laugh. "Everyone says you're a weird guy."

"Do they?"

"Yep. You sneak around with your little notebook, analyze our weaknesses, and use it to give yourself a leg up in battles."

I shrugged. O'Quinn and Mr. Howard walked ahead of us, oblivious to our conversation. "It's not against the rules. If anything, Principal Whittaker would pat me on the back and congratulate me."

"It's not against the rules," he agreed. "It's obvious you never belonged in the F Class and you're coming for what should be yours. I respect that. But..." His voice became frosty. "Passing it on to your F friends so they can cheat their way on the teams and take spots that don't belong to them is not right."

I stopped dead. "What are you talking about? I didn't help anyone cheat."

He spun around and faced me. The friendly smile was nowhere to be found. "We've seen you with the other Fucks, telling them what to do to win. That's not how it works around here. If they want something, they battle for it."

The flames of irritation stoked by weariness surged through my body. "That's not how it works around here? Are you kidding me? All the classes stick together, back each other up, and freeze the others out. You think I haven't noticed that my table is the *only* one in the entire cafeteria with a mix of people from all classes.

"You work together. You practice together. You study together. And if you discovered a weakness in me, you wouldn't waste a minute in running your mouth to your friends." I lurched forward and got in his face. "Don't tell me how it works around here, Prescott. I know exactly how it works."

We glared at each other, nostrils flaring, chests heaving, until a shout tore my eyes away.

"Zeke! What's going on?"

"Nothing, ma'am. We're coming." I sidestepped him and jogged the rest of the way to the gym. Coach waited for us in the middle of the shining, maple floors.

"Welcome, gentlemen. Let's get started."

I changed in the bathroom. The stalls were a tight fit. I leaned against the cool plastic as I wiggled into my gym shorts. I pulled my pants over my waist and wobbled. The dark blue barriers of the stall blurred and the world tilted.

Bang!

I cried out as my head smacked into the door. It wasn't the world tilting, it was me. Righting myself, I went out, splashed some cold water on my face, and came out to find Mason and Coach ready to go.

My vision centered on the ball and only the ball. I needed to win, get into the club, and make them pay.

Franklin tossed the ball up and we leaped. Mason soared over my head and caught it effortlessly. He smacked down and raced across the court before I could stop blinking. I never deluded myself into thinking this battle would be easier... and yet it was still harder than I thought.

Mason zipped up and down the court, sinking shot after shot. I was right on his heels—so close I breathed in his curious mix of sweat and cinnamon body spray. He jumped, hands poised to throw the ball, and I raced around him and knocked it out of the air.

I came down hard and my ankle gave out. Stumbling, I caught myself before I could hit the floor and dove for the ball. Then I was off.

Mason's shoes squeaked on the floor behind me. I skidded to a stop in front of my hoop and threw as his hand swiped across my vision.

"Wait for me!"

The mausoleum-white walls faded in a haze. People streamed around me, talking, laughing, carrying heavy shopping bags that hit me as I shoved through the crowd.

"It's me! Don't leave me!"

Pain exploded in my nose. A scream ripped from my throat and this time I couldn't stop my descent. I fell to the court in a chorus of whistles, shouts, and thundering footsteps. The last thing I saw before everything went dark was a bright red sign: "Holiday at the Chesterfield Mall."

"MR. MANNING? MR. MANNING, can you hear me? Mr. Manning?"

I cracked my eyes open and instantly regretted it. The harsh overhead lighting was a spike through my aching head.

I groaned. *Not just my head. Everything aches.*

"What... happened?" I slurred.

"What happened is the ball bounced off the hoop and hit you in the face," came a dry voice. "Why the hell didn't you move?"

"Quiet, Mr. Prescott," snapped O'Quinn. "I'm sure you have work to attend to. Off you go."

"O-off?" I got my hands under me and tried to sit up. Arms immediately came around me to help.

It took a minute for me to focus through the cloud of pain. My hands shook badly, visibly, and the thought came to me that I should hide them before someone noticed but the mere act of closing my fists felt impossible. My fingers twitched and I did not know if it was from the effort or the adrenaline-laced fear that rattled my bones.

It happened again. I was there. At the mall.

"Mr. Manning? Mr. Manning, are you alright?"

Why? Why again? I haven't been thinking about it. I haven't heard the voices.

I also haven't been sleeping, another voice countered. *I've been a wreck and... it finally caught up to me.*

My stomach heaved at the thought. No, this could not be my punishment. I couldn't do this anymore. What would it take to make that day disappear from my memory?

"Mr. Manning?"

Slowly, I was able to make out Coach Singh, Dr. O'Quinn, and Mason and his teacher as they walked away. It jerked me back to reality.

"Wait," I called. "Where are you going? What about the battle?"

"The battle is over for you, son." Coach Singh pointed. "Look at yourself."

I glanced down and almost had a heart attack. Red stained my shirt like a crime scene. I touched my fingers to my chin and it came away sticky with blood.

"I'm pretty sure it's broken," Singh continued. "We can't hold a battle when a student is injured."

"But..." I tried to think through the pain. "Who won?"

Coach shook his head. "No one won. It's called off. We'll have to reschedule the battle."

"But we can't," I cried. "The deadline to get into the Future Leaders Club is this week."

"You can worry about that later," said Dr. O'Quinn. "What you will do now is relax, wait for the nurse, and then go to your dorm to rest. You have my permission to turn your homework in a day late, but I want you taking it easy tonight. Do you understand me?"

Even as a denial rose to my lips, I knew there was no point fighting it. Mason was gone. The battle was off.

"Yes, ma'am," I said instead.

The nurse arrived minutes after they moved me to the bleachers. She clucked and tutted as she checked me out and then helped me to her office to load me up with painkillers and splint my nose.

People stared openmouthed in the halls as I left and headed for the dorms. I walked out of the main building and turned instead of going straight. My feet carried me six flights of stairs to the Elite floor.

Peeking through the window, I spotted a straggler in the hallway. When he disappeared into his room, I took my chance and hurried to Derek's door.

Knock. Knock.

"What the fuck do you want?! I'm trying to read!"

The sound of Derek's dulcet tones brought a smile to my face. I knocked again.

"Dammit, Hunter! Get off my teat!"

I stifled a giggle as I knocked one more time.

A string of foul curses accompanied the sounds of stomps. The door flew open, letting out a wave of pine air freshener and Derek.

"I said go..." Derek trailed off as he took me in.

I waved. "Hey. Sorry to bother you, but I've got an unexpectedly free afternoon and it has been a while since we hung out. Why don't we—"

"Who did this to you?"

The sentence fell from his tongue in such a threateningly low hiss, it made me back up a step. I never heard Derek speak in that tone before.

"What? Derek, no—"

"It was that shit Mason." The muscles in his jaw popped as he clenched his teeth hard enough to crack. "He's always pulling something dirty, catching players with his elbow, and tripping them up on the court." He surged out the door. "When I get my hands on him, I'll—!"

"No!" I grabbed him and got dragged along a few feet. "He didn't do this, Derek. He didn't touch me at all. I did it to myself."

He spun on me, mouth gaping. "What does that mean? Why?"

"It wasn't on purpose." I dropped my arm and made for his room. By his footsteps, I knew he was following. "The ball bounced back and hit me in the face."

"How in the hell does that happen?!"

I toed off my shoes and climbed onto his bed. "I don't want to talk about it." Derek's sheets welcomed me like an old friend as I slipped beneath them.

"I'll tell you how it happens," he went on. "You're killing yourself with all these battles and it's finally caught up to you. Have you seen yourself, Zela? Even without the splint you look like microwaved death."

"You say the sweetest things to me."

"Well, it's enough." Derek marched up to me, and instead of shoving me out of his bed like I expected, he grabbed the covers and brought it up to my chin. "You're going to get some sleep."

"It's five o'clock in the afternoon."

"Shut up." He sat down on his side and reached for the book he abandoned on the nightstand. "Go to sleep."

"Why are you letting me sleep here?"

"Because your stubborn ass won't do it unless I'm watching you."

I rolled my eyes, but stopped fighting it. At least we were finally spending time together. I reached into my pocket and pulled out my phone. There was something I needed to do before I obeyed orders.

Me: I broke my nose and ended up with bandages covering most of my face. I hope it wasn't my looks that you liked about me.

His reply came back in seconds.

Landon: Stop texting me.

Me: If you wanted it to stop, you would have blocked me by now.

Yes, I had been texting Landon. The guy had given me no choice after opting to give me the silent treatment since that day on the food line. I still had his number from when we were friends and I sent him random, cute messages throughout the day. Most of the time he didn't answer. The other times he told me to stop. What he didn't do was block me.

Me: I won my wrestling match because of what you taught me. I never got a chance to properly thank you for

training me. Can you think of any ways you want me to show my gratitude?

Landon: I can think of a few...

My brows shot up to my fake hairline. Oh my goodness. Was he flirting back? What do I say?! I've never done this before.

Me: Tell me. Spare no details.

I bit down hard on my lip as I sent it. My eyes flicked up to Derek as though he could read my mind. The boy carried on reading his book.

Landon: I want you...

Landon: ... more than anything...

Landon: ... to...

I held my breath as I waited for the final text to buzz my phone. Want me to what? What, Landon?!

It buzzed again and I rushed to open the message.

Landon: Leave me the fuck alone.

My phone buzzed again as annoyance welled up in me. Landon was going to make me work for this.

I pulled up the message and saw it wasn't from him.

Melody: I promised you guys I would come up with a way to stop the expansion. As I see it, the board of education could never approve this system if they knew the truth about it. So we tell them.

Meet me tonight in front of the cafeteria. Midnight.

"What are you doing? I told you to go to sleep."

I sighed. "I am. My face hurts despite the painkillers and being unconscious would give me blessed relief from this headache. I just need to set an alarm."

"For what?"

"Melody wants to meet up tonight," I said as I set the clock for eleven forty-five. "She needs my help with something."

"Fine."

I finished and set my phone on the nightstand. Then I snuggled into Derek's pillow, warm and comfortable for the first time in days, maybe weeks. Despite the sun still peeking through the windows, I fell asleep moments after I closed my eyes.

BEEP. BEEP. BEEP.

Shifting, I cracked an eye open. The covers ended up over my head during the night. Derek stirred and his pajama-clad leg poked over to my side.

What was going on? Is that my alarm?

I shoved back the covers and morning light beat down on me.

"What the—?"

The noisy clock read seven a.m. What happened to my phone?

A groan sounded to my right.

"Derek?" I grabbed his shoulder and shook. "Derek, where is my phone?"

"It's in the drawer," he croaked.

"Why is it there? Why didn't my alarm go off?"

"I turned off the alarm when it went off at fucking midnight. You needed to sleep."

I gaped at the lump that was him. "But Melody was expecting me!"

"She'll get over it." He didn't sound even close to repentant.

"I was supposed to get some studying done for the battle today."

"You can stop complaining now and say thank you."

I huffed and flipped over. So what? My headache was gone and I felt a million times better than I did twenty-four hours ago, but still. I had a lot to do and no time to do it. I couldn't afford fourteen-hour semi-comas.

"Thank you," I muttered under my breath, barely above a whisper.

"You're welcome." The bed dipped as Derek climbed out. I heard him pad to the bathroom and then the shower turned on.

I didn't bother to wait until he came out. I got up and went downstairs to my dorm. Adam was awake and messing with his phone when I walked in.

"Hey," he said. "Where did you— What the hell happened to your face?!"

I winced. The bandage was an eyesore by itself but I was sure my face was purpling to go with it. "I was hit in the face with a basketball. It looks worse than it feels."

"You see why I hate that game?" he replied. "Wow. Is that why you were gone? Did you sleep in the nurse's office last night?"

"No, I slept in Derek's room," I said as I crossed to my trunk and took out fresh clothes.

"Oh."

Something about that "oh" made me look up. "What?"

"Zela... are we the kind of friends that I can ask if you two are hooking up?"

I laughed. "We're definitely those kinds of friends, dummy, and no. Derek and I are *not* hooking up."

"Are you sure?"

My giggles were louder and higher than they needed to be, but I was riding a wave of well-restedness. "I think I would know."

"Okay. I guess I believe you," he said, grinning. Adam glanced at his phone. "I have another question about the levels of our friendship."

"What is it?"

"Can I stay at your place this weekend?"

The chest snapped shut and almost caught my fingers. "What?"

He waved his phone. "Jordan says you guys are going to this fall festival thing and asked if I wanted to come. Your mom already said yes and my mom is cool with it too."

I blinked at him. "My mother? Andronika Manning? She said it was okay for you to sleep over at our house."

Adam shrugged. "Yeah. Why not? You stay over all the time."

"But when were you making these plans?" I asked. "How long have you had Jordan's number? Why am I the last to know?"

Adam hopped out of bed, dressed only in a pair of boxers. "Because you're always busy, my friend. So is that a yes?"

I shook my head. "I feel like for your sake I should say no. You've never dealt with all four of the Manning women for prolonged periods of time. There's a good chance you won't come out on the other side of this weekend."

He doubled over laughing.

"But I really want you to come," I continued, "so I'll be selfish and say yes."

"Cool, Zee." Adam swooped down and grabbed me around the middle. I shrieked as he lifted me up. "There's something else I need to know. Are you ticklish?"

"Adam, no! Don't you dare! Don't you—"

He attacked my sides until I was breathless from laughter. Eventually, I got free and we dressed and left for breakfast, messing around the whole way.

"Are we staying at your place or Jordan's?" Adam asked.

We passed through the doors of the dining room and the smell of sizzling bacon and cooked spices hit our nose. I about knocked a kid out of the way rushing up to the line. I hadn't swallowed a single bite of food in over fourteen hours. My stomach was pretty much eating itself at this point.

"It depends on my mom," I replied as Martha piled my plate high with scrambled eggs. "She may kick us out halfway through and we'll end up at Jordan's. She's got a hot tub, so that'll be fun."

"Hot tub?"

His voice stopped me cold. I froze with my tray held above my head.

"What's this about a hot tub? You can't go in one of those. Isn't exposing your body against your... beliefs?"

The hint of amusement in his tone made my skin crawl.

"You need to walk away, Zach," Adam growled. "Now."

"I just want to know—"

Adam disappeared from my side. "You don't want to piss me off," he said in a tone I never heard before. "Walk away. Now."

"The fuck is wrong with you?" Zach yelled. "I was only joking!"

Despite that, I heard him storm off. When he was gone, I lowered my tray and kept going. Our mood was more subdued as we found our table. I felt Adam's eyes on me and thought of a change of subject.

"I missed it last night," I said. "Did you meet with Melody?"

"Oh, yeah." His expression morphed from concerned to furtive in a blink. "About ten of us met up and Melody had us"—he glanced around—"I can't talk about it here, but you'll see. The board is going to see a whole new side of Breakbattle."

I leaned in, lowering my voice. "I'm sorry I wasn't there. Derek sabotaged me and I slipped into a coma."

"You say the strangest things like they're normal."

"But I'm all in. I'm using the battle system to my advantage right now, but I want it dismantled as much as anyone. I've seen firsthand how it's used to bully students and make lives harder. It should have been done away with after Becca Taylor."

My thigh vibrated with a text. I pulled back to answer it.

Landon: You and Moon look cozy.

I frowned. I read it once, then twice, then a third time. What is this? Code?

Looking up, I scanned the cafeteria and found their table near the front. Landon's light-colored eyes bore into me through the sea of bodies.

Me: What are you talking about?

His reply came milliseconds after I hit send.

Landon: If you're with him, just tell me.

My jaw dropped.

Landon: I don't care if you are.

Landon: But it's not cool for you to keep flirting with me.

Landon: You can't keep texting me, Zela.

Landon: Just tell me if you're with him!

I was genuinely too stunned to respond to the avalanche of texts. How in the world did this guy get it into his head I was dating Adam?

"Adam," I whispered.

"What's up?"

"I think Landon... is jealous."

"Jealous of what?"

"Of us." My lips barely moved as I met Landon's furious eyes again. So that was what the look he had been giving me for weeks meant. He was jealous.

"Us?"

"He thinks we're dating."

Adam snorted. "And here I was thinking my feelings for Melody were blindingly obvious." I saw him look in Landon's direction out of the corner of my eye. "Are you going to put him out of his misery?"

A smirk tried to appear on my lips, but I bit it back. Landon was still watching.

"No, I'm not." I put my phone on silent and set it on my lap. "I can work with this."

"You want to make him jealous?" Adam flicked from Landon to me. "And... you want me to help," he said slowly.

I reached for my fork and speared a bit of egg. "If you don't mind."

"I don't but how far are you going to take this?"

I gazed into Landon's angry eyes and smiled. "As far as it takes. I told you, Adam. He made me think he liked me, stole my first kiss, and then watched as I was beaten. I'm going to win him back... and then I will blend his heart like a smoothie."

"A disturbing image."

My eyes traveled to Cole next. He had a fork in one hand and a textbook in the other. "Then there's Reed," I whispered. "So obsessed with being on top. Everything he wants, everything he works for, I'm going to take it from him. Top GPA, captain of Archimedean Club, president of the Future Leaders. He will spend the next three years of his life as second best. And then, Michael."

The tawny Adonis sat next to his best friend, eating his yogurt like he had no worries. "For him, I'm going to take away the only thing he cares about."

"And Zach and Cameron?" Adam asked. "You never told me what you were going to do to those two."

My eyes narrowed into slits when they found Zach and Shannon making out at the Elite table. "I have something very special planned for Zach... but it'll have to wait until I can stomach the sight of him."

"What about Cameron?"

"Cameron is tricky," I said after a pause. "Everything I thought of didn't feel like nearly enough after what he did to me. I'm not sure yet what I'll do to Cameron Dupre, but this is like math. Solutions can't be rushed. When the time is right, I'll know."

"And I'll back you up."

"You're a good friend, Adam." I reached under the table and squeezed his arm. "Thank you."

We finally tore into our breakfast. Melody showed up at our table partway through me inhaling my scrambled eggs.

"Guys, they're here," she said without preamble. "Whittaker, Argyle, Dupre, and Macy are giving them the tour right now." The intensity in her gaze told me better than anything that something was up. "They're starting with the boys' side first. You should get there before them."

"They're going to freak," said Adam.

"That's the plan." Melody moved off to another table before I could get any questioning in.

"Will I find out what's going on soon?" I asked Adam.

"Very soon."

I accepted that and finished my food. Twenty minutes later, the warning bell rang and we picked up our trays and made for the F Wing.

"Hey, Manning. Manning!"

"You guys go ahead," I said to Tanner, Nico, and Adam. I turned around as a guy I never spoke to before ran up to me. "Yes?"

"You're Manning, right? You're the guy?"

"Yeah. I'm Zeke Manning."

He broke into a huge smile that compounded my confusion. "Awesome. I'm Noah Prentiss. Look, I don't know how it works but I can pay. I'm seeing this girl in the C Class and I want to take her to the dance."

I stared at him as a string of words I didn't understand poured out of his mouth.

"But I'm in D, so I can't go," he continued. "I was going to battle every guy in the C Class if that's what it took, but then I heard about you."

"About... me?" I repeated.

His head bobbed excitedly. "You've been training the Fs to get on their teams. You're good because you use your crazy math skills to figure out how to take the higher classmen down, and that's why you've been dominating in battles." He thrust his fist at me. "That's wicked cool, man."

I bumped the outstretched hand because I didn't know what else to do.

"They're calling you the Battle Doctor."

"They're doing what?"

"And you're exactly what I need," he went on. "Tell me which C to pick and how to beat him and I'll pay you whatever you want."

"Okay, wait." I put up my hands. "Hold on. I don't—"

"Don't what?"

"I don't— don't— I don't do what you're saying," I burst out. "I battle a few people to get more studying and practice time, and yes, I helped a few friends with their soccer game, but I don't go around picking the weakest member of the herd and offering them up for sale."

His face fell. "Are you serious? Manning, come on."

"I have to get to class." I gave him my back and made to walk off. A hand on my arm stopped me.

"Please. I really like her and we never get to do anything together. Her parents won't let her date and there's this stupid separate campus stuff. I just want to take her to the dance."

I chewed my lip, willing myself to keep walking. It didn't work. "Ugh! Fine."

"Yeah?" The excitement crept back into his voice. "Thanks, Manning. I'll do whatever—"

"Listen up." I turned back to face him. "I won't pick someone out for you to target but I will help you improve your game if I can. What are your best subjects?"

"English and wrestling."

"Alright. I can work with that. Meet me in the gym next Thursday."

"Thank you. Thank you." He backed away, pelting me with gratitude as he melted into the crowd going upstairs to the D Wing. "Thank you!"

"—can recognize a few faces of the alumni." A smooth voice echoed through the hall. "Our students have gone on to build companies, create new innovations, and give back to their communities in extraordinary ways."

Whittaker rounded the corner trailed by Argyle, three respectable-looking people, Cameron, and Macy.

"My father was an alumnus of this school," Cameron said. He wore his standard uniform, but today his hair was slicked back and wrangled into submission with gel. His polished leather shoes gleamed in the artificial lights. He was working overtime to make a good impression. "If you ask him, he'll say he owes his success to Breakbattle Academy."

Whittaker's laughter boomed off the walls. "He honors us."

The board members nodded and smiled, clearly taken in by these two. I turned to leave when one of them spotted me.

"Hello, young man."

I waved. "Hi."

Whittaker's smile twitched. "Mr. Manning, shouldn't you be in class?"

"On my way now, Principal Whittaker."

"No, please," the woman called. She was handsome in a blue blazer and skirt. She gave me a charming smile as she beckoned. "I see you're one of the students in the F Class. We're going there now for the start of the observation. Join us. We'd love to speak with you."

The other two board members murmured in agreement.

Cameron stepped in front of them. "Actually, he can't—"

"What a great idea," Argyle said quickly. "Please, Mr. Manning. You lead the way from here on out."

Why does this feel like I don't have a choice?

"Okay." I stepped forward and held out my hand. Cameron's glare bore a hole in my head. "My name is Zeke Manning. Nice to meet you."

The board members introduced themselves as Sue Jeong, Rolando Martin, and Nathan Zabel.

"Tell us more about yourself," Sue asked.

"I'm rather boring," I replied. "I was worldschooled by my mother up until I entered the academy. We lived in over twenty-six countries and I learned a few languages along with how to wield a machete, chop a coconut, and haggle even the toughest stall owner down. So you know, typical childhood."

The board members laughed. Whittaker caught my eye and inclined his head imperceptibly. I could turn the charm on when I wanted to, and it seemed I earned his approval this time.

"Boring indeed," Sue teased. "What influenced the change to traditional schooling?"

"My mother wanted me to have a chance to learn advanced mathematics."

"Advanced math?" Rolando's brows drew together. "You are in the F Class, correct? Are advanced courses a part of your curriculum?"

I opened my mouth.

"Due to circumstances out of his control, Mr. Manning was unable to complete the placement test," Whittaker cut in. "As a matter of policy, he was placed in the F Class, but he has proven himself above and beyond our expectations."

Sue frowned. "If that is the case, why has he not been transferred to the proper class?"

I opened my mouth again.

"Transfers involve a specific process that we plan to discuss in detail later on in the tour," Whittaker answered. He leveled me with a smile. "Mr. Manning, continue telling the board how you have excelled here."

I'm not sure what was more unsettling—the singeing of my neck hairs from Cameron's glower or the blinding grin from Whittaker.

Our group passed out of the main hallway and rounded the corner for the F Wing.

"The school has a math club," I explained. "I battled for my spot and I get to do the math I came to learn. Mrs. Peterson is a wonderful teacher. I'd say she was my favorite, but you're not allowed to when your mother is in the running."

They laughed again and Whittaker gave me a look of such approval, I got worried he was starting to like me.

"What are your plans for the future, Mr. Manning?" asked Mr. Zabel.

"I hope to..." I trailed off as something caught my eye. Someone ran past the windows of the doors to the F Wing. I squinted.

They weren't the only person running. There was a flurry of activity when by now students should be in their classrooms.

"—quickly. Get those down!"

I darted forward and threw open the doors. Nico streaked in front of me, making me jump back. His arms were loaded with paper and he ran up to Dr. O'Quinn who snatched it from him and tossed them into the trash can.

I wished that was the strangest sight. What actually made my eyes widen were the hundreds of garish red flyers covering the walls of our wing. The white paint couldn't be seen for the volume of paper that had been taped to the walls, but the F students were doing their best to rectify that.

"What on earth is going on?" Mrs. Jeong breathed.

I bent down and rescued a flyer that flew between my shoes. In big, black blob letters across the top it read:

The Battle System: Bad for Breakbattle, Bad for Education.

Beneath the title was a list.

"Is there a problem here?" asked Mr. Martin. "May I see that, Zeke?"

A hand reached over my shoulder and took it before I could speak. I turned slowly as Mr. Martin read the title aloud. I had scanned the first few bullet points. This was not going to be good.

"—bad for education," he read. "The battle system fosters jealousy, elitism, and bullying. The battle system encourages students to see themselves as better than their peers. The battle system led to the suicide of Rebecca—"

"Mr. Martin, if you please!" Whittaker moved so fast his hand was a blur. The flyer was crumpled and sent sailing over his shoulder in a blink. He moved in front of them, attempting to usher them back out of the doors.

Sue goggled at him. "What is the meaning of this? A suicide? Is that true?"

"This is merely the work of disgruntled— I can assure you there is no truth—"

"We'll have the custodians sort this out right away," Argyle threw in. She stepped in front of Mr. Zabel when he tried to peer over Whittaker's shoulder. "A harmless prank by the students."

"A prank?" Sue Jeong repeated.

"That's right." Whittaker latched on to the excuse. "We don't wish to get in the way of the cleanup, so let's return to my office, have refreshments, and you can observe the F Wing another time."

The principal and vice principal peppered them with re-assurances as they practically shoved them out of the door.

Cameron had peeled himself out of the pack long ago. He stood to the side, face expressionless as he read the list. He glanced at me over the flyer.

"Is this the best you can do, Manning?"

I scoffed. "I had nothing to do with this. I swear on my math books."

"But you know who did." It wasn't a question.

I met his stare calmly. "I don't know anything, Cameron, and if I did, I wouldn't tell you."

Cameron crumpled the sheet one-handed and opened his fist. The tiny paper ball bounced off the floor and landed on my shoe. "Nothing will stop this expansion." He closed the distance between us. Cameron held tight to my gaze, drawing me in and chilling me. "There are things at play here that you could never understand. These stupid pranks won't make a difference and you can let your little buddies know that."

Cameron gripped my chin between two fingers. His touch was gentle, but a ripple went through my body. "If there are any more problems, I will hold you personally re-sponsible... Zela."

The breath deserted my lungs. Cameron smirked as my eyes grew huge. *They told him. One of them told him who I re-ally am.*

"Do we understand each other?"

I nodded in his hold.

"Good." Cameron backed away. He threw me one last wink before slipping out of the door.

Chapter Six

"It's too late to get away."

Adam grinned at me over the hood.

"Remember that I tried to warn you," I said. "I can't be blamed for whatever happens."

"Zela, what are you talking about?"

I jumped. "Nothing," I said quickly. "Just joking around with Adam."

She gave me a suspicious look through the crack in the door. "Well, stop joking around and help him get his things inside."

"Yes, Mom."

Adam was really laughing at me as he handed over his duffel bag. "Your mom seems cool. This weekend is going to be fun."

"That's nice, Adam." I patted his head. "It's good to have dreams."

Rolling his eyes, he went on ahead of me and into our house.

"I know it's nothing compared to yours," I said as I trailed him. "But the guest room is cozy and I know how to make your favorite breakfast. You should be comfortable."

"Of course I'll be comfortable."

Adam paused in the entryway. Covering the walls were photos of me throughout my life. The one Mom took in Korea as I posed with my friends from Tae Kwon Do. My eleven-year-old self cheesing in front of the Eiffel Tower. A cute one with me sitting under a café awning in Cape Town, and a photo of a two-year-old Zela buck-naked in the bathtub.

Adam stifled a laugh. "You were so cute."

Red faced, I shoved him on. "Your room is up the stairs and on the right."

"Thanks, Zee. I'll text Jordan and let her know I'm here."

My brows shot up my head but I didn't say anything. Those two had been texting a lot lately and I wasn't sure what to make of it.

"So about Melody's idea with the flyers," I spoke up. "I take one prolonged nap and you guys take over the F Wing."

"It was great, wasn't it?" Adam opened the door to his room and we set his things at the foot of the bed. He took out his phone and typed while he spoke. "We were up all night putting those flyers on the walls and in every classroom, but we wanted it loud and in their face."

"They didn't get a chance to read it before Whittaker swooped in."

Adam grinned. "Melody snuck past Matron and slipped it under their doors while Whittaker and Argyle had everyone watching the classrooms."

"The girl is smart." I sat on the edge of the mattress and Adam joined me. "What do you think they're going to do? Do you think... the expansion won't go ahead?"

"I honestly don't know, but at least we gave them something to think about."

What will Cameron do if they got too much to think about and call the whole thing off?

"Zela!"

I hopped up and stuck my head out of the door. "Yes, Mom?"

"Jordan is here."

I hit the bottom step as Jordan walked inside. I blinked at the state of her. My cousin was beautiful every day, but today she was working the makeup, purple lipstick, curls, and tight jeans like I had never seen before.

"You got here fast."

Jordan squinted in the reflection of a picture frame and fussed with her perfect hair. "I was on the way. How do I look?"

"Like Adam is going to admit I was right by the end of this weekend."

She cocked her head. "What does that mean?"

"Nothing." I stepped to the side. "He's in the guest room."

"Thanks, Zee." She bolted past me in a wave of sweet pea perfume.

Despite my moaning, the three of us had a great time. We carved pumpkins at the fall festival, rode in a horse-drawn cart, and took silly pictures all over the place. Mom was on her best behavior and only delivered two lectures about the patriarchy. Adam nodded along and even joined in on the discussion. Afterward, Mom smiled and told me he could stay over anytime. It was the surprise of my life that Aunt Bev was the one I needed to worry about.

We waited in line for the caramel apple stand. The wind carried a sweet, tangy smell to my nose that made me salivate as I swiped the screen, looking for the perfect picture to send to Landon. I asked Jordan to cute me up for the festival and she leaped at the chance. I went from my normal dress, sneakers, and ponytail to makeup, a burgundy sweater dress, and black ankle boots. My hair she curled and let fall in soft ringlets around my face.

I skipped over the ones with me and Adam cheesing cheek to cheek and picked one with me smiling into the camera and him standing behind me, clearly in view. I stamped the photo with a little message.

"So you know my nephew is truly my niece," I heard Aunt Bev say.

Me: Fall is my favorite season. I love the leaves and food and colors and weather. I would have loved it more if you were here. This is Zela, by the way.

My heartbeat ratcheted up as I hit send. The mix of my natural attraction for Landon with the plans I had for him made our little texting game deliciously wrong. I never thought I was this person—playing games, teasing hearts, but then I also never thought I'd be beaten and violated on a cold locker room floor. Life had a way of surprising you.

"Yes," Adam replied. "She told me a while ago."

"And yet, you've been sharing a dorm room all this time."

My head snapped up. *Wait. What are they talking about?*

"And you two are very close."

Aunt Bev towered over my best friend and she did it well. She was no small woman and boasted at least three inches on him. Jordan tugged on her arm, hissing at her to stop.

"W-we're friends, ma'am."

She lifted a brow. "Just friends?"

"Absolutely."

"Even if that's the case, I don't believe it appropriate for you to be sharing a bedroom together and doing Lord knows what."

Heat flooded my cheeks. "Aunt Bev!"

"My sister got pregnant while she was in school and Zee is a gift we treasure every day, but she's got plans for her future and they won't be derailed for a few heated romps in—"

I jumped in between them. "Aunt Bev, can you skip the lecture and just kill me now!?"

She cracked a smile and flicked me on the nose. "No, kid, but"—she leveled her finger on Adam—"I will kill you if you don't keep your hands to yourself."

"Yes, ma'am."

I was proud of Adam. His voice only shook a little bit.

Satisfied, Aunt Bev went up to get our caramel apples.

"Come on." Jordan slipped her arm through Adam's. "Let's run before she comes back."

The two raced off, giggling. I made to follow when my purse buzzed.

Landon: I'm sure Moon told you how beautiful you are. I bet you guys are having a great time. You don't need me there.

A thrill surged through my body. It was wrapped in a few layers of jealousy and insecurity, but Landon still told me I was beautiful.

Me: You don't need to worry about Adam.

His reply bounced back in seconds.

Landon: Don't give me that bullshit. Every time I look, he's all over you.

Me: Adam was there for me when I needed him. He's still here for me while you're pushing me away. If you want me, Landon, take me.

Landon: And what if I do?

"Zee? Why are you so red?"

I jerked. The phone slipped through my fingers and fell onto the grass. "No reason," I squeaked.

"And where is Jordan?" Aunt Bev handed me my treat. "And your friend? And my sister?"

"I'll find them and we can meet at the car."

"Thanks, Zee."

I picked up my phone and went in search. The whole while, I tried to think of something to say but my brain was fritzing out of control.

"And what if I do?"

"LET'S GET ALL OF OUR representatives together, please."

I set down the box I was carrying and followed two guys to the front of the room. The multipurpose room had been transformed into a maze of booths, table runners, and garish signs. Career Day arrived, and throughout the day, tenth graders and up would be filtering in and out during their networking block to speak with the attendees. Except for me, I would be here all day to help with the set up, breaking down, and getting the guests whatever they needed.

I knew that part. What I didn't know was that Landon, Michael, and Cole would be student reps too.

I peeked at them through my lashes. They were smiling about something—even Cole. Smiles looked so good on him, but the truth was, frowns looked good on him too. He was definitely the kind of guy that made a scowl smolder. His uniform was neat and pressed and there wasn't a single strand of hair out of place. The same could be said for Michael and Landon. Landon lost the contacts and Michael's shoes gleamed with polish.

"Listen closely, everyone," Argyle began. "The attendees have arrived and are enjoying refreshments in the dining hall. This gives us a chance to go over a few things.

"It goes without saying that your behavior will reflect the very best of Breakbattle Academy. We have not yet discovered who played that prank in the F Wing during the board visit, but there will be no such antics today. Is that clear?"

"Yes, Mrs. Argyle," we replied.

"Your duties at first will be to get them settled and make sure they have everything they need, but afterward, feel free to walk around and speak to the attendees."

Argyle told us to come up and find out our stations and then she sent us off. Michael, Cole, Landon, and I all went in different directions.

I went to my station and continued opening the boxes. I already posted the banner, set out the chairs, and snagged a few cookies off the snack table and laid them out. Argyle stopped in front of my booth and swept over my work with a pleased smile.

"This is wonderful, Zeke."

"Thank you, Mrs. Argyle."

"You are a credit to your class," she continued. "Your marks are the highest in your grade. You've won a spot in the Archimedean Club, Science Club, and Future Leaders Club."

Oh yeah, I won those spots. I came back the day after busting my nose and insisted I could carry on with my scheduled battles and a rematch. It probably helped that I had some much-needed sleep and I would be keeping up that trend. No more voices or hallucinations.

"At this point, I feel we owe you an apology."

I paused with the box cutter stuck in the tape. "An apology?"

"You had nothing to do with those attacks against the Elite students. I see that now. You've embraced the system and you've handled every win and loss gracefully. You are not For All." Argyle looked me in the eyes. "We will find the true culprit and they will be punished for framing you."

I swallowed hard. I never thought I would hear those words from her. "Thank you."

She inclined her head and then moved on. I heard the doors open as I watched her go. The murmurs of low conversations and polite laughter filled the space. The attendees were here.

"You're going to be a good girl, right?"

"Yes, Daddy."

"And Mommy's going to come later and take us out to lunch."

"Yay!"

I looked up from the box as Maverick Beaumont and Esme strolled up to the booth. I held out my hands. "What do you think? Am I the best student rep or what?"

Esme grabbed a cookie and shoved it into her mouth without preamble. Maverick's laugh rolled out of his chest like the sound of a bass.

"You've certainly earned the title."

Maverick lifted a giggling Esme and placed her in a seat. The little girl stuck her tongue out at me the second he looked away. I'd given up on winning her over three kicks in the shin ago. The closer I got to Adam, the more she hated me.

"There were all of these boxes," I went on. "Was I supposed to open them for you?"

Mr. Beaumont crossed the short distance to my side. It still amazed me how such a powerfully built man moved so gracefully. "Some of them," he replied. "A few are going on display for the students to try. The rest in the back."

Maverick reached in and pulled out a sleek, all-black tablet. His finger glided over the surface and it came to life. "They're a new product made especially for students. We're giving them their first test run in Breakbattle."

"Really? They're for us?"

"Free of charge." He tapped home and a sea of apps flooded the screen. "You can do everything like a regular tablet, but it also allows teachers to upload homework and assignments. You can take tests on these and there are free subscriptions to databases and scholarly sources."

"This is amazing and—" My excitement leaked out of me. "It's only for Elites and As, isn't it?"

"No." Maverick grinned as he handed it over. "My terms were clear. These tablets are free for all students regardless of class, or we offer them to Chesterfield High instead. You can't do a proper test without a varied sample size."

I clutched the tablet to my chest, grinning ear to ear. MT tablets were expensive on sale. This was an incredible gift.

"Want to hear about the tech?" he asked.

"Actually, I'd like to hear about the math."

"Just as interesting. So what we did is..."

Maverick and I launched into a fascinating conversation about the math involved in computer engineering. It was the most fun I had in school in a long time and it came to an abrupt end when Esme shoved her way between us.

A tiny elbow caught me in the side. "Daddy, I'm bored."

"Okay, sweetie." He lifted her up and she wrapped her arms around his shoulder. "Let's go see Mommy before the kids come." Maverick addressed me. "Zeke, would you mind taking the rest of the tablets into the storage room?"

"No problem."

The door to the storage room was in the very back of the room. I weaved through the booths with my precious cargo, scanning banners on the way. The collection of talent, companies, and fields here amazed me. I couldn't wait to speak to the people I circled on my list.

Carefully, I pushed open the door and slipped into the dark room. I let my eyes adjust rather than scramble for the lights while holding the tablets. I made out an empty table in the back. I put down the box just as the door opened. The next thing I knew the storage room was flooded with light.

"I got it. Finish setting up the table."

I froze. *That voice.*

"Okay," he said to someone I couldn't hear. "Thanks."

The door swung shut. "What are you doing in here?"

"What does it look like, Landon?" I turned and faced his narrowed gaze. I made a show of looking him up and down before meeting his eyes. "No contacts today. I love the colors you go with, but can I admit your natural brown is my favorite?"

"No."

His blunt reply made me laugh. Now that I knew what to look for, I could see his attempt to appear uncaring was failing miserably. The muscles in his jaw ticked and his grip on the tablecloth was tight.

Slowly, I made my way over to him. He tensed like I was going to attack him.

I stepped into his space and was engulfed in a sweet scent that was all Landon. *I just might attack him.*

A smile spread across my lips. "You shaved today."

"I shave every day."

"I like your stubble," I whispered. Without thinking too hard, I trailed my finger along his cheek.

"Don't," he said, but his eyes fluttered shut.

I bit my lip. My nerves were humming hot and tingly beneath my skin. I could sense the effect I had on him and it was causing my breaths to come in shorter pants. I stepped closer, pressing my chest against his just to see what would happen. Landon put his hands on my waist and held me tight.

My finger followed the natural ridges of his jaw until they reached just below his lips. The memory of those lips on mine were ravaging my mind and I felt an entirely new sensation in my core.

"We're not doing this, Zela," he whispered. "It's t-too much."

His trouble speaking only thrilled me more.

"You're a boy, then you're not a boy. You're For All, then you're not. You're with Moon, then you're saying you want me. I can't fucking keep up!"

His words were barely penetrating. All I focused on were those lips.

"I'm not playing this game. I don't know what you're trying to do but—"

"Don't know what I'm trying to do?" I caressed his bottom lip. "I thought it was obvious."

Landon's breath caught at the same moment mine did. His fingers dug harder into my side. "Don't do that."

"Don't do what? Stroke your mouth?" I rose on tiptoe and brushed my lips against his jaw. "What do you want me to stroke instead?"

My cheeks burned as I uttered that question. I had no clue what I was saying but it sounded sexy.

A groan ripped from his throat. "Fuck this!"

I cried out when Landon's hand suddenly clamped my ass and lifted me in the air. I didn't have a chance to think before I was slammed against the wall and his lips crashed down on me. This kiss wasn't sweet or gentle or loving, but neither of us were going for that.

My hands stroked and tugged at his hair as our tongues clashed in a fiery battle we weren't willing to lose. Landon grabbed me under the knees and spread my legs. I gasped as he ground his bulge against my center. It throbbed with more than it could take; I didn't know what would happen if he didn't stop—

Landon held me with one hand and slipped the other through the waistband of my pants.

My head flew back and hit the wall. I was seeing stars for many reasons.

"Fucking h-hell, Landon." I found the top of his shirt and tore. Buttons flew everywhere.

"Come back here," he growled. He caught my lips again just as his fingers found a spot that made my toes curl all the way up.

Landon swallowed my moan. It was true I didn't have the first clue about sex, but so far so fucking good.

Bang!

"Landon, what's taking so lon—?"

Our lips tore apart, heads snapping to the doorway as Michael burst in. Michael took in the scene—me pressed against the wall, lips swollen, Landon's hand down my pants—and his jaw dropped.

He didn't say anything. Michael darted out of the room, slamming the door shut. The bang was the final death knell on the mood.

Landon pulled his hand out and put me down while I was still trying to register what was going on.

"I have to go."

Then the door slammed shut again and I was alone.

I fixed myself up with shaky hands.

What the hell was that, Zela?! We're trying to seduce and dump him, not lose our virginity in a storage room!

Flushing, I straightened my wig. That got way out of hand and I had no explanation. My brain went off-line the moment I touched him.

The door flew open. "Zela, you in here?"

I blinked at Adam. "Hey, uh, did Maverick send you for me?"

Adam took one look at me and grinned. "So that's why Landon ran past me with his clothes all torn up."

If I thought I was blushing before. "Is it that obvious that I—?"

"Yep."

"Do you think other people can tell I—?"

"Yep."

"Should I go outside for a little—?"

"Yep."

I nodded. "I'll go get some water and maybe change my—"

"Panties?"

"Shut up!" I swatted his shoulder as he guffawed. "I was going to say clothes."

"Sure you were."

"I hate you," I mumbled as I raced out of there. His chuckles followed me as I skirted the back of the room.

"It wasn't my fault, Dad."

The whispered voice made me slow down.

"Don't give me excuses, boy," snapped a gruff baritone. "The weak blame others for their failures."

"I know, sir. I'm sorry, sir."

I stopped completely. *Cameron?*

How could that be Cameron? I had never heard him sound so contrite. Slowly, my feet carried me nearer the booth. No one could see me. All the booths in the back row faced the front and oversized signs and tarps concealed my presence.

"Do you have any idea how embarrassed I was when I discovered my own son was recruited into the Network without my knowledge or permission? Then when those pompous, self-righteous dicks accept my generous offer to join, I find out you've been demoted."

"I messed up, sir." Cameron spoke a decibel above a whisper. "I'm sorry."

"I don't want to hear you're sorry, boy. I want to hear you're going to get your position back."

"I'll get it back."

"Good." I heard shuffling, then the sound of something smacking the table. "I've been overhearing whispers about the Network for years, but never knew who was involved. Now they are coming to me because those bastards realized they're sitting on a gold mine. It could be so much more than a club of favors," said the man. "I will monetize the Network and see the top leaders, and myself, making millions. That all starts with the expansion."

"It'll happen, Dad. I escorted the members of the board of education myself. They were impressed with what I've been able to accomplish because of Breakbattle."

A low growl sounded on the other side of the tarp and my hair stood on end. Was this person man or beast?

"They weren't impressed enough, or I would not have received notice this morning that they are suspending their decision on adopting the system into public schools until the next school year."

"But that's not—"

"What went wrong?" he demanded.

"There— It was— Some stupid Fs posted about the battle system being bad for everyone and that it caused Rebecca Taylor's suicide, but they didn't take it seriously," Cameron added quickly.

"You should have told me this immediately."

"It wasn't my fault—" Cameron cried out.

"What did I say about excuses?"

I surged forward and burst through the stalls. The man dropped Cameron's arm. "What do you think you're doing? Who are you?"

I breathed hard as I faced a man I had only ever heard about, and not in good terms. Dominick Dupre was nothing like I pictured. I expected light brown eyes and the soul-bending beauty of his son, but this man wouldn't be considered a beauty to anyone but his mother.

The light shone off his bald scalp. I traveled down the length of his face to eyes that were too small, wide-set nose, and thin lips twisted in a frown that made them look like a jagged slash across his face. His eyes pierced me, sharp and unsettling for their dark brown bordering on black. I saw the cold intelligence in those eyes. I saw the contempt in those twisted lips, and I saw Cameron take a step back.

My gaze traveled over his head to the banner. Dominick Dupre was typed in huge letters. In smaller font, it read Dupre Financial Holdings.

I cleared my throat and willed my nerves to settle. "Hello, Mr. Dupre." I held out my hand.

Dominick didn't look at it. "What do you want? I'm a busy man."

"I wanted to ask you about your company," I said. My hand returned to my side. "I'm interested in financial mathematics."

If possible, his sneer deepened. "Like hell you are."

I stiffened. *What did he just say?*

"You're an F," he stated. "I doubt you can spell financial mathematics, let alone follow the conversation. Move along."

"Actually," I snapped, all pretense of politeness burning away. "I'm quite capable of understanding the application of mathematical methods to finances and using probability, economic theory, and statistics to problems. I was most interested in hearing how you apply those methods to portfolio structuring and managing risks, but since you're too busy to do what you came here for, I'll take my questions to Waterstone Financials. They're one of your competitors, right?"

Dominick's face gave nothing away. I had a feeling a man like this didn't expose an emotion he did not have complete control over. Which is why I didn't know what to make of it when his gaze turned assessing.

"You're no fool," he replied, "and you're not afraid to mouth off. Maybe you will make something of yourself."

"I will. There's no question about it."

Dominick smirked and the act threw me harder than his sneer. "Come back later, boy. I'll answer your questions." He closed his hand around Cameron's neck. "First, I need to finish a discussion with my son."

I looked from Cameron to his dad. "Actually, that's why I came over here. Mrs. Argyle wants to see him about something."

"Fine. You may go."

Cameron escaped his hold and fell in beside me. He spoke when we were a few feet from his father. "What does Argyle want?"

"Nothing. I made it up."

I saw him scowl at me from the corner of my eye. "What the fuck? Why are you wasting my time?"

I didn't reply. Cameron swore and strode off, but I noticed he didn't go back to his dad's booth.

Maverick, Esme, and Miss Val were sitting in the stall when I returned from freshening up. I immediately went back to my task of moving the tablets to the storage room. My mind was a tangle of confusing thoughts and emotions as I tried to sort through everything that happened.

Landon's hand down my pants. Dominick's behavior with his son. The Network attempting to monetize. What did all of this mean? And what would I do next?

I spotted Derek on my final trip to the back. He was talking to a tall man with thinning blond hair and a trim suit.

The box slid through loose fingers and nearly crashed to the ground. I bent, scrambling to catch it without taking my eyes off of the two of them.

Derek's attention flicked over to me as though he sensed my presence. He said something to the man and then walked over.

"Zee. What are you doing?"

"I'm..."

What the hell am I doing? I glanced down. "I'm taking this to the back."

"I'll help."

I let him take it from me without protest. "Who were you talking to?"

Derek peered over his shoulder. "My dad."

"Can I meet him?" I took a step forward and bumped into Derek as he crossed my path.

"Not right now. He's heading out."

"He is? But isn't he here for Career Day?"

"Nope. He swung by because I forgot something at home." Derek took my hand and led me away. "He never does things like this. People just come up and ask a million questions about Mom—most of them disgusting."

Tripping after him, I glanced over my shoulder just as his father reached the door. Why did I have a feeling there was more to Derek not wanting to introduce me? No matter how many books we stayed up all night reading or how often I split my chocolate treats with him, would there always be this wall between us that I couldn't climb? What was it going to take for him to let me in?

Those questions joined the others plaguing my mind, offering me no relief.

"YOU'RE OVEREXTENDING yourself, Noah," I called.

The boy from D Class and a friend he got to practice with him rolled around on the mat while I took notes and gave the suggestions Landon would have given himself. On my left, sat Adam.

"Get closer when you do the takedown so you don't lose your balance."

"Got it."

"Are you sure that's what he said?" Adam asked, picking up our conversation.

"I'm sure. Dominick Dupre said that he and the top leaders of the Network would make millions if the expansion goes through. How could they do that?"

"I don't know. The way Cameron explained it, the Network is about having a bunch of guys ready with a recommendation or something like that. I don't see how they could make millions off of it, or how spreading the battle system to more schools would help."

"Cameron's dad knows," I replied, "and he wants to see it done no matter what."

He shook his head. "I don't know about the Network or any of that but I know Cameron's dad is not a good guy. Do you remember that stuff Derek said during orientation? That night in the woods?"

"You mean when he accused Dominick Dupre of dealing in shady money? But Derek only said that to make their fight look real. It was all a part of their sick test."

"No way," said Adam. "I bet they had a plan to fake a fight, but in typical asshole fashion, Derek went for the jugular. All that stuff he said are things Dominick Dupre has been accused of. The guy has been investigated like three times and nothing ever stuck. If he's behind this, then it's even more reason to put a stop to the expansion."

"He said the board suspended their decision until next year. Do you think the expansion still has a chance?"

"If they do, we'll have a plan."

And if that plan works, what will happen to Cameron?

Noah pinned his friend and I let critiquing his technique pull me from my thoughts.

"That's great, Noah. If your challengee picks wrestling, you'll have them."

He beamed. Noah was a smiley dude, and whenever he did, it made him look ridiculously adorable. I don't know what he saw in his girlfriend, but I could see what she saw in him.

"Thanks, Zeke. I already know who I'm going to battle. I'll own him because of you." Noah stood and helped his friend up. "We're going to head out. Thanks, again."

I waved goodbye.

"All of this to go to the fall dance," Adam said as I packed up my things. "Are you going too?"

I tried hard to keep my face straight. "Maybe I would if someone asked me."

Adam shot me a grin. "Who do you think is going to do that?"

I shrugged. It had been three days since my run-in with Landon in the storage room. We hadn't spoken since, not even flirty texts. Every time I picked up my phone, I imagined my fingers running through his raven locks while he teased moan after moan from me. I'd promptly drop the phone as all the blood rushed to my face. That was my excuse. I don't know about him.

"Are you going?" I asked. We stepped out into the early autumn afternoon and I breathed deeply the crisp, refreshing air. Students raced across the lawn, playing a friendly game of football, and for a moment, Breakbattle felt like a normal school with normal worries and joys.

"I'd have to battle for it and there's only one person I want to go with."

"Melody."

"Do you know if she's going?"

"Melody Durant is the most popular girl in the school while also being the person least interested in popularity," I replied. "All of her friends are most likely going, but if she doesn't want to, she won't. You have to give her a reason."

Color stained Adam's cheeks. "I can't just ask her to the dance."

"Yes, you can."

"What if she says no?"

"She won't."

He let out a frustrated noise. "You keep insisting she likes me but she's never said anything. Ever."

"I don't think she could be more obvious if she tried."

"She could definitely be more obvious!" Adam ran his fingers through his hair, messing up his wild curls and still looking cute. "All we ever talk about is school and Stand Up."

"So next time you see her, talk about how much you want to be with her."

He gaped at me. "I can't do that."

"Again, yes, you can."

"Zee!"

"Adam."

He tossed his head. "You're being impossible."

I laughed. "I have to take my impossible butt to Archimedean Club. I'll see you at dinner."

I wasn't the first one to arrive. Cole and a few Elites and As milled at the back of the room. I met Cole's eyes but was the first to look away. I headed straight for Mrs. Peterson.

She rose from her seat and shook my hand warmly.

"I'm glad you'll be joining us this year, Zeke. Exciting things are happening."

"I want to be a part of all of it. I plan on taking real responsibility. Leadership roles, team contests, you name it."

"I'm happy to hear that. Our team plans to take first place in the regional mathematics competition next semester. With your skills, you'll be a top contender for captain."

"I'm also interested in the captaincy."

Mrs. Peterson started. She didn't notice Cole come up. I did.

"I hope to take on more responsibility too," he added.

"That's wonderful, Mr. Reed. I admire your dedication." She clapped. "Let's find our seats, everyone. We'll begin soon."

I brushed past Cole, leaning in to whisper, "Is admiring your dedication as important as admiring my skills, Mr. Reed?"

He tensed at my digging in the fact that she was on a first-name basis with me and not him.

"I'm going to be captain," I said as I moved around him. "The homeschooler has come to play."

MY TIMING WAS PERFECT. I stepped off the stairs seconds after Adam rounded the corner for the dining hall.

"Adam, hold up."

He slowed down for me to join him. "How'd it go?"

"Cole glared at me the whole time."

"You sound happy about that."

I tapped my temple. "I'm in his head, Moon. He'll watch me take everything he wants academically, while you crush him in swimming."

"I'm not in it for the competition," Adam admitted, "but what Cole and the others did to you... If beating him hurts him as much as he hurt you, then I'm not holding back. Those extra swimming practice times I battled for has me putting up the best numbers of my life. Coach Nelson won't say he's impressed with me, but I can tell. He'll make me captain for sure."

"When will he make his decision?"

"There is a swim meet a week before the end of the semester. He'll decide then."

Together we walked into the dining room and got in line for roast beef sandwiches and cauliflower soup. Melody and her gaggle of friends entered the dining room as we headed for our table.

"Hey, Melody."

"Zeke. Adam. How was class?"

"The same except everyone is talking about the fall dance," I said. "Are you going?"

"No."

"Argh." Melody's friend, Ainsley, pushed through the pack. "Will you guys talk some sense into her? The dance is going to be epic, Mel. You have to come."

"The dance is on a Friday night. I'd rather be home than propping up another elitist event this school made exclusive for no reason. It's a school dance. Everyone should be allowed to go."

"Mel, come on. We'll dress up, dance, and have a good time."

"I'm not going, Ainsley."

I piped up. "Adam is thinking about going."

The stubborn fix to Melody's chin melted away. "You are?" she asked him.

"Yes," I answered. "He just needs someone to go with."

Melody took a step toward him. "Who were you thinking of going with?"

I opened my mouth again. "He was thinking—"

"Zee, aren't you starving? I remember you saying you were starving. You should sit down and eat." Adam clapped a hand on my shoulder and firmly sent me on my way.

Laughing, I continued on to my table. My mirth dried up when I laid eyes on Landon.

He was sitting at his usual table although Cole and Michael hadn't arrived yet. As if he could feel my gaze, he lifted his head.

Landon looked at me as the flush crept up my neck. I felt his hands on my body like phantom fingers ghosting over my skin. I tasted the sweetness of his lips as though it was only moments since we kissed. And if the tight grip of his fork and the lip caught between his teeth meant anything, he felt something too.

I wanted him to stand up, come to me, talk to me, tell me that this peek-a-boo game was over and he wanted to be with me as much as I knew he did.

But Landon didn't do any of those things. He lowered his head and went back to dinner. Landon didn't look up again.

After a minute, I picked up my feet and kept going.

"We're going to the dance," I announced after Adam sat down. "Let me say that again: Adam, please go to the dance with me."

"With you? But I thought..." Adam looked in Landon's direction. "Is this about him?"

"Yes," I forced through gritted teeth.

"Then let's go to the dance."

It was difficult not letting my eyes drift over to him. A tray plopped down next to me and I looked up at Derek with relief.

"Hi."

He grunted in my direction.

"Hi, Zeke," Hunter said more cheerily. "I never got a chance to tell you how cool your protest was."

"My protest?"

"The flyers you put up in the F Wing, forcing the board members to see what the battle system is really about."

He was careful to keep his voice soft but I looked around just in case. "I can't take credit for that," I said after ensuring no one was listening in. "It was a good idea but it only bought us time. The board will make their decision next year."

"How do you know that?" His smile disappeared.

"Heard it from a reliable source," I said simply.

"What do they need to decide on? This system puts crazy pressure on people and a girl already died because of it. Why would anyone want more of that?"

I put my hand over Hunter's clenched fist. "Are you feeling pressure? If you are, you can talk to me."

He ducked his head. "It's n-not that. I just—"

"Let's go." Derek pushed back his seat. "Walk with me, Hunter."

Hunter picked up his food and followed Derek without hesitation. I assumed he was going to talk with him and he didn't want the cafeteria seeing him be a nice guy.

"So for this dance..." Adam nudged my shoulder. "Just how far are we taking this thing because I should let you know my virtue is off-limits."

I barked a laugh. "Just your virtue? What about the bases? Can I cop a few feels? Make out a little?"

He hummed. "I'm good with some over-the-clothes action but I'm no cheap date. You have to at least buy me dinner before things start coming off."

"What the fuck are you two talking about?"

We saw Justin's and Owen's slack-jawed expressions and practically fell out of our chairs laughing. At one point, I rested my head against Adam's shoulder as I caught my breath. A quick look at Landon told me he was watching... and he wasn't happy.

THE DAY OF THE DANCE dawned dark and gloomy. Heavy, gray clouds hung over the academy, promising to unleash its wrath. Adam didn't stir as I dressed in the dark and slipped out. I preferred to run at night, but with the skies the way they were, the track was sure to be empty.

I inhaled deep lungfuls of clean, moist air as I stepped out. I loved the rain. I loved thunderstorms that rattled the windows and smudged out the sun. I loved feeling the damp cling to my skin as much as I loved curling up inside with a book, a blanket, and the thunder as my soundtrack. I couldn't think of a better time to run, and if I catch a little rain, I'd enjoy the sharp splashes on my skin.

I jogged up to the bleachers, water bottle swinging from my hand by a strap that was beginning to fray. I'd need to get a new one soon.

I didn't notice the lone figure on the bench until it was too late.

"Are you kidding me? What are you doing here?"

Michael paused in tying his shoes. "I'm going for a run like I do every morning."

"But it's raining."

"That's not stopping you."

"Fine. I'll run tonight."

"Zeke, wait," he called. "You don't have to go. We can share the track."

"No, thanks." I turned to leave.

"Zeke. Zeke!" Footsteps sounded behind me. "Can you wait for a second?" He took hold of my arm. "I need to talk to you."

"There's nothing to talk about." I yanked out of his hold and kept walking.

"I'm sorry!"

That made me stop. Michael ran out in front of me, blocking my path. His usually serene, perfect face was nothing but. Beads of sweat collected on his forehead and his eyes were huge.

"I'm sorry, Manning, and I know I should have said that before."

Michael reached for me. I shot away and tripped over my soles. I caught myself before I could fall but my skin felt raw like I smacked the turf anyway.

"You're sorry?" I repeated. "Sorry for what, Michael?"

"For everything. I'm sorry I went along with Cameron's plan and challenged you to those battles. I'm sorry I didn't believe you when you said you were framed. I'm sorry I let those guys hurt you."

"You *ordered* those guys to hurt me, Michael!" My heart beat an irregular, rapid pattern in my chest. "I'm supposed to believe you're sorry now!?"

"I was sorry then! After I realized that you were— After I found out—"

"That I'm a girl," I rasped. "You felt bad after Zach stripped me. Is that what you're trying to say? It was okay to beat Zeke, but not Zela."

He tossed his head. "Nothing that happened was okay no matter what I thought. I'm not this guy, Zela. I've never been this guy. I don't bully people and get revenge and... hurt my friends."

He took a tentative step, trying again to close the distance between us, and I let him.

"You were my friend," he whispered, "and I should have believed you." Another step. "I'll do anything to make it up to you."

Michael threaded his fingers through mine. I gazed into his eyes, mind spinning, as the first raindrop splashed on his cheek. It traveled down his face, reminiscent of a tear.

"Just tell me... and I'll do it."

"Anything?" I croaked. The rain struck me, falling harder and faster and soaking me through to the skin in seconds. Backing away, I pulled out of his hold. "I'll let you know."

Michael was still standing there when the door closed behind me.

"HOW DO I LOOK?" ADAM did a little spin.

"Gorgeous, as usual."

The corner of his lip quirked up in a grin. "As usual?"

"Don't get smug," I replied. "It's one of the things I don't like about you. You're way prettier than anyone has a right to be." I smiled to let him know I was kidding.

He laughed. "People could say the same about you."

"Can they?" I muttered as I took a turn in front of the mirror.

Adam's suit for the dance accentuated all the gifts competitive swimming and good genes gave him. He did something with his curls that made them look effortlessly tousled instead of wildly adorable.

I, on the other hand, went with my school pants, black suspenders, and a white button-up shirt. I didn't do anything with my hair other than put it on.

"I feel bad you have to walk in with me as your date," I said. "At least Melody won't be there."

"Are you sure Landon will?"

"Yes. Derek told me he's going."

"Then let's do this."

Adam offered his elbow and I chuckled as I slipped my arm through his. Together we stepped out of our dorm to a silent hallway. The F dorm had emptied out, leaving us weekenders and dance-goers behind.

Stepping out onto the quad, our soles squished in the damp, muddy earth. It stormed on and off all day, and through the windows of Dr. O'Quinn's class, I saw the volunteers running and screeching in the rain as they set up the dance. We walked into the gym and saw right away it was worth it.

I barely recognized the space I once wrestled in with Landon. Standing tables covered in soft orange tablecloths and single glowing candles surrounded a dance floor swirling with spotlights. The decoration committee went all in on the fall theme. The serving table had small, fake autumn leaves between the punchbowl and snacks. String lights hung from above, casting red and yellow glows down on the dancers. For my first school dance, this already blew past my expectations.

"Let's get something to eat." Adam held tight to my hand as he led me to the refreshment table. If he noticed the curious looks people were giving us, he gave no sign. "Do you see him?" he asked under his breath.

I scanned the sweet-scented, high-heeled, bow-tied crowd for a boy with multicolored eyes and a suit that was sure to blow everyone away. I didn't see him anywhere.

"No," I said. "We can snag a table near the door so we'll see him when he comes in."

"You mean so he'll see *us* when he comes in."

"That too."

We loaded a plate up with stuffed mushrooms, pita chips, tomato hummus, wontons, and jalapeño deviled eggs. A weird culinary mash-up but everything was delicious. Adam and I chatted while we ate, but I kept one eye on the door.

Cameron strolled inside twenty minutes later with his entourage. Santiago and Heath flocked him, but this time the three of them were accompanied by three gorgeous girls draped over their arms. Santiago appeared seconds away from passing out from boredom most days, but as the bespectacled brunette gazed up at him...

"Oh my goodness," I breathed. "Is Santiago smiling?"

"I did not know his face could do that."

I laughed.

"We're not staying here until he shows up," Adam announced. "It's a party. Let's dance." He grabbed my hand.

"Whoa, whoa, whoa." I cried, digging in my heels. "I cannot dance. I'm serious. If I go out there, it won't be pretty."

"Just do what I do."

"Adam, you don't understand."

"You don't understand"—he yanked and I found myself flying into his chest and scooped up bridal-style—"that I'm not taking no for an answer."

I laughed even though it was wrong to encourage him. Adam carried me out to the dance floor and the crowd cleared a path for us, most likely to avoid getting knocked by my feet.

The speakers were thumping with a rap song I'd never heard of but everyone else was singing along to. Adam put me down and I stood stock-still.

"Relax," he called over the music. "Have fun!"

"What's fun about making a fool of yourself?!"

"Everything!" Adam grabbed my hips and jerked them side to side as he devolved into this wild, flailing dance like a man electrocuted. I laughed so hard tears ran down my face.

"Come on," he shouted. "Do it!"

I tried to copy him and soon we were both laughing and jumping around the dance floor, scaring everyone around us away. My nerves loosened up enough that when Adam began dancing for real, I joined in.

The guy did know how to dance. He rode every beat and knew all the dances down to the last step. Every time I got shy and tried to stop, he'd take my hands and dance with me.

The music shifted to an old-school TLC song and knowing the words injected some confidence in me. I took hold of him and Adam spun me into his chest and twirled me back. The room swirled in a blur of reds and golds. On the second spin, I saw him.

They probably weren't holding a spotlight on them, but in my mind, the world was converging on three single points named Cole, Michael, and Landon.

Cole went with a black tuxedo and black shoes, but tonight his blond locks were swept to the side and falling over his eyes, an understated effect that had me almost weak in the knees before I moved on to Michael. So unconcerned with fashion, Michael wore a simple pair of white pants and a red shirt with a white tie. He looked like cupid come to steal my heart, but when he glanced at me, I pointedly looked away.

His apology ran through my mind all day and I still didn't know how to feel about it. I swore I would make him pay for what he did and Michael laid himself bare and asked for the punishment.

My mixed-up feelings faded for a moment as I took in Landon. I knew his outfit wouldn't disappoint. His jacket color-shifted as he moved, changing from a dark burgundy to midnight black. Landon didn't opt for a shirt and the deep V exposed his sculpted chest to the feasting eyes of the crowd.

Landon glanced around. Maybe he was looking for me, too, because he stopped when our gaze connected. My breath hitched.

I wondered if he would always have this effect on me. Even while anger flickered in my soul like stoking embers—even though I wanted to see him cry like I did every night for weeks—Landon Foster made me feel like my heart would either burst or float out of my chest. It tried to do both as we looked at each other across the dance floor.

"Perfect timing," said Adam.

Adam's hands slid down to my waist. He pulled me close and draped my arms around his shoulders. Landon watched the whole thing.

With more strength than I knew I possessed, I turned away from him. "We can stop when he's not looking."

"Okay."

We danced to a few more songs and then Adam gave the all clear. "He went into the bathroom. Want to grab a drink?"

"Sounds good."

Adam kept an eye on Landon for me, which allowed me to sneak glances at Cole and Michael. I couldn't help it. Every time I looked at Michael, I found him looking back at me. Cole was a constant presence at his side as they found a spot on the wall and propped it up.

"You okay?" asked Adam.

I tore my eyes off them as he handed me a cup.

"Are you sure you still want to do this?"

"I have to do this," I said softly—so softly he might not have heard me.

The tempo slowed and couples came together like magnets, holding each other as they swayed to the music. In the corner of the room, I spotted Noah kissing his girlfriend and it buoyed my mood. Something good had come out of my crusade.

"He's back," Adam said. "Do you want to go back out there?"

I drained my punch and then plastered a smile on my face. "Let's do it."

Adam and I returned to the dance floor. His hands found my hips and I rested my arms on his shoulders as though it was the most natural thing in the world. On the outside, we looked like the cutest couple.

"If we're doing this," Adam spoke up, "we have to sell it."

"What does that mean?" The question was barely out of my mouth before he bent and captured my lips.

"Urgh!" I cried, eyes bugging out.

It wasn't a bad kiss. Adam's experience came through as he pressed a gentle, sweet kiss to my lips, not taking more than I could give. Not bad, but it was so unlike the feverish, mind-melting kisses with Landon that I knew Adam and I truly were meant to be friends.

A gasp pricked my ears.

Landon. He saw.

"A-Adam?"

Adam ripped his lips off mine. That voice was distinctly not Landon.

Melody stood in front of us, beautiful in a strapless, pink dress and shimmering glitter dusting her skin. She had come... and I was the worst person who ever lived.

Adam's head swung from me to her. "Melody, wait— It's not what it looks like!"

Her face crumpled. Melody spun on her heels and ran.

"Melody!" Adam took off after her.

Idiot! Idiot! Idiot! What did I do? I've been telling Adam she liked him all this time and then I told Melody he was coming to the dance. I saw her face light up. I should have known at that second that she had changed her mind.

My stomach twisted. *Why did I get Adam involved in this? He was willing to go as far as he had to be a good friend and now I might have cost him the girl he loves. What do I do?*

Go! a voice shouted. *Explain it to her. Fix this.*

I took off running before the thought fully formed. The skies opened up once more on Breakbattle and I burst through to stinging rain and sweeping, chilling winds. In the distance, pink and black figures raced to the main building.

I darted after them. I had to find them and back Adam up. Both of us telling her that we didn't have feelings for each other would fix this. It had to.

My wet shoes slid on the polished floors. I twisted around, searching for them, but the hallway was empty.

"Where are you? Did Melody go back to the girls' side?"

I glanced down at the pool of water I slipped in. I immediately searched for more water droplets and found a trail leading around the corner toward the administration hallway.

I picked up the pace. Everything would be fine. I would not be responsible for those two not getting together, not after sabotage, near-expulsion, Cameron Dupre.

The trail led toward the nurse's office and then veered around another corner, leading away from the girls' side. The water droplets led me to the door of the library.

Melody ran in here?

Pressing my ear against the wood, I tried to listen for the sound of voices. Nothing came through the solid oak. I grabbed the handle and inched open the door. Quietly, I crept in.

"Adam..."

My eyes flew to the figures at the back of the room.

Oh no.

"It's you," Adam breathed. "I've only ever wanted you."

"Oh, Adam." They attacked each other in a kiss that was the polar opposite of the one he gave me. Adam lifted her and placed Melody on the table, giving her better access to continue ripping off his clothes.

My smile split my cheeks. Apparently, they didn't need me to explain. They were working out the misunderstanding just fine.

Melody's breasts sprang free and she threw her bra over Adam's shoulder. My smile disappeared in an instant.

I really need to get out of here.

Moving fast, I half tripped over my feet, ducking out the door and hurrying down the hall. He grabbed me the moment I ran around the corner.

I cried out as strong hands gripped me and shoved me against the wall. The haze cleared and Landon appeared before me—whole, beautiful, and spitting angry.

Hot pants ghosted over my face. I was breathing his raw emotions in and the part of me that hungered for him came to life.

"What are you doing?" I cried, chest pounding.

"You said if I wanted you, I had to take you."

"Wha—"

Landon captured my lips in a kiss that was almost punishing. Maybe I deserved it for teasing him with Adam.

Maybe I liked it.

My body responded to him in an instant. I crawled up his body and wrapped my legs around his waist, welcoming it when he ground between my legs.

We broke apart, drawing ragged breaths, and he put me back on the floor.

"Well, I'm taking you."

I didn't have a chance to ask what that meant before he swooped down and grabbed me around the waist.

"Landon!"

The boy hoisted me over his shoulder and strode off.

Chapter Seven

"Would you mind telling me where we're going?" I asked into his back.

"Where do you think?"

Flushing had a whole new meaning when you were upside down. All the blood had no trouble rushing to my face. I knew where we were going. It was obvious when he stepped inside the dorm building.

I should not go up to that room.

He's not giving me much of a choice, warred my internal voice.

This is what I wanted. Seduce him, drive him crazy, and then dump him like hot trash the same way he did to me.

A swat landed on my bottom.

"Hey!"

"You're not with Moon anymore," Landon stated. "You're with me."

His tone left no room for argument. This was a side of Landon I had only seen on the mat. Strong, decisive, masculine, handsy. It was so ridiculously sexy, my heart throbbed harder than my left butt cheek.

Landon threw open his door and crossed to the bed. He flipped me over and dumped me unceremoniously on the sheets. My legs were splayed on either side of me. Cool air wafted over me from the vents, causing goose bumps to erupt on my wet skin.

"Take it off," he rasped. "All of it. I want to see the real you."

My fingers moved of their own accord, pulling my suspenders off my shoulders and then my wig. Landon's tongue darted out and licked his lips as my hair came loose and fell around my shoulders.

I moved to my buttons next and Landon stayed glued to my fingers, watching as they revealed my bindings and then took them off.

It felt like hours, but in reality, it was only minutes until I was before him in nothing but my tank top and pants. The real Zela.

"Your turn," I whispered.

Landon stripped off his jacket, revealing his bare chest. He was slim, but every inch of Landon was hard, wiry muscle. I ached to rub my hands over the bumps and ridges of his chest, so I did.

He sucked in a sharp breath as my finger stopped at his belt.

Get it together, Zela. Common sense beat back the haze. *You lose your head whenever you're in the same room as this guy. You're not going to get carried away like you did in the storage room.*

I took a deep breath. "Landon, I think we should—"

He leaped and suddenly over a hundred pounds worth of boy was on top of me. Landon pulled me in for a kiss that seared all rational thought into cinders. We rolled on the bed, scrabbling and tearing at each other.

He flipped me and we fell onto the pillows. I tore my lips away, coming up for air.

"L-Landon," I moaned. "I think we should— we should—"

Landon's hand slipped through my waistband. I promptly forgot what I was going to say.

He claimed my lips again. My body was humming with so many sensations I thought my nerves would overload. The ball of pain and fury I had been nursing felt small in the face of it.

I gasped as he found a particularly interesting spot. I had to stop this now or I never would. "Landon, please. We should—"

"Don't worry." He kissed down my cheek, leaving a burning trail to the shell of my ear. "I have condoms."

My eyes popped. That woke me up better than a bucket of water to the face. Losing my virginity was definitely not a part of this revenge plot.

"Landon, we need... t-to talk."

Damn, it's so hard to think when he's doing that!

I untangled my fingers from his hair and bit back a moan when he latched on to my neck. Landon took his hand out of my pants, allowing me to untense my body.

"Okay," I whispered. "I was saying—"

Landon pulled my pants down in one smooth move and I freaked. I reached behind me, grabbed a pillow, and smashed it into his face. He let out a muffled cry as I flipped him onto his back and straddled him, holding him down.

"Okay," I cried. "How about we take a minute and just— just— slow down."

I was talking to myself more than him. My breaths were coming in short, ragged pants. My lips swollen and tender. The cold air touched my ass and I tried to recall how I ended up half-naked on top of him.

"Uh, Zela." His voice was muffled. "I need to breathe."

"Shush! No one is doing anything." I swallowed a few times, finding my voice. "Landon," I began. "I think we should take things slow. It's been a rough start for us to put it lightly and it's important that we don't go too fast before we're ready."

It's important my heart is left intact after I crush yours, I added internally.

"What hm hmmm hm."

"What?" I lifted part of the pillow, revealing his mouth.

"What does slow mean?"

"It means we won't be needing *condoms* anytime soon."

"If that's what you want," he said to my surprise. "We don't have to have sex if you're not ready."

My heart slowed a fraction. "Thank you."

"There's plenty of other things we can do," he went on. "You seem to like being fingered." His hands found my bare ass. "Just wait until I give you head."

I shoved the pillow back down on his face. "Fucking hell, Landon!" I burned so hot I would have melted my clothes away if most of it wasn't off already. "Hands where I can see them."

I heard him laugh as he lifted his hands to his head. This guy was trouble in designer slacks.

"Everything below the waist is off-limits," I said. "It can't be all about the physical stuff with us. I want us to talk, get to know each other, and"—a thought suddenly occurred to me—"we're not exclusive."

Landon grabbed my wrist and raised the pillow. "Why? So you can hook up with Moon?"

I heaved a sigh. "Will you let that go? I'm not into Adam. I was *never* into Adam. I only did that stuff to make you jealous."

"Are you serious?"

"Yes. I'm being honest with you because that's what I want us to do. The problem with you and me is that we never trusted each other. We can't be in a real relationship until that changes. Okay?"

Landon didn't reply right away. After a minute, he said, "Can you stop smothering me now?"

Hiding a smile, I climbed off of him and pulled up my pants. I rested against the headboard and Landon sat up and did the same. We gazed at each other across the pillows.

"Okay," he finally said. "If that's what you want, that's what we'll do." He smiled and such was his magic that it pulled one to my lips. "We won't hook up tonight. We'll talk."

"It'll be nice. There's so much we don't know about each other."

"Where do you want to start?"

I shrugged. "We could talk about your family or the places you've been or..."

Landon put his arms behind his head and my attention snapped to his chest as it flexed.

"Or we could talk tomorrow," I said quickly.

"Good idea."

We reached for each other at the same time.

I WOKE WARM AND COMFORTABLE the next morning. Landon's nose was buried in my neck. His gentle exhales tickled me. Slowly, I came into my own.

His arm was draped over my waist, holding me securely to his chest. I wore only my bra and panties, but in my defense, my clothes were wet. It made sense to take them off. A lot of things made perfect sense to my Landon-addled brain last night.

Landon respected my wishes and didn't let his hands stray below the waist. Instead, he thoroughly tested all the wiggle room in the rules and had his fun above the belt.

I carefully extracted myself from under his arms and dressed quietly in the dark. It was Saturday. It would be easy to spend more time in bed with him and I was weak enough to say yes if he asked. Better not to give him the chance. I needed time to myself to think about last night and what, for a moment, I was going to let happen.

The F dorms were a ghost town. Feeling the freedom, I grabbed my towel and headed into the bathroom for the longest, hottest shower I had ever taken in that stall. The hot water soothed my muscles, but had no effect on my spinning mind.

I padded out of the bathroom to my room. I slowed down when I noticed something leaning against my door.

A present?

That's what it looked like. A rectangular blue and purple gift bag would be packing a present, but I approached it cautiously. I nudged the bag with my toe and it overturned. A metal water bottle covered in tiny colorful butterflies rolled out.

Hmm. This is nice. I picked it up and checked it over. *I've been meaning to get a new one anyway. Is this from Landon?*

I checked in and around the bag. There was no note or anything to indicate who it was from. I shrugged and took it inside anyway.

Shedding my towel, I dressed in a simple pair of shorts and a loose tee. I didn't bother to don my Zeke suit. I wasn't leaving my room anytime soon. I wanted to be comfortable.

Our door opened minutes after I climbed into bed. Adam came in dressed in his clothes from the night before and the goofiest grin. He might as well have been wearing a sign that said he got laid.

"Heeeyyy," I drew out. "Good night?"

His grin widened. "Pretty good. Sorry about running off and leaving you. Did things work out with Landon?"

I ducked my head. "Yeah. They worked out."

"Are you still going to dump him?"

"Nothing has changed."

Adam nodded and his face scrunched up in a wince. He pressed his fingers to the base of his neck, kneading it as he toed off his shoes.

"Sleep badly?" I asked. "That's what happens when you bed down in a library."

His eyes flared. "What? How did you know?"

"I followed you."

It was Adam's turn to drop his head. "You didn't see..."

"I saw enough to know you lied about not wanting to lose your virtue last night."

He chuckled. "That was the plan, but then I remembered I lost that over a year ago, so why hold back?"

I patted the mattress and Adam sat down. Rising up, I searched out the knot in his neck and massaged it. He groaned under my touch.

"You really are my best friend."

"Are you and Melody together now? Has it finally happened?"

"We're taking it slow. As of thirty minutes ago."

"Slow is good. Landon and I are doing the same thing."

"You've got him on the hook, Zee. He was looking at me like he wanted to light me on fire and toss me in a pool full of gasoline."

"Ouch."

"He wants you," Adam warned. "And you want him despite how mad you still are. Protect yourself or you'll get burned along with him."

"I will." I pressed harder and Adam let out a pleased sigh. "Let's talk about something else."

"I noticed you and Derek reading those Pendergast books and picked some up. Can we talk about that last one?" he cried.

"Oh my gosh, yes. Was your mind blown because mine was? We're talking splattered on the pavement."

Adam and I spent the rest of the day goofing off in our room, and if we stopped once in a while to grin at a text, neither of us needed to ask why.

MONDAY MORNING CAME much too quickly. Adam and I dressed and headed out to breakfast. The smell of home fries and sausages reached us before we got to the doors.

Justin, Owen, Tanner, and Nico were digging into their food when we joined them.

Nico threw down his fork. "Guys!"

"Good morning to you, too," I said.

He waved that away and leaned across the table. "You were at the dance. Did you see it? What happened after?"

"What are you talking about?"

Nico was ready for the question. He slid his phone across the table. "That's what I'm talking about."

Adam and I bumped heads leaning in to look. I squinted at the photograph.

The decorations and the lights. This is the dance and... what's on the projector screen? It looks like an—

"Upside-down A," said Adam. "For All."

"Oh no," I whispered. "Did something happen?"

Nico shook his head. "It showed up on the screen for a few minutes during the slideshow and that was it. There was no prank or attack against the Elites." He frowned. "How did you guys miss it?"

"We left the dance early," Adam replied. "We didn't hear anything."

"What do you think it means?" asked Justin.

Tanner swept his long, brown hair from his face. "Isn't it obvious? It means he's back."

"READ THE NEXT TWO CHAPTERS for homework tonight," announced O'Quinn. "One last thing before you go."

I paused with my finger on my backpack's zipper. Her voice was laced with more than her standard seriousness.

"By now you all have heard about the incident at the dance," she said. "The students are fine and no one has reported harm or that their things were tampered with, missing, or stolen. The attacks by this For All have so far been focused on one group, but in light of recent events, the principal wishes us to remind you of these safety methods to ensure there are no more incidents."

O'Quinn reached behind her and picked up a sheet of paper. "First, students should not leave their belongings unattended. Second, if you have reason to believe your belongings have been tampered with, find a member of staff immediately. Keep your door locked when you are out of your room."

O'Quinn rattled off the safety instructions. I couldn't believe this was happening again. Argyle knew I wasn't behind the attacks, so what did Cameron have to gain by starting them up again?

"That's all," said our teacher. "You may go now."

Adam and I walked out to discover someone waiting for me.

"I'm going to get in some pool time with the meet coming up," Adam said. "I'll see you after, Zee. Bye, Landon."

"See ya," Landon called, sounding downright pleasant. He was cool with Adam again now that he knew our relationship was a ploy to make him jealous.

I did not take into account how smug he'd get about it.

Landon grinned and put his arm around me. He boldly kissed my cheek.

"What are you doing here?" I asked.

"I'm walking you to your meeting."

"That's sweet of you." I nuzzled into his shoulder, breathing him in.

"I have ulterior motives. I was hoping you would come up to my room tonight. We can give that talking thing another try."

I tilted my head back to look at him. "Just talk?"

"And some other things?"

I chuckled. "We should put the *other things* on hold until after the talking and studying. That way it will actually happen. Finals are in two weeks. We have to focus."

"Whatever you want, Zee. As long as the night ends with you in my bed."

My heart dangerously skipped a couple of beats. There was no other way for the night to end when he said things like that.

Landon deposited me in front of an Elite classroom and then leaned in.

"Are you sure?" I whispered. "You're kissing Zela, but everyone else thinks you're kissing Zeke. If you're not ready for people to know, then don't feel like you have to because of me."

Landon kissed me so thoroughly my knees went weak. I wobbled as we broke apart.

"It wasn't so much a secret as it was no one's business," he whispered against my lips. "I don't care who knows." Landon pulled back and winked. "I'll see you tonight."

"Isn't that nice?"

I stiffened.

"You've managed to fool Foster again. I knew he wasn't over you." Cole stepped in front of me. "What are you going to do to him now? Blind him for good?"

"I'm not For All, Cole. How many times do I have to say it? I wasn't even there when his mark flashed at the dance. Landon will tell you the same thing. I'm innocent." I stepped closer. "Deep down you know it, but you won't let yourself believe it because it'll mean admitting you made a terrible mistake, and we can't have people think Cole Reed isn't perfect."

Cole didn't flinch or back down. Just the opposite. He moved in until our chests bumped. "I won't admit shit because there's something off about you and there always has been. No one else sees it, but I do.

"You follow Derek around like a little puppy when no one in their right mind would put up with that dick. You pretend you don't care about being an F, but it bothers you that you're not seen as the smartest anymore. That's why you have to prove it every day and this Battle Doctor stuff is just more of the same."

I swallowed hard and pulled my fists into the sleeves of my jacket. I wouldn't let him see them shake.

"You want me to believe you," he said softly. "Tell me what you're hiding. The truth—right here, right now.

"Right now!"

I went rigid. The room twirled and the white walls morphed into a merry-go-round of women pushing strollers and packs of teens loaded down with bags.

"Come back here right now! I said no candy."

The toddler wailed.

"Wait!" There was so much noise—screaming, crying, laughing, arguing. The tiny voice tried to rise above the din. "Wait for me!"

"That's what I thought."

Gasping, I stumbled and crashed into the wall. My whole body shook. If the wall wasn't holding me up, I might have collapsed to the floor.

Why is this happening?! They haven't been that vivid in a long time. Why is it all coming back?!

I heard a door slam shut. Cole had left me and went to the club meeting. I forced myself off the wall.

It's okay, Zela. It's not real. It's not real.

I repeated that to myself as I trudged inside. It was time for the Future Leaders Club meeting. I needed to focus on what I was here to do.

"Good afternoon, gentlemen." Mrs. Clancy waved us in from the front of the room. Her classroom fit the excellence one would expect from the Elite. Ten desks, ten chairs, and all of it more expensive than the entire F Wing's budget.

"Please, take your seats."

There were fifteen students in the club, so a few of us had to double up. I took a chair and placed it directly next to Cole. He scowled and got up from his chair.

"I said take your seat, Mr. Reed."

"But, Mrs. Clancy—"

"Sit."

He sat down, scowling harder.

Clancy cleared her throat. "Now, let's begin. Today we're voting on our club leaders. We need to choose a president, vice president, secretary, treasurer, and parliamentarian. You will take on real responsibility, so if you don't feel you can devote the necessary time and effort to the position, do not put your name forward.

"First, raise your hand if you'd like to be president."

Two hands shot into the air. Cole threw me a withering glare.

"What are you doing?" he snapped.

I raised my hand higher. "What does it look like?"

"Okay," said Clancy. "Mr. Reed and Mr. Manning for president. On to vice president."

Clancy collected the names. In the end, it was down to three for vice president and two for president. She had us each come up and make a speech.

"I'm the obvious choice for president," Cole began. "I'm an Elite student who proves every day that I can handle a rigorous schedule on top of athletics. My opponent can't even handle making it to the placement test on time."

I clenched my jaw as the other guys snickered.

"You know me. You know that I'll get the job done. Vote for me."

That was it. Short and sweet.

Cole sat down to applause. I got up and claimed my spot in front of Clancy's desk before the room.

"Cole is right," I said clearly. "I missed my placement test. I got put in the F Class. I sleep in a cramped dorm and don't get any privileges.

"Who gives a shit," I said clearly

Some of the guys stifled a laugh, looking at me in surprise.

"Keep it clean, Mr. Manning," Clancy warned.

"I'm serious," I went on. "Does any of that matter as much as the fact that I got into this club anyway? Beat out the precious A that was supposed to be so much better than me. Does it matter as much as me having the highest GPA in our grade and that I'll beat out Cole this semester?"

Cole surged to his feet. "The fuck you will!"

"Language, Mr. Reed!" Clancy barked.

He plopped down, red faced, and I gave him a wink.

"Does it matter as much as me having the qualities of a leader?" I went on. "If I want something, I not only go for it, I make it happen. You guys know me, too. You know I'm not afraid of a challenge. You know I turn a defeat into a success."

I held out my hands. "If all of that is not enough, consider that I'll truly make the club my first priority, while Cole Reed's priority will always be the swim team, and he doesn't hide that fact. He'd drop the club for a meet or practice without hesitating."

Cole's flush deepened. He couldn't jump around shouting at me for this one. Just last week he missed a meeting for the swim team.

"My last and most important point... I'm much nicer than Cole Reed."

Cracking up, the club applauded me to my seat. His glare could have flayed the skin from my face, but I smirked.

The votes were tallied. Zeke Manning was the president of the Future Leaders Club.

"YOU SHOULD HAVE SEEN his face, Adam. Next, I become captain of Archimedean and claim top spot in our year. He'll lose his mind."

I held open the door for Adam as we walked into the dorm building. "That would do it for sure."

"What about the meet?"

Thursday had rolled around, which brought the day of the swim meet. Nelson didn't make a formal announcement, but it was an open secret among the team that he would choose the captain on the results of the competition.

"I wish I could be there to see you."

Adam squeezed my shoulder. "I know you're cheering me on wherever you are. Stay. Study. I'm going to hold up my end of the plan."

A smile stretched across my lips. "Thanks."

"What about Michael?"

The smile didn't hold. "Michael is a different situation now," I said as we went down the hall. "But I've decided what I'm going to do about him."

"He apologized to you. Has Cole or even Landon done that?"

That was a good point. "It's okay," I finally said. "I know how I'm going to handle it."

"What are you— What is that?"

I followed Adam's fingers to the gift lying in front of our door. I crouched down. "It doesn't say if it's for me or you," I said.

"Why would anyone leave us this?" He opened the door and went in. I picked up the present.

"There was a gift here the other day too," I said as I closed the door behind me. "A water bottle. I think it was from Landon. He probably left this too."

"You think?" Adam bent before his trunk and pulled out his swimsuit. "Did he say anything to you about it?"

"No."

"So it could just as easily be from someone else... like For All."

"Cameron," I stated. "Why would Cameron give me a water bottle? How would that fit into a revenge plot?"

"How does taking your mattress pad fit into a revenge plot?"

"Alright," I mumbled. "Point one to Moon."

"Settle it right now and ask Landon if he gave you the gift."

"Okay."

I took out my phone and shot him a text.

Me: Did you leave a present in front of my door today and after the dance?

He came back right away.

Landon: Nope, not me.

Landon: When are you coming up here? I want to do that thing again with your

I stopped reading right there and shut off the phone. I knew what he was alluding to and seeing it spelled out would have me fire-engine red for the rest of the day.

I really need to get a handle on this guy. Rules are not slowing him down.

"It's not from Landon," I said to Adam's questioning look. "What if it's from Melody?"

He shook his head. "Melody's not risking a month of detention getting caught in the boys' dorm just to leave me something she can hand me at breakfast. Dump it in the trash."

"But it could be from one of our other friends," I protested.

"Do you think it was Tanner, Nico, Justin, Owen, or Derek that picked out that pretty purple wrapping paper and bright blue bow?"

"Fine," I sighed. "Another point to Moon." I moved over to my bin and dropped the gift in the trash.

"Hopefully it's not a bomb."

Adam laughed. "It's not. Cameron doesn't want to kill us... right?"

We both eyed the bin.

"Maybe I'll put it in the dumpster outside," I offered.

"Good idea."

Adam got ready and took off for the meet. I decided to stay in the dorm to get some studying in. I had to ace these finals to have a chance of getting anywhere near the Elite scores, let alone Cole Reed's.

I worked until the sun went down, only breaking once to take the pretty gift out to the dumpster. When I came back, Adam was standing in the middle of our room with a towel slung over his shoulder. He grinned.

"Don't tell me," I said as my cheeks split. "Are you...?"

"You're looking at Breakbattle swim team's newest captain."

I screamed. Adam grunted as I threw myself at him and wrapped my legs around his waist. "Revenge aside, I'm so happy for you."

Laughing, he hugged me tight. "I am too. It's all because of you, Zee. You and I make a good team."

THE NEXT MORNING, I woke before my alarm. It was dark in the room. The beginnings of sunlight peeked over the horizon, not yet strong enough to chase away the gloom. I dressed and went outside.

I knew he would be there. He was always there and he was always a sight to behold. I sat on the bleachers and watched him. It was a wonder if he was real. His body was a sculpted masterpiece made for one purpose: to fly. Gazing at him, it appeared as though his feet weren't touching the track.

Michael broke step when he saw me. Veering off, he jogged over to the bleachers. Sweat glistened on his wrinkled forehead as he hovered over me. One thing I always liked about him was that he wasn't a drippy, sweaty dude that soaked through his clothes if out in the sun for longer than two minutes.

No matter how hard, or fast, or long Michael Young ran, he'd walk off the track covered in a light sheen that only made him look sexier.

He's perfect, I thought. *He's the perfect guy. The perfect student. The perfect athlete. And now, he wants to give me the perfect apology.*

Michael knelt before me as the silence stretched. "Zee? You okay?"

He wants to make everything right so he can go back to being the quiet, unassuming prodigy who never made a mistake and never had to pay for it.

Not this time.

"Did you mean it?" I whispered.

"Did I mean what?"

"You told me you'd do anything to make it up to me. Did you mean it?"

"Yes," he breathed. Michael reached out and took my hands. To anyone looking on, we must have appeared a sweet pair. "I meant it. I'll do anything. Just tell me."

"Lose."

His brows drew together. "Excuse me?"

"That's what I want you to do." The words fell from numb lips. "Lose."

"I... don't understand what that means."

"Lose, Michael." I stroked his hands with my thumbs, almost lovingly. "Every single race. I want you to lose."

"What?" He pulled away like I burned. "You— I— I can't do that!"

"Then, I can't forgive you."

His jaw worked. "But, Zee, I have a team relying on me. Coach. My mom. They all expect me to—"

"And I had friends that I relied on to have my back, not watch while Zach stood on it. This is what I want you to do."

He leaned in, eyes huge and shining. "Anything else, please. Scouts watch our games. This is my future we're talking about."

I stood. "Goodbye, Michael."

"Wait. Don't— Zee!"

I walked off and didn't look back. Michael's shouts followed me until the door slammed shut.

ADAM WAS AWAKE AND on his phone when I returned to the dorm.

"Morning," I said. "Talking to Melody?"

"Nah. It's Jordan."

I heaved a sigh. "I swear you talk to my cousin more than me these days."

"And don't think she's not pissed about it. You should call her. She wants to talk to you."

"I'll call her on the way to breakfast." I flapped a hand at him. "Close your eyes. I'm going to change."

Adam clapped a hand over his eyes and I quickly got dressed. We left after he was ready and I made good on my promise to call my cousin.

"It's about time," she said. "Do you have any idea how long I've been waiting to hear the details?"

"Details about what?"

"Don't try that mess. I know you've been getting hot and dirty with one of those Breakbattle boys."

My eyes bugged out.

"And you said you weren't interested in manflesh," said Jordan.

I whipped around. "Adam Moon!"

Cackling, he burst into a run and expertly dodged my swat. I huffed as he disappeared through the door.

"What exactly did my ex-best friend tell you?"

"Who cares? I want to hear it from you. I also want to know why you didn't tell me sooner."

"Because I didn't know what to say. It was"—I glanced around to make sure no one was listening—"Landon."

"Oh."

With that one "oh" I knew she understood.

"How far did you take it?" she asked.

"Not too far. I stopped it before that."

"But still, you did *things* with him, right? I know I said I was on board with this plan, but don't make choices you're going to regret."

"I know what I'm doing."

"Do you? You had feelings for him. You can't just turn those off and things can get pretty blurry when clothes are falling on the floor."

"It won't get blurry. Those feelings are gone."

"Really?" She did not sound convinced.

"I may be attracted to him physically but... that's... it..." I trailed off as I rounded the corner.

A group of B boys blocked my path, shuffling and yawning as they took up the hallway.

"Are you trying to convince yourself or me?" asked Jordan.

"Hold on." I rose on tiptoe to peer over their heads. The line continued down the hallway and stretched around the corner. "Jordan, I have to go. I'll call you back."

"You better because now that I've imparted my wisdom, I can hear every detail and squeal without shame."

"Got it."

I hung up and pushed through the crowd, looking for Adam. I spotted his curly mop of hair halfway down the hall. He was speaking to his mom.

"Adam. Miss Val. What's going on?"

Miss Val brushed Adam's hair back. "That's what I came to say. Go and get your things, baby. You're going to come with me."

"Okay."

She clapped. "Attention, everyone. Listen up." The noise dropped to a dull roar. "The dining room is closed. I repeat, the dining room is closed. Breakfast will be served in the basketball and wrestling gyms. Boys will go to the wrestling gym."

The hallway began to empty out as the boys trudged off with no questioning. I had a few questions.

"Why are we having breakfast in the gym?"

Miss Val gave me a look I couldn't decipher. "Wait until they've gone."

By the time everyone left, Adam returned. Miss Val grabbed our shoulders and led us to the side. "There was another prank."

"Another prank?" Adam said. "What happened?"

"Someone got into the kitchen last night and unplugged the fridges. We can't serve food to students that hasn't been properly stored. It all has to be thrown out and now the staff is scrambling to serve up something else."

"But why can't we go into the dining room?"

"Because whoever did it spray-painted an upside-down A over the head table."

Adam and I shared a look.

"What?" Miss Val asked. "Do you know something about this?"

"No," I said. "But I don't get it. What does Cameron have to gain by spoiling breakfast?"

"Something that we can't see yet," Adam said. "Like with you."

"Maybe."

Miss Val sighed. "I've spoken to Cameron Dupre twice and he maintains his innocence. We can't prove he committed those acts last year or today. No one saw anything and they wouldn't. We don't have cameras or guards patrolling the hallways. I'm going to speak with the principal and vice principal again because this can't go on."

She kissed Adam's cheek. "But for now, you'll eat with me until the cafeteria opens. The perks of having a mom on staff."

I mumbled goodbye and walked off. My mind was spinning. I didn't know what was going on, but something did not feel right.

I stepped outside and a shadow fell over me.

"I want to make things right, Zee."

Stiffening, I didn't turn around. "Then you know what to do."

"I can't lose on purpose."

"That's your choice, Michael. You have a track meet after break. I'll be there. You decide."

I walked off. Michael didn't follow me.

Chapter Eight

By some miracle, I got through finals. By an even bigger miracle, I walked away from them with a straight A average.

I smirked at Cole all through our last day of the semester. He got all As too, so technically we were tied, but it didn't stop him looking fit to throw a table.

"How'd you do, Cole?" I sidled up to him as he headed for lunch. Yes, I waited for him to come down.

"Fuck off."

I tsked. "This has not been your year, has it? Lost the presidency, lost the captaincy, and I beat you for highest average."

"You didn't beat me," he snapped. "We tied."

"Oh?" I quirked an eyebrow. "How would you know that? Did you check up on a lowly F's grades?"

The muscles in his neck bulged with the effort of holding himself back.

"I didn't know you cared that much."

"I don't care."

Cole picked up the pace and I was practically running to keep up with him.

"But that's the problem, isn't it, Cole?" I said in his ear. "You don't care about anyone but yourself. But what you're feeling right now—that feeling like no matter what you do or how hard you work, you can't get what you want. You care about that, and I'll make sure you feel this way until you've learned something."

Cole lengthened his strides and finally got away from me. I let him go.

My family would be here in minutes to pick me up for two weeks of Christmas cookies, presents, music, and complete freedom from the world of Breakbattle. Words couldn't convey how much I was looking forward to it.

I ran out the gates at two o'clock on the dot. Jordan pounded the horn, screaming her head off, while Mom waved from the driver's seat.

We drove home with the music blasting and us singing along at the top of our lungs. Jordan and I did the singing. That Mom let us do it showed what a good mood she was in.

Christmas break was everything I wanted and more. We baked those cookies, opened dozens of presents, and Adam invited us to his annual Christmas Eve party where I stole baby Jessie and narrowly escaped a beating from Esme.

A huge part of me did not want to go back to Breakbattle when the day finally came for Mom to drive me back to school. It was hard to kiss her goodbye in front of the gates, but there were some perks to being back.

I pulled away, leaning back on the headboard.

"Where are you going?" Landon snaked an arm around my waist and drew me in.

I pressed my swollen lips to his throat so he couldn't claim them again. "You were saying something and I interrupted you. Finish telling me."

His chuckle rumbled against my lips. "I didn't mind the interruption."

I wasn't too proud to admit keeping my hands off of Landon was impossible, and he knew it. We were a few days into the first week and had been all over each other. The guy told me a story about his winter break while slowly removing his uniform to change. I jumped him before he got his pants all the way up.

Twisting around, I glanced at the clock.

Thirty minutes making out. Eight minutes talking. Zero minutes studying. Doing great, Zela.

"I'm serious," I said. "I want to hear the rest."

He sighed. "It's not that interesting. I spent the last week in Europe with Declan. I modeled for him. Did a few photo shoots."

"That doesn't sound boring to me."

"It is." Landon leaned back and took me with him. He enfolded me into his side, draping his arm around my waist. "Declan works the whole time but he doesn't trust me to walk the city alone, so he makes me stay in the hotel. When I'm not being shouted at by photographers, I'm sitting in my room all day watching Netflix."

"Oh." I rested my head on his chest. His heart beat in my ear, steady and soothing. "Well, it's sweet that he wants his son to be a part of his work."

"Only because I fit his brand. Henrietta has no use for a boy since she sells makeup, so her total number of bring-your-kid-to-work days are zero. If I'm ever horribly mangled in an accident, Declan won't have use for me either."

I raised my head to meet his eyes. "Does that upset you?" I was genuinely asking. Landon sounded so matter-of-fact it was hard to tell.

"Nope." He shifted to smile at me. "I bitch a lot, but they're decent parents. They don't let me wander around strange cities, but when I'm home they let me do whatever I want. There's always food in the fridge, money in my account, and they didn't blink when I came out. Can't ask for much more."

I think you could ask for a little more, I thought, but I didn't say it out loud.

"My mom and I have a weird relationship too," I said. "I know she loves me, but she puts a lot of pressure on me. Like she gave up a lot to raise me and I have to prove I'm worth it."

Landon's finger skated along my skin as he brushed a strand of hair behind my ear. "You're worth it."

Breath catching, my heart fluttered. My internal voice shouted a warning but it faded in the background as our lips met. This wasn't our usual passionate tongue battles. Landon kissed me slow and sweet. The opposite of the wild pounding in my chest. We broke apart and Landon dropped little kisses along my jaw.

"I have a question." His hot breath warmed my ear, making me shiver. "Are you going on the spring break field trip?"

"What... field trip?" I whispered.

Landon kept kissing me, leaving a burning trail down my neck. "After finals, Elites and As are going on a field trip to Orlando. Water parks, amusement parks, five nights in a hotel." Landon reached the strap of my tank top and slowly pulled it down. "I want you to come."

"I... don't know." I bit my lip hard as Landon moved to the other strap. I was highly aware of his hand on my hip, his thigh between my legs, his sweet scent, and his lips pressed to my skin. He was overloading my senses and my brain worked overtime attempting to supply me with words.

"Even if I win a spot," I continued. "I'd have to pay for it. A trip like that... sounds expensive. My mom might not go for it."

"Convince her." He was teasing me now. Landon dropped kisses on my collarbone instead of going where I expected him to go.

"I can't convince my mom to do anything she doesn't want to do."

He chuckled. "It'll be worth it to try. We'll have fun, ride the rides, stuff our faces, and we could even break a few rules."

I formed my lips to ask what rules until Landon raised his head. He gazed at me through heavy-lidded eyes and my pulse quickened.

"Come on, my sweet, sexy genius. Find a way to be with me."

This is just a physical attraction. The feelings I had for the strong, funny guy with the jelly bean eyes don't exist anymore. He means nothing to me. All I care about is making him feel the pain I felt. Nothing else.

I grabbed his face and pulled him in for a kiss that had us both panting when I pulled back.

"Okay. I'll be there."

FOR A RELATIONSHIP that wasn't really a relationship, it looked a lot like one.

Landon walked me to class every morning and waited outside for me at the end of the day. We went back to wrestling together and he joined me on my run most nights. He sat with me for breakfast, lunch, and dinner, and at night, breached the edges of the rules when we should have been studying. A week of this and it got hard to remember a time that wasn't Landon, Landon, Landon.

I pulled in my chair and picked up my chocolate chip muffin. I dropped it on Derek's plate. "Here you go."

He grunted a thanks.

"What are you doing tonight? I feel like it's been forever since we hung out."

"I'm busy," he clipped.

"Really?" I hooked my arm through his and gave him a little shake. "But I thought we could go back to your room after the meet and watch a movie. We can do a short one."

"I said I'm busy." Derek slipped his arm out of mine. "I've got mentor stuff with Hunter."

"Tomorrow?"

"We'll see."

I frowned. Derek didn't make eye contact with me throughout the whole exchange. "Are you okay?"

"Yep."

"Then why don't you want to hang out? We don't have to watch a movie. We can just sit on your bed and read."

Derek finally turned to me. The look on his face made me reel back. "My door isn't fucking open whenever you can be bothered to remember I exist."

"What are you talking about?"

His eyes drifted over my head. "Besides, I think you're busy tonight too."

"Hey, baby." An arm snaked around my neck. Landon took hold of my chin and tilted it to receive his kiss. When he let go, Derek was gone.

"Derek? Derek?" I twisted around and spotted his retreating back as he walked out of the dining room. I made to stand up.

"Where are you going?"

"I have to go after him." I tugged at his arm to get free. "I think Derek is mad at me."

Landon heaved a sigh. "What's he got to be mad about? You're the only one who tolerates his bullshit. He should be running after you."

"Landon, I have to go."

"Leave him." He sat me firmly back down. "If he's really mad, he needs time to cool off. Catch him at the meet. You're going, right?"

"Yes." Reluctantly, I sat down. Landon had a point. It was always better to approach Derek when he was calm.

"Good." Landon buried his nose in my neck. His breath tickled as he spoke. "I'll save you a seat. Afterward, we'll go up to my room to study."

"Only if we actually study," I said. "I got among the top grade point averages last semester. This year, I'll be number one. No ties."

"You have strong competition, Zee."

He kissed my neck and a shiver thrummed my spine.

How do I make that stop happening? Why does he have this power over my body?

"Cole says he's gunning hard for it. First week back and he spends every spare minute in the library."

And it won't be enough.

I gazed across the room at Michael and Cole. Landon still hung with them, although they sat at their table alone these days. Every now and then, I'd look up and find one or both of them staring at me, or staring at me and Landon.

"You guys are so cute," Melody spoke up from the circle of Adam's arms, but she was one to talk. She and Adam had been all over each other since the dance. Adam couldn't sneak into her room as easily as I could go into Landon's, but he went somewhere every night. My best friend had a permanent goofy smile on these days.

"Adam said you were planning to go on the field trip," Melody went on. She leaned her head back and gazed up at Adam. "You should come too. The four of us can hang out."

"Perfect," Landon replied. He squeezed me tighter. "Tell me you got your mom to agree. I don't want to go if you're not there."

"She called me back this morning. She said yes."

Landon stole a kiss and I could feel him smiling through it. His excitement bubbled over and engulfed me, filling me with an emotion that had been plaguing me since that night in his room.

He's so happy just at the thought of spending time with me.

Good, said another voice. *That's what we want. He has to fall hard for you, so letting him go will break him. This is what we want.*

I returned his kiss without holding back.

This is what I want.

OUR GROUP TRUDGED ACROSS the grass behind the people leading the way to the stands. It was time for the track meet against Chesterfield High and a few other high schools. I wished Jordan was here. I wished I wasn't. Michael wasn't going to throw the race. His reasons for running were bigger than me—bigger than our brief friendship. As much guilt as he may have felt, he did not care about me enough to sacrifice this. Today would only prove it.

"You okay?"

"I'm fine, Nico."

"We can bail if you want."

I shook my head. "I said I would be here. I have to see this through."

"Whatever, man."

The stands were beginning to fill up. Most of the seats were taken, except for the one next to Landon... and Cole.

"I'm going to sit with Melody," Adam said before taking off.

Tanner waved at someone in the stands. "I'll sit with the team."

Nico's face fell as his best friend took off. "I'll sit in the back and wonder how I became the pathetic one with no boyfriend, girlfriend, or friends at all."

Laughing, I snagged his collar as he tried to take off. "You're sitting with me, Nico, and you'll like it."

He beamed. "I'm cool with that."

I spotted the boys in the second row. Cole scowled when we approached. "Sit somewhere else."

Nico turned around.

"Not you, Kazan." Cole narrowed his eyes on me. "You."

"Zee isn't going anywhere," Landon said. "I told you about this. We're together. Get over it."

"You're fucking," Cole clipped. "There's a difference. Did *Zee* ever tell you why he doesn't want to be exclusive?"

"That's none of your business," I said.

"My theory is you're holding out hope that Derek will go out with you," he plowed on. "Give it up. He doesn't do relationships and he never will. The guy has the emotional depth of a teardrop."

"You can be as horrible as you want, but you're not driving me off." I plopped my butt on the bench to prove it.

Nico was slower to sit down. He perched on the edge of the seat like he was poised to run.

Speaking of poised to run.

My eyes found Michael on the side of the track, speaking to his coach. He looked good, but then he always looked good. His track uniform was loose on his body and yet it was meant for him. His strong, ropy arms. Calves I could hammer a nail with and skin that reflected the sunlight. Michael Young was perfect, and this is what he was meant to do.

Landon put his arm around me and drew me close. "You're spending the night with me, right?"

"We can have dinner," I said. "Afterward, I'm going to find Derek. I need to make sure we're okay."

Landon pulled away slightly. "What is it with you and him? For real, Zela. Is Cole right about...?"

"Cole has never and will never be right about anything."

A low hiss told me Cole heard that.

"I'm trying to have a relationship with Derek and that relationship is a friendship. As I'm sure you can guess, he doesn't make that easy on anyone, but it's worth it. He was there for me when I needed him."

Landon dropped his eyes.

"So if he needs me right now, I'll be there for him."

"I get it. Don't bug you about Derek."

"No, don't." I nudged him to take the sting out of it. "I'll stay over tomorrow night."

"You better." He gave me a quick peck. "Or I'll find you, throw you over my shoulder, and take you where you belong."

I giggled. "So I belong in your bed?"

"I'd never let you leave my bed if I could get away with it."

"If I could get away with it, I'd let you keep me in bed."

Landon's grin was wolfish. His eyes were pink tinged with silver today and they heated up as my lust ignited. "You should stay at school this weekend. We'll spend it together."

"I—"

"You should both shut up," Cole snapped. "The meet is about to start and you're making me sick."

I rolled my eyes but did shut up. Cole was right about the meet starting.

Michael took his place on the line. It was hard to tell from my seat, but I imagined his expression was the same as when we ran together. Serene calm belied by laser focus. It was the face of someone who knew he could achieve anything he wanted. He only had to take it.

I used to like that about him. Michael made me feel like I could do anything too. He encouraged me to do better, breathe harder, run longer. I felt like I was getting close to him in a way no one other than Cole ever did.

The horn blew and the runners took off.

But I was wrong.

Michael raced ahead of the pack. The others were light-years behind him as he rounded the first bend.

Sighing, I dropped my head. *There it is. I have no choice. I have to move on to Plan B.*

The thought stirred nothing in me. It didn't waken the tight ball of pain and rage that had been my constant companion.

"What the fuck?" I heard Cole say. "What is he doing?"

I looked up. Michael wasn't light years ahead of the pack. He was hardly inches ahead of them. As he reached the last bend, Michael slowed to a pace that was near enough to crawling for him.

I rose from my seat, eyes widening.

The other runners huffed and puffed, vigor renewed, as their sole competition came within their reach, and as I watched, every single one of them ran past him.

Chesterfield High crossed the finish line and roared. The winner jumped up and down, lapping up the cheers from his team.

Our students were silent.

He did it. Michael lost... for me.

THE STANDS WERE LONG empty. I sent Landon on with a kiss and promise we'd see each other at dinner. It was only me and Michael.

"Disgraceful!"

And Coach.

"Did you fall asleep out there, Young?!"

"No, Coach."

"You must have! That's the only explanation!"

I could see the spittle flying from my seat.

"You quit, Young! You quit on me, on this team, and on yourself!"

"I just felt off, Coach. I'm sorry."

"You take your tummy aches to the nurse! When you're on the track, you give nothing but your best! Do you understand me?!"

"Yes, Coach."

Coach stormed off. Michael stood still until he slammed inside. I tensed as he closed the distance between us.

For a long time, we just stared at each other. Michael's handsome face was the picture of serenity I once admired. He looked like he could do the silent game all day and never tire. I wasn't that patient.

I burst out, "If you're waiting for me to apologize for getting you chewed out, I—"

"I'm waiting for you to say you forgive me."

Michael took a step and I scrambled to my feet. I sucked in a breath as he cupped my face.

"I'm waiting for you to say we can go back to how things were."

My heart beat loudly in my ears. *What is he doing?*

Michael stroked my cheek, soft and gentle and terrible for the confusing mess of feelings it caused. The anger was still there. The betrayal simmered beneath the surface, but among that, was the crush I thought I buried.

"I can't say that," I whispered. "Not yet."

Michael pressed his forehead to mine. "Then I'll lose. I'll throw every race until you can."

My eyes stung. I don't know why. It was stupid to cry over him getting exactly what he deserved. "Why are you doing this?"

"Because I want— I need you to trust me again. I told you that I'm a good guy, but I've acted like a complete shit since we met and the locker room..." He sighed and his breath tickled my nose. "If I'm a good guy, then I'd face the consequences of what I've done. That's what I'm going to do, Zee."

He stepped away, dropping his hand, and I stumbled. I hadn't realized I was leaning on him, drawing closer to his body like a gravitational pull.

"And you're going to forgive me."

I watched him go. Minutes after he stepped inside, I summoned the strength to pick up my feet. What was I supposed to do now? There was no fight. No argument. No calling me an evil bitch who should get over herself.

Michael was willing to give up what mattered to him for me. How could I know how to handle something I never thought would happen?

My feet carried me up to the sixth floor on autopilot. I walked past Landon's door and knocked on Derek's. It flew open without the customary shouting to go away.

He took one look at me and frowned. "What are you doing here? I told you— *Oomph.*"

I hugged him tight. "Whatever I did to upset you, I'm sorry. I know we haven't hung out lately, but I haven't forgotten you exist." I pulled back and flicked him on the nose.

"Hey," he cried.

"But if you want to talk or spend time with me, you have to say so. I'm not into this one-sided thing where I put in all the effort and you pout whenever I get busy."

"I don't pout."

"You know where I sleep, eat, and study." I wrapped my arms around him and rested my head on his chest. "Come to me when you need me."

"Stop hugging me," he mumbled.

"No."

His chest rumbled with a soft laugh. "I get it. I just don't like seeing you with Foster. Not after what he did. You said you were going to take a stripe out of his ass, and instead you're sleeping with him. In no universe does he deserve you."

"Why does everyone think we're sleeping together?"

"Because you're in his room every damn night. I know you're not studying."

"Well, we're not having sex either," I said. "Also, nothing has changed. Landon will pay for what he did to me."

"Yeah," he drew out. "I can see you're really making him suffer."

"Leave Landon to me. All you need to do is stop being a weirdo and watch a movie with me."

"Later, Zee. I can't tonight." He grabbed my arms. "You have to go."

"Right now? But I can wait until Hunter—"

"What's this?"

Derek's grip on me tightened.

"You're already catching some off Landon," said a loathsome voice. "Now, you're trying it on with Derek."

I turned my head. *What is this?*

Santiago, Heath, and Cameron stopped in front of us with varying expressions on their faces. Cameron wore his usual dislike. Santiago looked like he couldn't be bothered to care, and Heath smirked at his nasty comment.

"Want us to come back later so you can bang it out?"

"Shut the fuck up, Dowell." Derek moved me to the side and stepped out of the room. "Let's go."

"Go?" I spoke up. "Go where?"

The three set off without another word to me and Derek followed.

"Derek," I called, taking a step. "Do you need me to—?"

"Stay here, Zee."

Something in his tone made me stop. The four of them left and didn't come back for hours. I knew because I waited until well into the night before finally giving up.

THE NEXT MORNING, ADAM'S alarm woke me.

Groaning, I blinked blearily at the noisy thing. What happened?

What happened is I stayed up so late waiting for Derek that I didn't finish my homework until two in the morning. Then I passed out without setting my alarm.

"Zela?" Adam croaked. "What are you doing in bed?"

I buried my face in the pillows.

Eventually, the two of us got dressed and out the door. I stumbled on a tiny, wrapped package sitting on the carpet.

"I got it." Adam picked up the present and put it under his arm. I knew where he was planning to relocate it.

"Maybe we should open it," I offered. "See who it's from first."

"No one we know has a reason to drop gifts in front of our door. We're not opening it, Zee."

"Anyone ever tell you that you're overprotective?"

"All of my siblings," he replied. "Even Jessie, but she babbles it."

I chuckled. "Fair enough."

Adam deposited the gift in the trash on the way to the cafeteria. "About the field trip," he said as he joined my side. "Did you challenge the A that you're going to battle?"

"No, but I know who. Landon and I have been practicing again and he thinks I'm good enough to take on Penn Yu."

"Good idea. He gets cocky on the mat and collects A minuses in English. You should challenge him on that subject."

I hummed. "And they call me the Battle Doctor."

"You've earned the title. Tanner is kicking ass on the field. He loves you now."

"Didn't he love me before?"

"Nope." He bumped into me. "We guys don't give it up that easily. You have to work for it."

I snorted a laugh. "Am I still working for your love?"

"Yes, and you better step it up."

We stumbled through the doors of the dining room laughing our heads off. The noise almost blew us back out.

"Can you believe this?!"

"It's fucking sweet!"

"My sister is going to freak out when she sees this," Nico cried as he ran up to us. He waved his new prize in our faces. "Guys, look. They were on the tables when we came in. New MT tablets. One for everyone."

Nico shoved it in my hand. I recognized the tablet right away. "Um, yeah. Adam's dad did say they were for the whole school so—"

"Whoo!" He snatched it back and raced off to celebrate with Tanner.

I looked around at everyone showing off their tablets and grinning like Christmas came again. In a way it did. Maverick Technology tablets debut at prices north of a thousand dollars. Not a lot for the Evergreen kids, but for Chesterfield babies like me, most of our parents could never afford to buy us something like this.

"It was cool of your dad to let us be his guinea pigs," I said as we backed toward the food line.

"Yeah, but don't you think it's weird that—"

"The tablets were left out on the tables instead of passed out in class?" I finished.

He nodded.

"Yes, I do."

Tanner and Nico were still gushing over their tablets when we sat down. Landon took a more relaxed approach.

"Cool," he said as he tapped the screen awake. He patted his lap and I sat in it. I leaned against his chest as he wrapped his arms around me and rested the tablet on my knee. "I was going to buy this one anyway."

"Dad worked on this himself," Adam said. He paused to give Melody a peck on the lips. "It's ten times better than the last model."

"Are these ours or just for school?"

"They're—"

"That is enough!"

The bark caused half my table to jump. All eyes flew to the entrance as Whittaker stormed in. On his heels were Argyle and Miss Val.

Whittaker stopped in front of the head table. The man looked madder than I had ever seen him. His suit was perfectly pressed and not a strand was out of place, but the purplish hue to his face said all was not well.

"Students, you are to bring those tablets up here immediately!"

No one moved.

I looked around at my friends, mirroring their wide-eyed expressions.

"But." A tremulous voice broke through the silence. "Why?"

Whittaker turned toward the person. "Those tablets were removed from a locked storage room and given without permission. This is an extremely serious offense—tantamount to stealing. These actions against the school will no longer be tolerated. When this For All is found, they will be expelled."

"For All?" I repeated.

I glanced at the extra tablet sitting before my usual seat. *Cameron broke into the storage room and passed these out to us. Why?*

"But aren't these for us?" Tanner got to his feet. "How is that stealing? You were going to give them to us anyway."

Whittaker pushed back his jacket placing his hands on his hips. "They were to be given to the students, but only after it was decided among the staff how to incorporate the tablets into the privilege system."

"Privilege?" Tanner repeated. "But they belong to us. You can't—"

"Mr. Grady, they were given to the school," Whittaker stated. "Given with the caveat that you all have access to them, but that access will be determined by me."

"But—"

"I do not suggest you argue with me on this. It's a battle you will not win."

On any other day and any other topic, that response would have ended the conversation.

"I don't understand," Melody said as she rose from her chair. "Mr. Beaumont told me himself that the tablets were free to all the students with the rule that they be kept *out* of the system. If not, they would be given to Chesterfield. Isn't that right, Miss Val?"

Adam's mom stepped forward. She raised her chin and said clearly, "Yes. That was my partner's intention. The only string attached is that you share any glitches or ideas for improvements as he readies it for the market. But they are a gift and they belong to you."

If Miss Val noticed the look her boss threw her, she gave no sign.

Melody folded her arms and met the principal's eyes steadily. "If that is what Mr. Beaumont wanted, then we get to keep them."

Whittaker's face was approaching a hue that appeared dangerous—for him or Melody, I wasn't sure. "Mr. Beaumont does not decide what happens in this school."

"No, but we decide what happens to our belongings," Melody threw back. "Especially after the school got in trouble for making our personal items a part of the battle system. It's my tablet, and I'm not giving it back."

"Yeah."

I didn't catch who sounded the first whoop but it was quickly followed by more. Soon, most of the room was clapping and egging her on.

Whittaker slammed his fist on the table. The cheering stopped instantly. "That's enough! You are to stand up and place those tablets on the head table or you will receive a month's detention."

Excruciatingly long seconds passed as no one moved.

Then Melody picked up her tablet, stepped away from the table, and walked out.

She disappeared around the corner by the time Adam picked up his and followed her. The rest of the dominoes fell.

Tanner and Nico walked out. Hunter was two steps behind them. Then went a group of girls I didn't know well, but recognized as Melody's friends. Whittaker watched them go in equal parts anger and disbelief.

I was roused from my shock by a kiss on the cheek. "Are you going after them, Zee?"

"Yes," I replied. "I am."

I climbed out of his lap, grabbed the tablet waiting for me, and made for the door. I took two steps before I realized someone was behind me.

Landon put his arm around my shoulder and marched next to me.

"Stop right there."

I skidded to a halt as a body stepped into our path. Argyle held out her hands.

"Tablets. Now."

I considered refusing, but she had a glint in her eye even scarier than Whittaker's. I had a feeling she wasn't used to blatant disobedience from her students, but she was prepared to deal with it harshly.

We handed them over. One by one, the rest of the students walked up to the head table and surrendered For All's surprise.

Landon and I were given a week of detention for our almost-walkout. The others got a month, but we all got our tablets back a week later with a few conditions.

Dr. O'Quinn handed me my device as she went down the row. "Since the news is out, I don't have to tell you much about what these are or who gave them to you."

"At least we finally get them back," Nico said.

"It's not that simple, Mr. Kazan. The staff have discussed it and we decided on the best way to incorporate it into the system and allow you to benefit the way Mr. Beaumont intended.

"Monday through Friday after school, we will have a study hall of sorts. You will come in, check out your tablets, and work quietly on the assignments I've given you. Seeing as every student has their own tablet, there is no reason to battle for them. That being the case, they are not a part of the battle system, but they are considered a privilege and privileges reflect class. In your case, your tablet time is restricted to two hours after school."

Tanner raised his hand. "What about weekends and stuff?"

"Unless I assign you weekend homework that requires the use of this device, you are not allowed to take it home."

"But the Elites can, can't they?"

O'Quinn didn't reply, which was answer enough.

"This isn't fair." Tanner ran his hand through his hair, making it stick up. "They're ours."

"You need to understand that they were gifted to the *school* as educational tools. Despite the numerous irate calls parents have made over the last few days, you have no grounds to claim these devices as your property." She pinned him with a look. "So let me be clear, any more argument on this and you will be in detention for the rest of the year."

Tanner cursed under his breath. In a louder voice, he said, "Yes, Dr. O'Quinn."

I didn't think it was fair, but I could say that about everything in Breakbattle Academy. I had to choose my battles and nothing was more important right now than beating out Cole, enticing Landon, and seeing Michael lose. Those last few weeks until spring break, every part of my plan was going perfectly.

Michael lost two more track meets and Coach screamed himself hoarse. Landon and I spent almost every free minute studying, wrestling, or making out. Cole watched me run Future Leaders as president and be chosen by Mrs. Peterson as captain of the Archimedean team.

Cole glared at me as I tossed my backpack under the bus.

"It's a wonder your face doesn't stick like that," I said. "Frown lines are a real thing. You're too pretty for them."

"Fuck you. You're real smug, but we both got straight As and do I need to remind you my classes are ten times harder than yours? Tying for top spot means nothing. Neither does sucking up to Peterson until she handed you the captaincy."

"Hmm." I straightened and flashed him a grin. "If it means nothing, why are you so mad?"

A vein in his forehead ticked. "I'm mad because you're fucking with me. You've joined all my clubs and you've fucked with my friends." He advanced on me, stopping only when we were a hair apart. "You think I don't know what you're making Michael do? When are you going to let up? When he gets kicked off the team? When he loses a chance of getting a scholarship? When his and his mom's dream is flushed down the toilet?"

My fist clenched within the sleeves of my sweater. "Michael made his own choice. I'm not out on the track with a gun to his head. You ever think there are more important things than athletic dreams? Like maybe... being a decent person."

"No," he hissed. "I don't."

Cole's hair brushed against my forehead as he got in my face. His eyes blazed with intensity, but there wasn't a day when they didn't.

It's like he wants things more, feels things harder, and experiences life deeper than the rest of us, and I only need to look in his eyes to see what he can't hold back.

"You're going to stop this. You will let up on Michael, step down as president of Future Leaders, quit the math club, and stop playing whatever game you're pulling on Landon."

I swallowed hard through a throat that was suddenly dry and scratchy. "Why would you think I'm playing a game with Landon?"

"Because if you're fucking with me and Michael, then you're definitely fucking with him. He's too in love to see it, but I warned you. I see right through you."

"You think so?"

"I know so."

We must have been an interesting sight. Both of us puffed up, eyes flashing, and in each other's faces.

"And if you don't stop," Cole plowed on. "I'll make you."

"How are you going to do that? Show up with five of your closest friends and jump me?"

"I would never hurt you again!"

I stepped back at the force of his response.

"I wouldn't have someone else do it either, but you and I both know, there are plenty of ways to get at a person that aren't physical. End it now, *Zela*."

Cole turned his back on me.

"Did you ever think this would stop if you learned your lesson? You've never said sorry, Cole."

He paused and I eyed the tense muscles of his back as I waited for him to say something. He picked up his feet and kept going.

"Great talking to you too," I called. He ignored me and stomped onto the bus.

I climbed up too. This was it. This bus was driving through the night to take us on the big Elite and A Class field trip. Five days and four nights in an Orlando resort and every day a different theme park.

Landon was beside himself about me going. After I won the battle for my spot, he scooped me up, kissed me, and heavily implied things would go down in his hotel room.

The bus was still filling up, so I grabbed a seat near the back. Adam and Melody came up next and grabbed the row across from me.

"One to ten," Adam said. "How jealous is Jordan that you're going to Orlando without her?"

I groaned. "Sixty-two. Aunt Bev is getting sick of her begging to transfer to Breakbattle."

Melody asked, "Who is Jordan?"

"She is Zee's cousin," Adam said. "She's terrified of roller coasters and gets crazy motion sick, but she told me to step in if Zee has too much fun without her."

"Feel free to ignore that order," I put in.

Derek and Landon stepped onto the bus. I waved them over. Derek came down the aisle and threw himself on the seat next to me. Landon stood over him.

"I was going to sit there, Derek."

"And now I'm sitting here."

"Get up."

Derek laced his fingers behind his head and leaned back. "Why doesn't Zee tell me to get up?"

They both turned to me. Biting my lip, I glanced up at Landon. "We can ride together on the way back."

His jaw clenched.

"You heard him," said Derek. "Move along."

Cursing, Landon took the seat behind me while I gave Derek a look.

"You don't have to make trouble, you know."

"Who's making trouble? I'm just hanging out with my friend Zee."

I rolled my eyes but didn't say more about it. The truth was we were hanging out like we used to but we weren't talking much. Derek refused to explain what he was doing with Cameron, Heath, and Santiago that day. I wouldn't tell him what I had planned for Landon. As a result, we spent most of our time reading books inches away from each other while I felt like we had never been further apart.

On the ride to Orlando, we kept things light. We read, watched movies, joked around with Melody, Adam, and Landon, and made a plan on how to tackle the trip.

"First, Islands of Adventure. Second, Universal Studios. Then, Magic Kingdom, Animal Kingdom, and Epcot." Landon reached through the seat and stroked my arm. "You're not afraid of roller coasters, are you?"

"Don't know. I've never been on one."

Derek lifted his eye mask to give me a crazy look. I balked at him when he pulled it out. Sometimes I'd forget what a pampered prince he was and then he'd remind me.

"You've never been on a roller coaster?"

"I've never been to an amusement park either."

"How is that possible?"

"Mom wasn't into them, so she never took me."

Landon's finger glided along my skin. "I'm glad I get to experience your first with you."

I was saved from having to find an answer to that by Mrs. Clancy. "Alright, everyone. We'll be at the resort in ten minutes. A few things before we get there. If your parents paid for the upgrade, you will have your own room. Otherwise, there will be two people to a room and you may choose your roommate.

"We have seven a.m. wake-ups to beat the lines. Be awake, fed, and in the lobby at eight thirty sharp. You're sixteen and seventeen years old. We expect you can handle being on your own, so you will have our numbers, but will be allowed to roam freely. As long as you don't leave the parks, we want you to have fun."

It did sound like fun. Exploring some of the best theme parks in the world with my friends was an incredible field trip and it made it worse that most of my friends couldn't come.

The bus lumbered under the hotel portico and turned us out. Together our group entered a dazzling lobby of marble floors, indoor palm trees, and glittering chandeliers that cast light on our tired faces.

"Everyone, get your room assignments," said Clancy. "Then off to bed."

Adam's parents sprung for the upgrade while my mom didn't. He smiled guiltily as he accepted his key. "Sorry, Zee. I'd let you sleep with me anyway but"—he peered over his shoulder at Melody—"I can't."

"Don't worry about me. I'll be fine."

A hand draped over my shoulder. "You can sleep with me like you *always* do."

Just as quickly, Derek's arm was gone. Landon pressed his body against me. "Zee is staying with me."

"Zee is sleeping in his own room and will see you all in the morning." I untangled myself from Landon and took off.

"Zee, wait." Landon caught up to me at the elevator and took my hand. He pressed something in my palm. "In case you change your mind." He kissed me and then left for the elevators that would take him to the single suites.

I pressed his room key to my chest as I waited. *I know what he wants to do. He believes we're ready to take things to the next level. Landon feels this is real. He cares about me.*

Which makes this the perfect time to dump him.

The plastic cut sharply into my skin as my fist clenched. *This is the plan. This was always the plan. I have to do this or he gets away with what he let those boys do to me. I have to do this.*

The words repeated on a loop as I rode up to the sixth floor. I found my room at the end of the hall. It was a cute space with two full beds, a small fridge, and a big-screen tele-

vision. I tossed my backpack on the bed and then threw myself after it.

My face buried into the comforter. I relaxed as I inhaled
the fresh, downy smell of detergent. I didn't have to decide
what to do about Landon right this minute. All I needed to
do now was sleep.

I heard the door open.

"Hey," I said. "I hope you don't mind I took the bed by
the window."

"It's all yours."

I shot up so fast I tipped and fell off the bed. "Michael?!"

"Are you okay?" Footsteps and then two hands lifted me
up.

"I'm fine," I muttered. I tugged free and reclaimed my
spot on the bed. Michael sat down across from me, and for a
while, we just stared at each other. I broke first. "Why didn't
you get a single room?"

He shrugged. "Want the truth?"

"Of course not, I love lies."

Michael cracked a smile. "You might. You do lie to people every day, Zela."

"I think we're veering away from the point."

Sighing, Michael stretched out on the sheets. "I didn't
get a single because I figured you wouldn't either. I asked
Clancy to put us together."

"Why would you do that?" I chuckled. "Are you planning to smother me in my sleep?"

Michael heaved himself off the bed. "I'm going to shower."

"Michael? Michael, I'm going to need an answer to that question. Michael!"

His laughter was the last thing I heard before the bathroom door shut.

SOMEHOW, I MADE IT through the night. I shivered as Landon pressed a kiss to my neck. "Use the key tonight. I have something special planned."

My heart thumped too loudly in my chest. "Special?"

"Trust me," he whispered. His nose skated over my skin as he traveled up to my ear. "You'll like it."

"Morning, everyone," called one of the chaperones. "You've waited long enough. Let's hit Islands of Adventure!"

Excitement pumped through my veins as we piled onto the bus and took the short ride to my first theme park. Landon stuck close by me this time as we got off the bus together, holding hands.

"Do you guys want to be alone?" Melody asked. "Or ride the rides with us?"

"Let's do it together," I replied. "We Es and Fs don't get to hang out enough."

"We'll come with." Michael stepped up to our circle. He looked handsome today. I thought that when he dressed in front of me and it crossed my mind again. Michael wore a pair of tight-fitted jeans, a black sleeveless tee, and a soft-looking brown jacket. Cole trailed him several feet behind, looking irritated as usual.

"Well, I survived through the night, so I guess that earns you the benefit of the doubt." I glanced around. "Where did Derek go?"

"There." Adam pointed across the parking lot to where Derek was getting in line for the park.

"Let's go," I said.

Our mishmashed group made it through security and the ticket line but Derek was nowhere to be seen when we stepped out.

"Don't worry about him. We'll see him around." Landon laced his fingers through mine, then brought my knuckles to his lips. "Let's just have a good time."

That seemed guaranteed. There was so much to see and do. Landon had the park map out and our itinerary planned. The six of us didn't waste another minute.

My mouth fell open at my first look at the park. Despite the time, the place was packed with shrieking children, fans donning their favorite cosplay, and tourists with their hydration packs and oversized wallets. A sweet mix of caramel popcorn and cinnamon buns wafted over us as we passed a stand on the way to the first ride. It was a virtual superhero game that promised thrills without gut-busting drops.

"Only a half-an-hour wait," said Adam.

"Only?"

He laughed at me. "Get ready, Zee. This right here is going to be half our day."

We winded through the ropes to reach the end of the line. I'm pretty sure it took longer than thirty minutes for us to climb into the ride and buckle ourselves in but we passed the time talking and goofing off—except for Cole. He stood at the back, arms folded, and alternated between glaring at me and rolling his eyes.

It was a real pleasure when I ended up squished between him and Landon. "You going to be like this all day, Mr. Pouty?"

"Fuck off."

"Your standard answer to me. Can we get something else out of you? How about a smile? Hm? Hm?" I attacked his sides with tickles. Cole jerked like my fingers were electrified. "Let's get a smile."

"Stop!" he wheezed. He caught my wrists and held them fast. "What the hell are you doing?"

I laughed. Wide-eyed, slack-jawed surprise wasn't what I was going for but this looked cute on him too. "Seeing if I can get a laugh out of you." I wiggled my fingers at him. "I can do this all day."

"Don't tickle me."

"Try and stop me."

Cole twisted around. "Michael, switch seats with me."

"No."

Cursing, Cole put my hands firmly in my lap. They were there for all of five seconds before I went for him again.

"S-stop!" he cried, and this time I heard it, a tiny breathless laugh.

"Uh, babe. I'm over here."

Landon followed that statement by pulling me closer to him. I shook my head but leaned against his shoulder anyway. He was quite possessive for someone who agreed to a non-exclusive relationship.

Soon, the ride rumbled to life. I held Landon tighter as we slipped into a darkened passage. I came out smiling on the other side.

"What did you think of your first amusement ride?" Melody asked.

"Loved it."

"Then let's do this for real," said Adam. "The Hulk ride next."

The rest of them cheered. Cole even offered a half grin.

"What do you mean do this for real?" I asked.

"Drops, twists, turns, head dangling upside down. Time for your first roller coaster."

Everyone took off. The line for this ride was even longer but they happily hopped on it. Twenty minutes in, Landon and Adam were up front locked in conversation and Melody was in the back talking with Cole. Michael sidled closer to me.

"Are you okay? You look nervous."

"I'm okay."

He cocked his head. "Seriously, Zee. You don't have to do this if you don't want to."

I looked down. "It's not that. It's just these rides make Jordan sick. Doesn't fill me with much confidence."

"You might not get sick. If it is too much, there are plenty of slower rides we can do. There's a water ride in the back that's good. We can brave that if you're not scared to get soaked."

I blinked at him. "We?"

A small smile played at the corner of his lips and it dimpled his cheek. "I'm not a big fan of roller coasters either. Believe it or not, I don't always like to go fast."

I chuckled. "I don't believe it. Does this mean you'll be screaming your head off in the next seat?"

"Yes."

A full-blown giggle burst from me and tangles of anxiety loosened. "Okay. If I'm not a fan, we can take on the slow rides."

Another forty minutes and we finally reached the front of the line. The attendant strapped me in between Landon and Michael. My palms were slick on the green restraints. Landon wanted front seats, but all I could see through the hole was clear sky. My grip tightened as we inched forward.

"Ready for this?!" Landon shouted.

I opened my mouth to reply and we shot forward. The world blurred in a haze of colors, screams, and whoops. I ping-ponged in the seat. I was so slight, my butt lifted off the chair every time we flipped and the fear that I would fall through the bars made me cling to the handles for dear life. It was too much.

I need to get off. I need to get off. I need to get off!

The coaster hurtled to the earth and my stomach shot to my throat.

"Wait for me!"

The fuzzy world of shrieks and roller coasters blinked out.

People streamed around, bumping and shoving as they rushed to do their Christmas shopping.

Ding! Ding! Ding!

The elf rang his bell. "Right this way, kids. This way to Santa's workshop." The tiny bells on his shoes tinkled as he stepped toward me. "You ready to see Santa's workshop, princess?"

I shook my head, making my ponytails smack my cheeks. "No."

Across the bubbling fountain, a blue cap bobbed among the sea of people.

"Sweetie," said the elf. "Where are your parents?"

I pointed.

"Well, go to them. All of you can come and see Santa."

I took off, chasing after the blue cap.

"Whoo! Yes!"

I gasped. I was wrenched out of the memory with the force it took to propel the roller coaster.

"Wasn't that amazing, Zee?" Landon shook my thigh. "We should do it again if we have time at the end."

My fingers shook as I scrambled for the restraints. My body twitched and shook under the restraints.

"Wait for me! Wait!"

A soft cry escaped my lips as I yanked at the belt. I needed to get out now.

Then a hand crossed in front of my eyes. Michael unbuckled me and lifted the restraints off. "Zee, you okay?" Concern laced Michael's voice.

He took my hand and I clamped down—too hard if his wince was anything to go by. Taking it in stride, Michael helped me down and pulled me to his side. I leaned on him as we walked away from the ride to our group.

"Baby, what's wrong?" Landon brushed my fringe from my sweaty forehead.

"You look really pale," said Adam. "Let's go out so you can sit down."

"I've got him." Landon tugged me out of Michael's grasp.

I tried for a laugh but it sounded more like a whimper. "Apparently, I share more than just blood with my cousin."

"You're motion sick," Adam stated. "Jaxson gets that too. You'll feel better now that we're on the ground. We'll get you some water."

The five of them led me to a superhero-themed café in front of the ride and fussed over me. It was Cole who set the cup of water in front of me. I might have reached for it but my hands were still shaking. I balled them in my lap so they wouldn't see.

"Thanks, guys," I said. "You can go now."

"Go?" Melody said. "We're not leaving you."

I tried to laugh again. This time it sounded more like one. "I'm done with the fast rides and I don't want to ruin your day. Please, go. I'd feel so bad if you didn't have fun because of me. I'll hang out and you can text me when you get in line for the slow ones."

Landon knelt at my knee. "Then I'll stay with you."

"No way. You were most excited of all for today. Please don't worry about me. I'll be fine here."

"I'm not going to leave you by yourself."

"I'll stay with him," Michael spoke up. "I'm not a fan of roller coasters either."

"See," I said. "I won't be alone. Landon, go."

I could see how torn he was. "Are you sure? I'm happy to stay with you."

"We have the whole trip and after to be together, but we're only at this park for one day. I want you to do everything you planned."

Landon let out a sigh. "Okay, but I'm going to call you after we get off Doom and we'll do Popeye's. It's nice and slow."

I nodded. Landon gave me one last kiss on the forehead and then he, Melody, and Adam left. Cole didn't follow them.

"I'll be at Harry Potter world," he said to Michael. "Catch me up there."

"Sounds good."

After his friend left, Michael pulled out a chair and sat before me. His knees brushed against mine as he scooted closer. "What is really up with you?"

"What do you mean?" I reached for my water and took a small sip.

"You didn't look sick when I helped you off that ride, Zee. You looked... scared."

I lowered my head until my hair obscured him. "I'm fine. All those flips just made me queasy."

"If that's all it is, why are your hands shaking?"

I turned away from him, face burning. "Please, stop."

Michael was quiet for a moment. "Okay, I'm sorry. After you finish that, we'll get out of here."

"What? Why?"

"Because it looks like a comic book threw up in here and smells like it too."

A tiny laugh escaped my lips.

"If you're not feeling well, this is the last place you want to be."

"Alright." I drained my cup and the two of us left the café.

The muted sounds of the park turned up to maximum as we stepped outside. I tensed but Michael didn't notice as he led the way.

"We can just walk around," he said over his shoulder. "We'll grab something to eat if we see anything good. Or we could catch up to Cole. The butterbeer is insane. You have to try it."

His words washed over me. The noises, the shouts, the smells were all pressing on me.

"Wait, Dad!" A kid bumped into me as he chased after his father. "I want to buy cotton candy."

"Wait for me."

My head spun. There were so many people, moving in and out of frame, blurring around the edges of my vision. Maybe I wasn't far off with the motion sickness because my stomach was heaving.

"No!" A scream cut through the air. "No! I don't want to go!"

My sight cleared on a little girl a few feet in front of me wearing Gryffindor robes. Tears ran down her face as she yanked at the hand around her wrist. "I don't want to go!"

"Stop!" A shout shattered the scene. It took me a second to realize it was ripped from my own throat. "Stop! Leave her alone!"

Michael whipped around, eyes wide. "Zee?"

Everything was spinning. Noises from the past mixed with the screams from the present and bile burned as it surged up my throat. "Stop!" I sprinted past Michael's outstretched hand.

The man's eyes bulged as I advanced on him. Jerking back, the hood of his Ravenclaw robes slid off his head, revealing a portly, sunburned face.

"Get off of her!" I screamed.

Tourists halted in their tracks to watch the scene I was creating.

"Excuse me?" the man cried. "Who are you? What do you want?"

He pulled the girl closer and I leaped forward. "Leave her alone!"

"What are you doing?!" he bellowed as he stumbled out of my reach. "Get away from us!"

"Daddy!"

The cry pierced me. The little girl clung to her father looking terrified... of me.

"Zee," Michael shouted. Hands grabbed me from behind. "What's wrong?"

My head whipped around at the shocked, scared, and disgusted faces.

They're all looking at me. They think I'm crazy. I'm not crazy!

The man flinched. "You seem crazy to me!"

I hadn't realized I shouted it.

I couldn't be here. I had to get out.

I ripped out of Michael's hold and ran.

Chapter Nine

B*uzz. Buzz. Buzz.*

I ignored the vibrations in my pocket. Tears ran down my cheeks and soaked the knees of my jeans. The tiny corner of Seussland that I tucked myself away in was a cramped little space between the side of a gift shop and some hedges. I could see families walking past. Children ran among the colorful rides and cheerful music, looking like they had never been happier.

I lowered my head, encasing it in the circle of my arms as I choked back a sob.

It's been so long since I've reacted this badly. Why is this happening now? What will it take to make it stop?

"Zela?" I lifted my head and met Michael's eyes. He shoved through the tiny space, carefully making his way over to me. "There you are."

I gaped at him. "How did you know I was here?" My voice was barely more than a croak.

"I didn't know." Michael sat down and stretched his long legs through the hedges. "I've been looking everywhere for you for the last thirty-five minutes. You didn't pick up your phone. Are you okay?"

"How can you ask me that?" I hugged my legs to my chest. "You saw my show."

"Do you want to tell me what happened?"

My nails dug into my thighs. "I just... heard her screaming," I whispered. "I thought he was hurting her."

"Oh. Well, it's good that you wanted to help."

I shook my head roughly. "There's nothing good about going off like a crazy person."

"You're not crazy." Michael pushed my hair from my face. "Don't say that about yourself. But, Zee, you don't look well."

"There's too many people." Fresh tears collected in my eyes. "So much noise and shoving and I don't know where anyone is, or who anyone is."

"You don't like crowds."

"I can do crowds, but Mom was always with me. She's not here." I wasn't making much sense now, but the words tumbled from my lips. "She held my hand."

"Okay. I understand." Michael caught my hand as I reached up to scrub my face. "Come with me."

"No." I recoiled when he tried to pull me up. "I can't go back out there."

"Zela, trust me."

I'm not certain what it was. It might have been the gentleness in his voice. It might have been the thumb tenderly stroking the inside of my palm. Or it could have been both that allowed him to bring me to my feet.

Michael led me out of our hiding space. I went rigid the moment the people and noise assaulted my senses.

"Hold on to me," he said.

I didn't get a chance to ask why before the crowd blinked out. Michael enfolded me under his arm and his jacket draped over my face. I looked up at him and he smiled.

"Ready?"

It took a minute, but I wrapped my arms around his waist. "I'm ready."

Michael didn't rush. He walked out of there calmly while I buried myself in the haven that was beneath his coat. I couldn't hear much with his arm covering my ear. I could see only a sliver through his coat, and the smell of burned popcorn couldn't penetrate the sweet, spicy scent that was Michael.

Eventually, my tears slowed. My heart stopped trying to escape through my mouth and my twisting stomach settled.

"Thank you," I whispered.

"You're welcome."

I had no idea where he was taking me, but I knew we left Seussland when the music changed. Someone bumped into me and I jerked.

"Sorry," Michael said. "I'll be more careful. We're almost there."

"Where are we going?" I should have pulled my head out and looked, but at that moment, nothing seemed more un-appealing to me than to trade what was out there for what was in here.

"Away from all of these people."

How can we? We'd get in massive trouble if we left the park without permission.

But I didn't voice my thoughts. I didn't care how. I just wanted him to make it happen.

We walked for a little while more, then came to a stop. "Two, please."

"That's one hundred and ten dollars."

I made a noise from the depths of his jacket. "A hundred dollars? For what?"

"For you."

Cheeks warming, I snapped my mouth shut. What was I supposed to say to that?

My anticipation built as Michael led me on. Peeking through, I saw metal bars.

Are we getting in line for another ride?

"Okay. You can look now if you want."

I lifted the flap of his jacket and blinked. Looming before me was the Hogwarts Express.

He grabbed my hand when the doors opened. "Come on. You'll like this."

Together, we followed a charming man in a red and gold uniform to a compartment toward the end of the train. He closed us in and I knew right away why Michael brought me here. Eight comfortable, plush seats but they were only taken by the two of us. We were alone in the softly lit space. All the noise and people from the park were completely shut out.

I relaxed as the train took off. A scene played on the screen of what outside the true Hogwarts Express would look like.

"We can ride for as long as you want," he said. "If they kick us out, we'll just get back in the line."

A tiny smile formed on my lips. It wobbled for a moment and then disappeared, but still, it was a smile. "Thank you for this. I'll pay you back."

He shook his head. "Don't be ridiculous. I'll spend more than that on souvenirs this week."

We fell quiet. For a moment, all you could hear was Harry Potter's and Ron Weasley's voices filling the compartment. I shut them out as I gazed at Michael.

I don't understand. Why is he doing this for me?

"Why are you being so nice to me?" I asked, finally voicing my thoughts. "You should hate me for forcing you to lose."

Michael frowned. "How can you ask me that? You know why, butterfly."

"Butterfly?"

Michael gave me a strange look that I'm sure matched the one I was giving him.

"Why would you think I hate you?" he asked. "I told you it was my choice to lose and one I was willing to make if it meant you'd forgive me. You're the first person other than Cole I've gotten close to in a while and I... did what I did. All I want is to make things right with my butterfly."

A flush crept up my neck. "Why are you calling me butterfly?"

"Why are you pretending you don't know?"

"Why can't you see that I'm not pretending?"

He cocked his head. "Seriously? You didn't read my letter?"

"What letter?"

"The one on top of the chocolate wings."

I looked at him blankly.

"The present that I left in front of your door?"

"Present in front of my...?" I sucked in a breath. "You mean you left those?"

"Yes. The water bottle, shoes, and chocolate wings."

My mouth formed a tiny "o" as realization dawned. "I got the water bottle."

"What happened to the other gifts?"

"Adam threw them away."

His jaw dropped. "He did what?"

"There was no name on them and For All's been active again. We didn't know what to think."

"If you had opened the chocolate, you would have seen my name!"

I giggled. Michael was so outraged I couldn't help it. "That's what I said."

"The last gift I revealed it was me and wrote you a whole letter telling you how I feel."

"How you feel?" I repeated. My pulse began to quicken after all the work he'd done to bring it down.

"I also explained," he continued, "that I call you butterfly in my head because sometimes when I watch you run, you'll put your arms out and flap them like you're about to take off."

I blushed hot and fierce. "But I— You— I only do that when I'm alone! Where were you hiding?"

He chuckled—a smooth, deep sound that drowned out the fake adventure pouring through our speakers. "You run at night to avoid me, but sometimes I go out late if I miss my morning run. I saw you the first time and a few other times since. It's not just that you pretend you're flying. You hide who you are behind this cocoon, but beneath it is this strong, smart girl who never gives up. A butterfly... is you."

"Oh." I lowered my eyes and silently wished my wig was longer to shield me from his penetrating gaze. "What else did the letter say?"

"You'll have to fish it out of the garbage to find out."

"That's not fair," I said in between laughing. "It was Adam who threw it away. I voted to keep our suspicious packages."

"Too bad." I could practically hear him smirking. "Maybe if you're lucky, I'll write you another letter someday."

Lifting my head, I didn't think too hard as I replied, "Then, I hope I get lucky."

Michael rose and the cushion dipped as he sat next to me. He put his arm around me and I was plunged into his spicy, sweet aura once more. "Your chances are good."

MICHAEL AND I RODE the train back and forth five times. I felt like myself after the second time, but kept riding with him for reasons I didn't let myself think about. On our fourth ride, Landon blew up my phone asking where I was.

"Tell them to meet us at the Confit Grill," Michael said. "You must be hungry."

Actually, I was starving. We left the area for the Hogwarts Express and returned to the fray. Michael didn't tuck me into his jacket again, but he did take my hand and hold me close as we weaved through the crowd. I should have pulled away, but I found his presence too comforting to give it up. I couldn't stand it if I freaked out again.

The crowd thinned out as we left Harry Potter land. We turned down a path and amusement rides fell away in favor of food stands and restaurants. I knew he chose this place for me when we stepped inside the Confit Grill and were treated to a quiet, traditional eatery. No screaming, no buffets, and no sticky, soda-stained floors.

"Can we have a booth at the back, please? The rest of our friends are on the way."

"Of course. Right this way."

We slid into our booth and just got our hands on the menu when Adam, Melody, Landon, and Cole showed up.

Landon didn't sit right away. He stared hard at Michael, clearly wanting him to give up the seat next to me. Michael pretended not to see him.

"Were you guys bored waiting for us?" asked Melody.

We shared a look. Michael didn't push me to talk about the little Gryffindor girl and I did not offer more information. I felt like we both silently agreed not to speak about it.

"No," Michael replied. "We rode the Hogwarts Express back and forth. It was cool."

"Damn," said Cole. "Why didn't you text me? I told you I was around."

"We're hitting Universal tomorrow. We can do it then."

The conversation shifted to what we wanted to do after lunch.

"No more roller coasters or fast rides for me," I said.

"We can do the slow ones," said Landon. "If that's too much, there are shows we can watch too."

"We?"

Landon cut eyes to Michael as he addressed me. "I'm not leaving you alone. I don't want to. Doom was no fun without you. We can do the rest of this together."

He didn't look like he would be argued with, so I let it go. The rest of the day was great with the four of us hanging out together. Cole and Michael left us soon after lunch, but it was still a good time. We left the park a little while after sundown.

"Hey." Landon leaned across his seat. The bus was quiet with half-sleepy teenagers and he whispered as he pressed his lips to my ear. "I don't want you to feel pressured, but I'd like it if you came up to my room tonight."

I turned so I could face him. Our noses brushed in the process. I made no attempt to move back. "I'm not sure if I'm ready to break any rules, Landon."

"Trust me." His breath tickled my lips. "You won't regret it. Room 745. Okay?"

I hesitated. It had been a hard day in more ways than one. My reaction to my first roller coaster threw me and I didn't know if I had caught myself yet. "Okay."

Beaming, he caressed my lips with his before claiming a kiss. If he noticed I was hardly kissing back, he said nothing about it.

That night, I got ready before the bathroom mirror while Michael watched television. He rested on top of the covers in nothing but a sleeveless shirt and boxers. The screen flickered endlessly as Michael flipped through the channels on a loop.

"You look like you're going somewhere," he called.

"I am." I put on nice clothes for Zela, and then threw on a hoodie and sweatpants for Zeke. "Don't wait up."

I felt Michael's eyes on me as I grabbed my things and walked out the door. I felt them, but I didn't have the headspace to acknowledge what he might be thinking, or even how our relationship had changed in less than twenty-four hours. My thoughts were consumed by Landon Foster and what I had to do.

Dump him, Zela. Let him get hot and heavy and think he's going to get some. Then, tell him you'd never be with a guy who did what he did. Dump him.

He deserves it, doesn't he? All he wants from you is sex.

I held those thoughts in my mind as I rode the elevator to his floor. It buoyed me on the walk to the door. I knocked and it opened immediately.

"Zee, there you are." A crisp scent of tart plums and sweet vanilla wafted out of the door. I had a wild thought that the scents were us. Sweet and tart. Opposites that only make sense when they are put together.

"Landon," I began. "There's something I need to talk with you about."

"Okay." Landon stepped back. "Come inside."

My breath caught at the sight that awaited me. There were no lights on in the room. The soft, flickering glow was the results of dozens of vanilla plum candles scattered through the space.

Slowly, I stepped over the threshold to take it in. Landon's suite may have had the same beige wallpaper, gray carpets, and damask comforter, but the bed he led me to was huge—more than enough space for two people.

Landon took me in his arms and threaded his fingers behind my back. I felt the duvet bumping the back of my knees.

"I'm glad you're here." He kissed my forehead. "Tonight will be perfect."

I took a breath, held it, and then softly let it go. "I need to talk to you about something, Landon. I said I wasn't ready for sex. I'm also not ready for—"

"Shhh, Zela," he whispered. "I know."

"You know? What do you know?"

"I know you're not ready. I didn't ask you up here for sex. I asked you up here so we could talk."

I could not have heard him correctly. "To talk?"

"Yes." Landon pushed back my hair and my eyes fluttered shut at the touch. "You've been asking to get to know each other, and tonight, that is what I want to do. No rules, no sex. Just you and me."

My mouth suddenly felt dry. I gazed around the room as his words burrowed inside of me. I thought all he wanted out of this trip was to get into my pants, and the whole time he was planning to curl up and talk to me.

What do I do now?

"Okay," I said softly. "Let's talk."

Landon guided me back and I dropped onto the sheets with his hands still around me. Together, we inched up the bed until we fell onto the pillows. Landon reached for my wig first and gently took it off. I held still as he loosened my hair from its wrap. He moved to my clothes and disappeared as he pulled the sweatshirt over my head.

He promised nothing sexual was going to happen tonight, but reclining here while he unwrapped Zela made my nerves zing with electricity. Of all the moments we shared, this felt the most intimate.

Landon pushed the sweatpants down my waist and then all that was left was my striped shirt dress and stockings. He crawled back toward me, moving like a panther that had its prey in sight and my heart beat loudly in my ears as he reached for me.

If he takes off my dress too, I don't know if I'll be able to stop him.

Landon picked up the pillows and gathered them around me to make me more comfortable.

"One more thing." He flipped over and lifted a tray of tiny treats and goodies. "You like chocolate, so I told them to send up a tray of chocolate everything."

I giggled. "This is so sweet, Landon. It's honestly nothing like I expected."

"In a good way, I hope."

"Definitely in a good way." My lips quivered and I took a bite of tiramisu to cover it.

He grinned a happy, lopsided smile. "Where do you want to start?"

"You start first."

"Me first?" Landon blew out a breath as he leaned against the headboard. "Where do I begin? How about we tell each other something... real?"

"Real?"

"It doesn't have to be a deep, dark secret, but something that matters."

I nodded rather than answering.

"Good. Then, I'll go first as promised." He curled his hand around mine. "Did I ever tell you that Cole, Michael, Adam, and I used to be best friends?"

I sat up a little straighter. "You were?"

"Yep."

"What happened?"

"I happened." Sighing, he let his head fall back onto the pillows. "People have always assumed I was into guys because of my clothes and contacts, but what they were so sure of, I was still figuring out in middle school. I didn't have many people to talk to, but I did have my friends—specifically Michael and Cole."

I didn't know where this was going, but I refused to interrupt. I listened silently and tried not to shiver as his thumb lazily stroked my hand.

"You've seen how they are. They're pretty much joined at the hip and they were the same back in Evergreen. You couldn't catch one of them without the other and one day I thought…"

"That there was more to their relationship."

He nodded. "I only wanted to talk to them, but when I walked up to Cole and asked him if Michael was his boyfriend. He punched me in the face."

"He did what?" I breathed. "Why would he do that?"

"Because he's Cole. He'll take the smallest thing from zero to five hundred in a second. I asked him if he was hooking up with his best friend, and he dumped me. Michael didn't want to be in the middle, so he made it easy and chose Cole."

"What about Adam?" The question was pulled from me. I didn't want to hear that Adam had been horrible to him, but now that he was opening up to me, a bigger part of me craved to learn a new part of him.

"He never really dumped me. His mother started popping out babies like it was her goal to repopulate the earth and he took on more and more responsibility to be there for them. Suddenly, there was no time for movies, coming over to my house, sleepovers, none of it.

"Then, things heated up on the swim team. Adam and Cole were the only two worth looking at. It burned Cole up every time Adam beat him, or when he beat Adam and Adam acted like he didn't care and none of it was worth worrying about.

"It got tense with them. They stopped being friends and Michael stuck with Cole again." He laughed without mirth. "Adam can make friends with a rock, so he picked up a new crowd pretty quickly, but our group was done. I lost all of my friends within one year."

"I'm sorry. I can't imagine how hard it was." I turned my palm up and threaded our fingers together. "Did you lose Derek too?"

"Never had him. He had another group. Then some stuff went down with his mom and he had nothing to do with them or anyone else."

"Do you know what happened to his mom?"

"You should ask him about that. Somehow, you managed to become friends with him. If he'll tell anyone the truth, it's you."

I looked down. "Why are you telling me this, Landon?"

"Because I realized that I want to talk to you too. I want to know why pretending to be a boy was the only way for you to come to this school. I want to know why you love math so much. I want to know all of the places you've been and where you want to go."

Landon's eyes traced my face. I imagined him seeing through to my soul. "And because, more than anything, I don't want to be casual anymore, Zela. You were the first guy I ever had the courage to like, and now, you're the first girl I'm falling in love with."

I pressed my lips together. They trembled worse than ever, but my attempts to hold back the flood of emotions were not enough to stem the tears collecting in my eyes. Landon blurred as his sweet, perfect confession undid me molecule by molecule.

"Don't cry, baby," he whispered. He gently wiped away a tear from my lips. "I want you to know how I feel. It's okay if you don't feel the same way right now. I can wait as long as it takes."

"Landon..." I shook my head. I had to stop this. I have to tell him the truth of how we got here.

"I know it will take time," he continued. "What I did to you was awful and I don't deserve your forgiveness. It didn't matter that I was mad or what I thought you did or who I thought you were. We took it way too far and—"

"Landon."

"—I'm sorry." He brushed away more tears as they fell. "I've never said it before and now I'll say it as many times as it takes. I'm sorry for the locker room. I'm sorry I didn't stop Zach. I'm sorry I hurt you, and I promise whether we're exclusive or not, together or not, friends or not, I'll never hurt you again."

"Oh, Landon." One by one, he broke through all of my defenses. My body shook as though it knew how vulnerable I was. One more strike, and I was gone.

"It's okay, Zela," he whispered. "Just breathe. It's me and you."

He murmured that to me as my tears slowed. Then, he cleaned my face with a tissue. "Better?"

He kissed me before I could reply—a soft peck on the lips.

"So what did you want to tell me?"

I blinked as he slowly came into focus. "Tell you?"

"You said you needed to talk to me about something." He smiled that happy, beatific smile that punched me in the gut. "What is it?"

I had to tell you that I don't want to be with you anymore. That all of this meant nothing to me and we were over. I came here to tell you to rot in hell.

My throat constricted around the words. They choked me as I gazed at the boy who had given me everything I needed to break him and was so out-of-his-mind happy about it.

I opened my mouth to tell him what I came here to say... and a sob escaped my lips. Once free, the floodgates opened and nothing could hold them back. I cried heart-wrenching, gushing tears.

"Zela? Zela, what's wrong?" The alarm in his voice only served to make me cry harder. "Zela, I'm sorry. I didn't mean to make you cry."

I shook my head roughly. "I-it's not y-you. It's me. It's always me. I do everything wrong."

The roller coaster, the hallucinations, the little Gryffindor girl, and the pitying, repulsed looks of the crowd swirled in my head. The emotions tangled into one overwhelming mess that I couldn't pick apart.

"Baby, you haven't done anything wrong. You're perfect. It's me who messed up. I'm the one—"

"No! You don't understand!"

He took my face in his hands and he raised me to look into his wide, beseeching eyes. "Then help me understand. Tell me what to do. I'll do anything."

Landon must have thought that would bring me around. Instead, I cried even harder. Loud, hiccupping sobs that hurt almost as much as what I felt inside. I couldn't do it. I couldn't do what I came here to do and I couldn't stay.

I have to get out.

"Derek." The name tumbled out unbidden. "G-get Derek."

"Derek? Why? I don't under—"

"Please, Landon. I need him."

He didn't argue further. Landon climbed off the bed and bolted out the door without bothering to put on his shoes. All I could do was try, and fail, to slow my tears as I waited for them to come back.

"—want from me." His voice reached my ears before he reached me. "You better have a fucking good reason for dragging me here."

The door flew open.

"I don't have time for— Zela?"

I lifted my head. Derek took one look at me crouched on Landon's bed, eyes puffy, and face soaked with tears, and he launched at him.

Derek grabbed his collar and slammed Landon into the wall.

"Hey!"

"What did you do to her?! What did you do?!"

Screaming, I tumbled off the bed and raced to him. "Derek, no! Stop!" I grabbed his wrist and tried to pull him off. "He didn't do anything to me."

He whipped around, releasing his hold. "Then why are you crying?"

"Please," I rasped. "I have to go. Just take me out of here."

"Go?" The pain etched in Landon's face made me feel a million times worse. "Why do you have to go? What did I do wrong?"

"It's not you," I said. "I'm sorry. It's me. It's always me."

He stepped closer. "Zela, whatever it is. We can talk about it."

Derek encircled my waist and drew me to his side. "I will find out. If you did do something wrong, I'll be back to beat your ass."

His threat hanging in the air, Derek swept us out of the room. Landon watched us go from his doorway. I knew I should say something, but nothing would come out. We turned a corner, and my chance was gone.

Derek walked up to the elevators but didn't stop. We kept going to a door near the end of the hall. There was no vanilla plum haven waiting for me inside of this room, but as he pushed aside his mountain of books and placed me on the bed, I felt comfort of a different kind.

He got in next to me and brushed away the hair sticking to my face. "What happened?"

My response was to take a pillow, put it on his lap, and rest my head on top. I gazed at the black screen of the television while Derek continued to stroke my hair.

"Did he do something to you?"

The menace in his tone forced me to speak. "Landon was amazing. He was sweet, open, and patient. He said he wants to have a real relationship and he thinks he might be falling in love with me."

"What a bastard."

I almost smiled. Almost. "I went there to dump him, Derek. That was my big plan for revenge. To make him fall for me and then crush his heart like he did mine."

"But when you had your chance... you realized you had fallen for him too."

"Yes," I whispered.

His hand was warm and soothing as it ran through my hair. "What are you going to do now?"

"I don't know."

"What do you want to do, Zela? You don't have to dump him because you feel you have to be mad at him, but you also don't have to stay with him because you have feelings. It should feel right completely with the person you love. If you trust them and forgive them and... can't imagine not seeing them every day.

"If the best part of your morning is eating breakfast with him or sitting on your bed goofing off. Or if it breaks your heart when they cry and puts it back together when they laugh. If even when you're blindingly mad at them... they're still the person you most want to talk to. It's worth going after that no matter what's happened in the past."

I turned my head up, blinking at him in surprise. I had never heard Derek speak like this before. He caught my look and pulled away, returning his hand to his side. I smiled a little as he cleared his throat.

"I'm just saying... the real thing is worth it."

"The real thing?" I repeated as I turned back to the television. "How can I ever have something real?"

"You can."

"No, I can't," I said through numb lips. "I can't because no one knows anything real about me. I demand trust and honesty from Landon but Jordan was right. I don't let anyone in. I never have."

"You can let me in."

I didn't reply.

"Whatever it is, Zela. You can tell me. I'll understand. I'll listen."

Still, I did not answer.

Derek sighed. "Okay. Here goes."

Here goes? What does that mean?

"When I was in middle school, my best friends were Mateo and Edmund."

I frowned. *What is happening right now?*

"We did everything together," he went on. "They couldn't come to mine, but I went to their houses. We hung out at the Promenade. I thought we were solid."

"What changed?"

"My mother is Naomi Grayson."

I didn't know where that segue was leading, but I let him talk.

"She's used to fans hounding her, shouting at her in the street, trying to break into her dressing room, and once, sneaking past the guards and attacking her."

"Oh my goodness," I breathed. "Was she okay?"

"The deluded woman slapped Mom across the face for 'breaking Antonio's heart.' Antonio was the character she dated in a movie."

"Wow. I can't imagine dealing with that."

"Mom hates that part of her job, and when she's home, she wants to relax and take a break from being Naomi Grayson. That's why we've always had a rule that I wasn't allowed to bring friends home. She didn't want them fawning over her or asking for autographs."

"Oh. Is that why you wouldn't let me visit your house over the summer?"

"The guards wouldn't have let you past the gate... and I didn't want to explain why."

"Derek." I patted the part of him that I could easily reach—his knee. "You could have told me that. I would have understood. Your mother wants to be comfortable in her own home. I respect that."

"There's more to it, Zela."

Something in his tone stilled my hand. "What do you mean?"

"I mean... once, in middle school, Mom gave in to my begging and pleading and let Mateo and Edmund stay over."

I tensed. Somehow, I knew I wouldn't like what was coming.

"Did they do something? Hound your mom?"

"I wish that was what they did. That night, Edmund distracted me with video games while Mateo made up something about getting a snack from the kitchen. It took me a while to notice how long he was gone."

"Oh no, Derek. What did he do?"

Derek's hand fisted on my shoulder. "The filthy fucking piece of shit snuck into my parents' room and hid in the closet. When my mom came in to take a shower, not seeing the sick pervert peeking through the slats, he took pictures of her."

My jaw worked but no sounds came out. His best friends did this?! Even imagining Adam creeping around my house, violating my mom's privacy made my mind recoil. A friend would never do something like this.

"The pictures were all over the internet the next day. Mateo and Edmund walked into the cafeteria like they were gods. I beat them both into a two-week suspension. Not that it changed anything. Mom put on a brave face for the cameras and gave a speech about respecting women and not tolerating things like this, but at home, she cried every night for a week."

I placed my hand over his fist. I couldn't find the words to comfort him. I did not think there were any.

"That was it. No one she and Dad didn't know and trust personally was allowed near our house. And because I was so easily taken in by those shits, my parents stopped trusting my judgement and wouldn't let me spend time alone with people they hadn't triple-checked. Not that I would have fought them, I didn't trust anyone either."

"Derek, nothing that happened was your fault."

"Yes, it was," he rasped. "I begged Mom to let them stay and they did that to her. It wouldn't have happened if I didn't spout bullshit about her not letting me be normal. I guilted her and naked pictures of my mother ended up plastered all over the locker room. She was right to keep people away."

"So... now you keep everyone away?" I twisted up to look at him. Derek refused to meet my eyes. "You don't trust anyone."

Derek was quiet for so long, I settled back into the pillow, figuring our conversation was over. Then he spoke.

"I trust you, Zela."

I squeezed my eyes shut as Jordan's speech came back to me.

"I know you, Zee. You don't tell people very much about yourself, and it makes sense. You moved around so much, there was no point baring your soul to people you'd never see or speak to again. If you want Derek to open up to you, then you have to be willing to do the same. You might even have to do it first. That's how it works."

Well, it was Derek who did it first. He's opening the door to what I always wanted—for us to be close. I knew at that moment if I shut that door, Derek would never open it again.

Breathing slowly, I took deep breaths and then began. "The Chesterfield Mall holds a holiday bash every year. It's huge. There's Santa's workshop. Mini rides for kids. People come in from neighboring towns. Bands play. Decorations.

People get dressed up. It's a big deal and no matter where we were in the world, Mom would pack us up, put me on a plane, and we'd come home to spend Christmas with Aunt Bev and Jordan. Our Christmas celebration always included a trip to the mall."

"Okay." I could hear the confusion in his voice, but he didn't interrupt.

"One year when I was six, Aunt Bev and Mom took us to the holiday bash. The place was insane with people everywhere—bumping into us and being loud, but we were having a good time. We were headed to Santa's workshop when I saw the ice cream parlor and asked Mom if I could have some.

"Mom said no. The line was wrapping around the corner to sit on Santa's lap and she wanted to claim our spots before he stopped for lunch. So, Aunt Bev offered to take me while she went on with J-Jordan."

I paused as my voice broke and took a breath. *I can do this. It's time I did this.*

"We got in line," I continued after I felt stronger. "One by one, the people gave their orders and collected their cones. Finally, it was my turn, and when I stepped up to the glass, I looked up and saw... my father."

"What? Your father?"

I nodded. "My mother hated my dad and she never told me a single thing about him except for his name: Jeremy Holt. I looked up into his eyes that were so much like mine and the brownish-blond hair that peeked through his hairnet and I had a feeling. Aunt Bev said hello and called his name and I knew. I had finally found my father."

"What did your aunt say?"

"She didn't say anything, but I didn't expect her to. If Mom hadn't told me about him, why would she tell the sister she fought with more than anything? There was nothing from Aunt Bev, but Jeremy was so nice to me. He said I was the most adorable thing he had ever seen. When he asked me if I wanted pistachio ice cream like Aunt Bev, I said I hated pistachios. Jeremy scrunched up his face all funny and he said he hated it too. Last, he handed me my ice cream and winked. One wink and I knew that Jeremy recognized me. He knew that I was his daughter.

"Aunt Bev took me to a table and sat me down with my ice cream. I watched him the whole time. After a while, he disappeared into the back and then returned in his street clothes and a knitted, blue cap. He said goodbye to his coworkers... and he left."

"What did you do?"

"I couldn't do anything... until Aunt Bev stood and told me she had to use the bathroom. I bolted from the table the second she was gone."

Derek put his hand back on my head. "You chased him," he said as he ran his fingers through my hair.

"I took off in the direction he went and searched frantically for that blue cap. The loud noise and the crowd weren't fun anymore. They pushed and knocked me about as I got more desperate. I was almost to Santa's workshop when I finally spotted him."

My voice got hoarser as I spoke. My tone became lower and lower and Derek leaned over me to hear. I could have stopped here, but this was having a strange effect on me. It burned me like the poison was finally leaking out.

"I screamed for him," I whispered. "My little tiny voice calling among the racket of the music and the shoppers. I begged him to wait for me... his daughter... but Jeremy didn't slow down. He only got further away from me.

"Eventually, I was stopped by an elf asking where my parents were. When I got away and ran to the spot I last saw him, he was gone. I freaked out. I ran further—away from the people, further away from my family. I ended up in a nearly empty part of the mall, crying my eyes out, when a man came up to me and asked if I needed help."

Derek's hand stilled.

"I told him I was lost. My dad had left me and I didn't know how to get back to my mother. I told him that and... he took me."

"Zela?" Derek's voice shook. "What does that mean?"

"It means he kept his kind, helpful expression on long enough to promise he'd help me find my father. He took my hand, led me outside, and ignored me when I said I wanted to go back to my mom. We were almost to his car when I started screaming."

"Fucking hell," Derek cried. "What— Don't— Please, tell me he didn't—"

"He got me all the way to his house. The whole time he said I would never see my parents again and I lived with him now. The man locked me in the basement that was to be my new room. That night, the police busted in and rescued me. Someone had seen him stuff me into his car. They got suspicious, took note of his license plate, and were the ones to run to security when they blasted through the speakers that a little girl had gone missing.

"They saved me. The man never got a chance to touch me but... after they raided the place, the police found the bodies of two dead girls buried in the backyard."

"Holy shit, Zela." Derek bent over, pressing his forehead against my temple. He put his arm around me and squeezed me so tight I couldn't breathe. I let him. The tears weren't falling. Crying about what happened wasn't how my mind chose to process the trauma. Instead, it tormented me with visions and voices from the past. Never letting me forget for a moment that one day I chased after my father and almost lost everything.

No, I wasn't crying, but a hard pit lodged in my throat as I bared the raw, naked pain of my past for the first time to someone other than my family.

Derek was the first one I told, but as he held me and the pit loosened, I knew I had done the right thing.

It's right that it was him, I thought. *It was always meant to be him.*

"I'm so sorry, Zela," he said softly.

"It's okay. I got back to my mother, and after I told her what happened, she said that man wasn't my father. Jeremy Holt had died years before and it was just me and her now. She was always going to be there to protect me. It's just me and her," I repeated.

"And me," he said. "You have me too."

Despite the pain swirling inside of me, I smiled. "I know I do."

You're mine now, I thought as I closed my eyes. *You're finally mine.*

Chapter Ten

I knocked on Landon's door the next morning. It flew open as I lifted my hand for the second knock. Landon stood in front of me with messy hair, boxers, and eyes brown and natural. He never looked cuter.

"Zela? Are you okay?" He hugged me. "I was up all night worrying about you," he said into my neck. "What happened?"

"There's something I need to tell you." I put my hands on his chest and gently pushed him back. "Please, listen. You won't want to hug me after this."

His brows snapped together. "What are you talking about?"

I took a steadying breath. I made up my mind to do this. I walked down the hall certain that this was the right thing to do. I didn't take into account the impact of just seeing him.

I'm going to lose you the moment I realize you're all I want.

"Landon," I began. "I never got over what you guys did to me in the locker room, and if I'm honest, I'll never get over it completely. It's going to hurt sometimes. There will be days that I'll look at you and remember."

"I know, Zela, and I'll tell you every single day that I'm sorry if it'll make things better. More than that." He took my hands and pressed them to his chest. "I'll *show* you every day that I'm sorry."

"Landon," I whispered. "You don't have to. Despite everything, I've forgiven you. I don't know when it happened, but somewhere along the way, I forgave you. But if we're ever going to have something real, I have to tell you the truth."

The words tried to stick in my throat but I forced them out. "Landon, I got back with you to make you fall for me. The whole time... my plan was to dump you and break your heart."

Landon's smile melted away as color drained from his face.

"I wanted to hurt you as badly as you hurt me, but I couldn't... stop myself from falling for you... and..."

I ran out of steam. I didn't know what else to say and Landon's silence was not encouraging.

"I wanted you to know the truth," I finished. "So..."

Landon did not utter a sound.

"So, I'll go." I turned to leave.

"Was?"

I froze. "Huh?"

"You keep saying was and wanted." A shadow fell over me. "You *wanted* to hurt me. Does that mean you want something else now?"

Tensing, I swallowed hard. His tone was too even. It gave nothing away.

"Yes," I replied.

"What do you want?"

"Landon—"

"Tell me what you want, Zela."

"I just did." I squeezed my eyes shut and took the leap. "I want you."

A hand grasped my shoulder and spun me around. I didn't have a chance to open my eyes before his lips crashed onto mine. My shock lasted a millisecond and then my arms flung around him. We kissed hot and wild and frantic. Landon stumbled back into the room, taking me with him, and kicked the door shut.

Mrs. Clancy banged on the door forty-five minutes later, sounding the warning that Landon had ten minutes to get to the lobby or the bus would leave without him. He might have answered if his mouth wasn't busy at the time.

Eventually, we dragged ourselves out of bed, straightened up, and went downstairs in time to board the bus. I held tight to his hand, blushing at how many rules we had broken. We didn't have sex, but Landon was absolutely right about how much I would enjoy him giving me head.

We stepped up to the bus and looked for seats. Michael rose from his seat when he saw me. My heart skipped two beats as a breath-stealing smile stole across his face and he waved us over.

I squeezed Landon's hand. "In the spirit of honesty," I said. "I want to be with you one hundred percent, but I may also have feelings for someone else."

"Derek," he stated like it was a foregone conclusion.

"No," I ground out. "Not Derek and don't you dare say Adam," I added when he opened his mouth.

Landon chuckled. "I don't care who it is. All I heard is you want to be with me one hundred percent. I'm happy to share as long as I get a piece of you."

I buried my face in his back so he couldn't see how hard I was smiling. I didn't think I could be happier than I was at that moment.

"Morning, butterfly," Michael said as I sat next to him with Landon on my other side. He trailed his finger along my thigh. "We'll do only the slow rides today. Me and you. I won't leave you alone."

I bit my lip. Okay. Maybe I could be a bit happier.

THE REST OF THE TRIP was a lot less eventful. I stayed away from roller coasters and any rides that triggered anxiety. There was no chance of staying away from hordes of tourists, but Michael kept his promise and stuck to me like glue, much to Cole's annoyance. The need did not arise for me to burrow under his jacket again, but it was nice talking to him and getting to know him for real.

Friday night, Mom, Jordan, and Aunt Bev waved from the gates as I climbed off the bus. I said goodbye to everyone and got a hug from Adam, wave from Melody, kiss from Landon, wink from Michael, and a grunt from Cole. Cole didn't tell me to go fuck myself, so I was calling that progress.

Squealing, Jordan ran and scooped me in a tight hug. "I'm pissed at you for going to Orlando without me, but I hope you had a good time."

"I'll tell you every last detail when we're alone," I whispered.

"Oooh. Sounds juicy."

Aunt Bev gave me the same strangling hug and Mom a soft peck on the forehead. Outwardly, I was happy about my trip, but inside, my heart was in turmoil.

"So you couldn't go through with it?" Jordan asked as we stayed up in my bed. The television was on loud enough to drown us out to anyone passing by the door.

"No. My grand plan to break Landon's heart ended with us locked in his room, spilling our guts, and stripping off our clothes. I clearly didn't do so well with the execution."

She snorted. "It went as well as your plan with Michael. The guy lies down and takes your punishment and then saves you from a crowd of tourists. He sounds very—and I don't use this word lightly—gallant."

I brought my knees to my chest and rested my chin on them. "But does it make up for what they did?"

"Only you can answer that, Zee. It's your forgiveness to give."

"But what would you do if you were me?"

"I'd cut their balls off."

I barked a laugh. "Of course you would."

"You're not me." She stroked my hair in a way that was reminiscent of Derek. "The important thing is if you think they'll ever try to hurt you again. If yes, crush those feelings and stay away from them. If no..."

Jordan trailed off but she didn't need to say more. The message was clear and it banged around in my head all weekend and up until I returned to school.

I woke early Monday morning to run with Michael. Afterward, I cleaned up and went to the Elite floor to meet up with Derek.

He growled at me as I walked inside. "Don't be mad," I said. "Your alarm clock was set to go off in five minutes anyway."

"Like that's the point." He fell back on the bed and closed his eyes. "What is it?"

"There's something I want to talk to you about."

"I'm listening."

The bed dipped as I sat down. "What was going on with you, Cameron, Heath, and Santiago that day?"

"How did I know you wouldn't let that go?"

"Because you know me." I nudged his leg with my foot. "What's up? Why don't you want to tell me?"

"It's Network business. We agreed not to talk about that stuff."

"You agreed."

He cracked his eyes open to give me a look. "Zela, it's not a big deal. We were talking about the expansion and what we can do to sway them."

"Next year?"

"Now. We know which members of the board will be making the decision. Instead of them coming here and risking another prank, we're going to them. The senior members expect us to handle this. There is only so much they can do before it looks like bribing. When they come back next year, their tour and observation will be a formality."

I gaped at him. "Why are you going along with this?"

"We've all got our orders, Zee."

He made to get up but I grabbed him and pulled him down. "Derek, I'm serious. Is this because of Cameron's dad? I won't deny that he's a scary guy, but I would *not* follow any orders he gave me."

"I wouldn't either. I've got no problem telling Dominick Dupre, his spawn, and his buddies to fuck off. But that doesn't work with my dad."

"Your dad?" I repeated. "He wants this expansion too?"

He nodded. "Dad told me to do this. I don't have a choice and that's all I can say about it, okay?" Derek bumped my shoulder. "Wait here while I get ready. We'll go down together."

I was too mixed up to do anything but sit there as he got his stuff and went into the bathroom. What did it mean that his father wanted the expansion too? Was he one of the leaders hoping to make money off whatever deal Dominick had been brought in to handle?

Slow down, Zela. Dominick Dupre seems shady but we don't know him or anything about what they're planning. Just because he looks like a bad guy doesn't mean there's something rotten about the expansion.

And Derek wouldn't be a part of anything wrong, I thought. *He loves his dad. They may be out to make some money, but I have to believe they wouldn't hurt the students.*

Derek left the bathroom fresh and ready to go like he'd shed his worries down the drain. Try as I did, I couldn't do the same. Back and forth I went in my head, trying to convince myself the expansion wasn't something I needed to worry about, but all I could picture was me standing behind that booth while Dominick Dupre berated his son. It seemed to me like the expansion was already hurting one student.

TWO WEEKS PASSED BY and I still didn't know what to do. Derek stuck to his moratorium on Network talk and I didn't push him. I understood he was in a tough spot with his dad. Despite that, I enjoyed the nights we spent reading in his room, the even later nights in Landon's room, and the early mornings I spent running with Michael. Every day, I felt the raw lashings that night in the locker room left in me begin to heal a little more.

"What time do you leave for the competition?" asked Hunter. He blinked owlishly at me as he slurped his milk.

"Noon," I replied. "It's a four-hour drive. We'll get there before five, do the competition, spend the night in a hotel, and then be back before lunch tomorrow."

Landon pecked me on the nose. "Are you excited, my little nerd?"

"Your use of pet name tells me that if I say yes, you'll make fun of me."

His eyes danced. "There's a very good chance."

"Well, I'm saying yes anyway. I love this stuff. Math competitions are like my football."

"I hope you still have fun even though Cole's being weird," said Michael.

I looked at him, and then past him to where Cole sat at their table—alone. Michael had been sitting with me since we got back from Orlando. I'd seen, and heard, him invite Cole to sit with us numerous times but the blond boy said no every time. Then proceeded to glare at us all through our meal.

He couldn't shake that something was off about me, and I couldn't blame him. So far, he called me out on everything and had been right. That I had given up on my revenge against Landon, Michael, and even him, was something I'd have to prove to him—not that he made it easy.

"I will," I said to Michael. "I'm sorry I'll miss your track meet today. But you're going to kill"—I looked him in the eyes—"and you're going to win."

Michael winked. "I'll win for you." He stood, went over to Cole's table to say something, and then left.

We finished our breakfast and broke apart for class. My legs jiggled under my table as I watched the clock tick down to noon. When the bell rang for lunch, I was the first one out of the door.

"Good luck, Mr. Manning," called Dr. O'Quinn.

"Thank you!"

I hurried outside with my backpack slung over my shoulder. I packed it with everything I needed the night before.

"Hello, Zeke." Mrs. Peterson waved as I rushed out the main entrance. "Are you ready, *Captain*?"

"Heck yes." I punched the air. "Are you ready, team?"

Joey and Baker cheered, whooping it up with me. Cole, on the other hand, rolled his eyes and stomped off to the bus.

The ride to Villanova was pleasant. There wasn't a lot of us, so Mrs. Peterson read her book, Baker and Joey chatted in the back, Cole listened to music, and I watched the hills and trees go by outside of the window. Eventually, those trees were replaced by red brick buildings, traffic, and shopping mall parking lots. The regional competition was held in Villanova High School. Ten schools competed in a game show-style math quiz. The winners advanced to the next rounds until there was only one champion school left to represent the state in the national tournament. That team would be us.

I twisted around in my seat to gaze at Cole. What started as a way to drive him mad, resulted in more than I bargained for. My grades were so amazing Mom sent me to Orlando. I was in the best shape of my life due to competing in those battles to get on his level. I was captain of the best team on campus, and I enjoyed Future Leaders Club more than I thought I would.

Although, I'll most likely drop Science Club. Complete snooze fest. Other than that, riling Cole up has been good for me and I don't need to get into what I got by going after Michael and Landon. Jordan is right. It's my forgiveness to give and... it may be time to give it.

"Why are you staring at me?"

"No reason," I said without skipping a beat. Cole was four rows back. "Do you want to sit up here so we can talk?"

"Nope."

"I'll tickle you. You like being tickled."

Color stained his cheeks.

"Fuck off," we said at the same time.

"You have to come up with a new response," I added. "That one is getting stale."

His eyes narrowed. "It gets my point across."

I sighed. "One of these days, you're going to unwind that tight ball of grumpiness and intensity and remove it from your ass. You'll be a whole new person then."

Cole flipped me off.

Giggling, I said, "I've seen that guy and I like him. When he's ready to come back and apologize for what he did to me, let me know. I'd like to be friends with him again."

"I'm not friends with people I don't trust."

"You lost my trust first. If you want me to give it, you have to earn it."

"I feel the exact same way." With that, Cole popped his earbuds back in and shifted to the window.

I didn't try to talk to him for the rest of the drive. I wasn't going to beg. He might think he was wronged, but I wasn't For All, and I didn't have him beaten. When he woke up and realized who owed who the apology, I'd be willing to forgive him.

"Alright, team. We're almost there." Mrs. Peterson put her book away and got to her feet. "Let me run down the rules quickly."

We listened up as she explained how the competition would go down.

"… we'll be the winners," she finished as the bus turned into the school parking lot. "This is a great team and I have nothing but faith in you."

The bus pulled up to the entrance and let us out. My ears perked up as I climbed off. In the distance, I heard the faint, persistent thumping of a bass. Whoever was playing that music was playing it loud.

"It looks like we're the first school to arrive," Peterson said as she glanced at the near empty parking lot. "Not surprising as we're an hour early. Wait here, everyone, while I get us checked in. If we're lucky, we'll find a spot to run some last-minute drills."

"Okay," we replied.

She went inside while the rest of us hung out. Cole wandered a bit away from us as Joey and Baker looked around.

"So this is what a regular high school looks like?" Joey said. "Breakbattle has us warped."

"You'd rather go here than have a sweet dorm room, pizza for lunch every day, and movie nights on the weekends?" challenged Baker. "No one wants to go to a regular high school."

"I don't think it'd make much difference for me," I said.

Baker winced. "Right. Sorry."

"These regular kids have good taste in music though." Joey bobbed his head. "What's the name of this song again?"

The music was getting louder and closer. It reverberated inside of me, bouncing a beat off my bones. The windows rattled as the music got louder still. I turned away from the boys just as the car whipped around the corner.

"Cole!" I sprinted past the guys onto the street. Cole froze in the wake of the deafening convertible bearing down on him. Grabbing him around the waist, I yanked us back and we collapsed onto the pavement to shouts and cursing—most of it Cole's.

"Fuck! Fuck!" he bellowed. "They almost killed me! Zee? Zee, are you okay?!"

He scrambled off of me. Cole lifted me onto his lap with more gentleness than I knew he possessed. "Are you okay?"

I couldn't answer. Cole landed on me hard. His weight punched the air from my lungs and smacked my head into the pavement. Something wet trickled down my neck into my shirt.

"Zee?"

"I'm fine," I croaked. I tried to sit up and pain rocketed through my skull.

"Don't move. Wait for Mrs. Peterson." Cole raised his head. "Don't stand there! Get help!"

I didn't have the energy to fight him. I heard my team yelling their heads off for Mrs. Peterson. Then more yelling as the guys in the car spilled out, bleating that they were sorry and didn't know anyone was here and please don't tell their parents. Through it all, Cole held me and told me I was going to be okay.

"I'm so sorry. I can't apologize enough." Villanova High's principal fluttered behind the paramedics. "Students like to come on school grounds after classes and race around in the empty parking lot even though *I've warned them about this multiple times!*"

Her students cringed. Everyone was crowded around the back of the ambulance as the paramedics checked me out. Behind them, the other contestants of the math competition arrived and glanced curiously at the spectacle as they made their way inside.

The guys who almost mowed down Cole didn't look older than sixteen, but they did look like they were about to shit their pants.

"I will be speaking to your parents and you will all be suspended." They winced under her glare. "More so, if the paramedics don't clear this young man of injury, my first call before your parents will be to the police."

Now I think they did shit their pants.

One of the paramedics shone a light in my eye. "How are you feeling, Zeke?"

"I'm feeling fine."

"Head wounds bleed enough to scare people, but it looks like just a small cut." The paramedics noticed pretty quickly that I was wearing a wig, and they were good about closing the door while they patched me up. With that done, I gave permission for them to be opened again. "Did you black out at any point?"

"No."

"Do you feel dizzy?"

"No."

The man rattled off a list of questions and I answered no to all of them. He leaned back and addressed an anxious Mrs. Peterson. "He's going to be fine. I suggest he gets some rest."

"He will," she assured him. "I'm taking him back to school right now."

"Back to school?" I said. "No, Mrs. Peterson. He said I was fine. I want to compete."

She clutched her chest. "You boys can't compete after this. You were almost hit by a car."

"But we weren't hit. We've worked so hard and we've been waiting for months to earn our place in nationals. We can't miss our chance because these dummies wanted to play speed racer."

"I don't know..."

Baker inched closer. "If Zeke says he's okay, then—"

"Excuse me," Peterson snapped. "You do not get a vote."

"Sorry, ma'am."

Her lips pressed into a thin line as she studied me. "Are you absolutely sure he will be fine?" she asked the paramedic.

"At this point, I say yes, but if he develops any symptoms later on, pull him out."

"Fine. That's what we'll do." She leveled a finger at me. "If I get even the inkling that you're unwell, the competition is over and we're going back to the academy."

"Yes, ma'am. Thank you, ma'am." I hopped out of the back and hurried inside—too fast for Mrs. Peterson because she hauled me back and told me to walk with the team.

Together, we entered the gym that would be our competition space. Two tables were set up on either side of a podium. Above it all, Archimedean Regional Finals blazed proudly on the banner.

One after the other, our team faced the best students the schools in our region had to offer. One by one, we beat them.

"For the ten points and the title of regional champion," the moderator said. "Find the domain of the function x plus three over parentheses x minus one and parentheses x plus two. Teams, you have ninety seconds."

We almost bonked our heads leaning over my paper as I scribbled the question.

"The expression is not equal to zero," Cole offered.

Baker added, "Not if x doesn't equal one or negative two."

My mind worked faster than it ever had in its life. "I got it!"

Joey banged the buzzer before I could and I shouted the answer.

"Breakbattle Academy..." The moderator said.

We collectively held our breaths.

"You are the winners of the—"

We didn't hear the rest as we shouted our heads off. I jumped up and down with my team until Mrs. Peterson barked for me to sit down.

After receiving our trophy, we rode the bus to the hotel and she ordered me straight to bed with instructions for room service to bring up my meal.

My roommate, Baker, got on the phone to his mom to tell her about our win. I settled in bed and decided to heed Mrs. Peterson's order to rest. A night of Netflix and room service sounded nice after such an adrenaline-inducing day.

Knock. Knock.

I climbed out of bed to get my food. Cole greeted me instead.

"Cole? What's up?" I glanced over my shoulder. "Baker is on the phone."

"I'm not here to talk to him." He stuffed his hands in his pockets. "Can you come out here, please?"

More than anything, it was the please that pulled me out of the room. I've never heard Cole say that word before.

"What is it?"

He rocked back on his heels, looking everywhere but at me. "I just wanted to say... thank you for saving my life."

A smile tugged at my lips. "You don't have to thank me."

"I do. I also"—his eyes suddenly locked on mine—"have to apologize for the locker room."

My smile disappeared. "Are you only apologizing because you feel you have to after today?"

"I'm apologizing because I should have done it a long time ago," he replied, steadily holding my gaze. "You were right. You may be a little weird and you messed with my best friend, but all of that came after you were framed and I had you jumped. Either way you look at it, I started this." Closing his eyes, he took a deep breath and released it. "I'm sorry, Zee."

"Thank you, Cole," I whispered. Inside, I sensed that raw, aching pain lessen just a little more.

"I would have said it sooner," he continued, "but you may have noticed I'm an asshole."

He startled a laugh out of me. "I did notice that."

Cole closed the distance between us. "I doubled down rather than admit I was wrong about you. But today you saved my life and then kicked ass at the competition with a bashed-in head. You're badass, Zela."

"It's true." I saw my smile reflected in his eyes. "I am."

He chuckled. "Go inside and rest."

"Why? You worried about me or something?"

Cole backed away, grinning. "Fuck you."

THE NEXT DAY, WE ARRIVED at school and went straight to lunch.

"Heard you guys won," Adam said. "Congratulations."

Landon patted his lap. I shouldn't indulge him but I liked leaning against his chest while he kissed my forehead and whispered dirty things in my ear.

I sat down and he pulled me close. "We'll do some celebrating in my room tonight," he whispered.

Giggling, I rose up and kissed his jaw. "Sounds good to me."

"Whoa," said Justin. "Check it out."

Cole bypassed his table and stopped before ours. No one spoke as he pulled out the chair next to Michael and sat down. Everyone stared at him as he took a bite and then wiped his mouth with a napkin.

"So," he began. "Did Manning tell you we almost got hit by a car?"

All eyes flew to me. "What?!"

My friends and boyfriend grilled us until the bell rang. Classes gave me a bit of a reprieve, but the big brother in Adam prompted him to start up again after class was over.

"Are you sure you're okay? You should tell Coach Singh that you have to sit out."

"Mrs. Peterson will have told everyone what happened. If I have to sit out, Singh will tell me."

We rounded the corner headed for the dorm building. Adam held open the door for me to go in. I walked inside. A wall of stink the likes of which I never smelled before smacked me in the face. I retched.

"The hell?!" I cried. "What is that smell?!"

Adam clapped his hand over his nose. "Shit!"

"It's worse than shit!"

I heard gagging and then thundering footsteps from above. They had the right idea. Adam and I ran out of there and didn't stop until we escaped out of the main building.

Doubled over, Adam clutched his knees as he sucked in lungfuls of fresh air.

"What was that?" I asked. "Did a sewer line burst or something?"

He shook his head. "Didn't you see it, Zee?"

"See what?"

"The upside-down A on the hallway door."

I stopped retching.

For All did this?

BASKETBALL CLASS WAS canceled. Every student from both campuses was evacuated and ordered to stay in the cafeteria while the staff assessed the situation. We whispered among ourselves under Argyle's watchful eye.

"Why would Cameron do *that*?" Adam whispered. "You think there's a reason he wants us out of the dorm?"

"He and all of his friends are sitting over there. If he wanted us out, he's not taking advantage of the opportunity by being stuck here with us."

"Cameron has to have a reason. He has a reason for everything he does."

I studied the handsome boy as he messed with his phone. It's true. Cameron did always have a reason.

"Attention, students." Whittaker marched inside flanked by two custodians. All three of them were wearing face masks. "I apologize for the disruption to your day. The source of the smell was determined to be a bunch of aptly placed stink bombs on the first, second, and third floors of the dorm building.

"It will take time to make sure all of them have been re-moved and then for the... stink... to dissipate. Until then, it's uninhabitable."

"Where are we supposed to sleep?" a D student down in front asked.

"It's simple. The fourth through sixth floor were spared, so for tonight, students will have to double or triple up."

"Triple?"

"Yes. The As will move up to the E dorms. The Bs will move to the A dorms. The Cs will sleep in the B dorms, and the Ds and Fs will gather their things and sleep in the dining room."

A chorus of groans followed that statement, loudest of all from the two classes that would be sleeping on the hard, sticky floor.

"I will hear no complaints about this," Whittaker snapped. "This was another prank perpetrated by the self-named For All. You may blame him."

"I will blame Cameron," Adam bit out. "What is he try-ing to pull?"

I looked at Cameron. His face was twisted up in annoy-ance as he said something to his friends. Slowly, I shook my head.

"Nothing," I said. "Cameron isn't pulling anything, Adam. He's not For All."

"HOW CAN HE NOT BE BEHIND this?"

Adam and I laid out our comforters. More had been brought in from storage to make our stay in the dining room comfortable, but I had a feeling it would still be a rough night.

"It doesn't make sense," I replied under my breath.

"Cameron was the one who messed with the contacts, changed the uniforms, and drugged Michael."

"Absolutely."

"He came up with the For All sign to make it look like a math nerd was behind it."

"Yes, and it was pretty clever."

"He admitted what he did and threw in your face that you could never prove it to Whittaker and Argyle."

"Yep."

Adam stared at me blankly. "But you're saying he's not For All."

"No, he is For All— Or he *was* For—" I waved my hands. "What I'm saying is that Cameron was behind everything that happened last year, but this year, it's being done by a copycat."

"How do you know that?" he hissed as he stretched out on his makeshift bed.

"Because of what you've said. Cameron does everything for a reason. Last year, his reasons were getting back at me, punishing the boys, and proving himself to the Network. This year, I know what Cameron is after and not only does stink bombs, tablets, and spoiled food not get him closer, it might actually harm his chances of getting what he wants."

Adam nodded slowly. "You mean the expansion."

"Yes. How can you sell people that this is the best way to run a school when an unknown saboteur is running around protesting the system? It doesn't make sense any way you look at it for Cameron to waste his time doing these things. Especially when he loves this system. All signs point to the opposite for the new For All."

Adam grabbed the edge of my bed and pulled me closer. He glanced around to make sure no one was listening. "You're about to tell me how you know New For All hates the system."

"You're right, I am." I held up a finger. "The first prank with the spoiled food forced us into the gym eating pounds of takeout. The second prank gave us the tablets we were owed before Whittaker could find a way to ruin it. The third prank forced the hallowed Elite to open their floor to their lowly brethren. The lower classes got a taste of privilege when we got tablets and food delivered to us, and the Elites and As got to feel what it's like to lose a privilege. That's not a coincidence."

"Alright, I can see what you're saying." He flipped over and propped himself on his arms. "But if it's not Cameron, who is it and how long are they going to keep this up? Forcing me to sleep on the floor isn't going to bring down the system any time soon."

"That I don't know, but at least we know it's not directed at me or anyone in particular. We can sit back on this one and let the teachers handle it. It's their job."

"Good point." Adam dropped his head on the pillow. "Night, Zee."

He was out in minutes. I didn't follow him into dreamland quite so quickly. I stayed up long past when everyone else had fallen asleep.

So much has happened this year and none of it went the way I planned. Landon, Michael, Cole, Derek. Things are so different now.

But there is still something I have to do.

WE WERE WOKEN UP EARLY the next morning to gather our beds and trudge back to the dorms. I stepped inside and took a tentative sniff. "No rancid milk and dog shit smell," I called back to Adam. "Actually, they used so many air fresheners in here I can't smell anything other than morning pine."

"I'll take it."

We put our stuff away, changed, and returned to find the dining room back the way it was. With one difference, my table was packed with the recent additions to our group. I gazed at Landon, Michael, and Cole and thought of the events that brought us to where we are now.

I've forgiven what most never would. I've risen above the challenges everyone thought would beat me. I've earned the trust of Derek Grayson—probably the hardest of all three of those things. I've come so far. That's how I know this is what I have to do.

I walked up to our table and kept walking.

"Zee?"

I heard Landon but didn't acknowledge him. My eyes were fixed on one person.

Zach halted mid-laugh when he laid eyes on me. His mouth froze wide open in a way that was almost comical.

"What are you, lost? Get out of here."

"Zachary Fields, I—"

His lips twisted. "I'm not interested in what you have to say. Walk your ass back where you belong."

"—challenge you to a tournament."

Zach's sneer vanished. He blinked at me slack-jawed. Around him, the Elite boys fell silent.

"At the end of the semester," I continued. "Your spot in the Elite Class for my spot as an F."

He flinched hearing the final letter.

"Do you accept?"

"You can't just—"

"I'm not interested in what you have to say," I sang. "Not unless it's 'I accept the challenge.'"

Zach snapped his mouth shut. His eyes burned into me as the silence stretched.

Rhys nudged him. "Dude, you don't have a choice. The penalty for turning down a tournament is even worse than being knocked down a letter grade."

His friend's warning only made him turn redder. "Fine," he forced through gritted teeth. "I accept the challenge."

"Perfect. We can get it approved after school." I turned my back to leave.

"They'll never approve this, F, and even if they do, you'll never fucking win!" His voice got louder as I walked off without looking back. "You'll never be Elite! You'll—"

The door slammed shut on his noise.

"WHY DIDN'T YOU TELL me?"

I smoothed my blazer down and fixed my hair. I didn't know why I was primping. Something about this made me feel like I needed to look presentable.

"Because it took me a while to decide what I was going to do, Adam." The two of us stood outside Dr. O'Quinn's classroom, waiting for her to return. The end of the day arrived and Zach would be down any minute to make the tournament official. This was it. "In the end, it came down to something that Jordan said. I should consider forgiveness if I thought the boys would never do it again and if they felt true remorse.

"I feel that from Landon, Michael, and even Cole... but not Zach. I've left him alone but he's gone out of his way to be a bastard. I bet it never crossed his mind that he did something wrong in the locker room. If it did, he didn't care enough to apologize.

"The only one who deserves to be punished more than him is Cameron and it's past time I strike back." I pinned him with a look. "I don't like violence but I'm happy to take from Zach what he's wanted more than anything but never deserved. He's out of the Elite."

"And Cameron?"

I glanced away. "All in good time."

"Mr. Manning. Mr. Moon." Dr. O'Quinn strode down the wing. "I hear you have caused another stir."

I didn't have to guess. Her pride in me was obvious.

"A bid for the Elite Class. I cannot say I'm surprised, but I am sad to see you go. It's been a privilege to witness the wonders the battle system can achieve in a bright, hardworking pupil." She smiled at Adam. "Are you challenging a student to a tournament as well?"

"No," I began. "He's—"

"Yes."

I whipped around. "Adam, what are you doing?"

"I'm challenging Rhys Lewis to a tournament," he stated. "That's what I'm doing."

"But—"

"Excellent." Dr. O'Quinn gave him the fond pat she reserved for me. "I'm sure your mother will be glad to hear you're moving up to the proper class." She clapped. "Alright, boys. Let's get these tournaments approved."

O'Quinn said it like it would be easy, but it was no surprise that it was not. Clancy flat out refused to approve it. At the start of the year when everyone thought I was an upstart nobody, she might not have been worried about us beating them, but Adam and I had collected so many wins against the As and Bs, she knew we were real competition. Her reasoning, she would not allow two excellent students to be shuffled off into the F Class.

O'Quinn wasn't one to take no for an answer and she marched all of us to Argyle's office.

"She cannot refuse on these grounds," O'Quinn stated. "It is not in the spirit of this academy. Besides, if she fears her students will lose to mine, that is only proof they do not belong in the Elite Class."

Rhys flushed bright red. "*They* don't belong in the Elite Class! They—"

"I will handle this, Mr. Lewis," Clancy cut in. "Vice Principal, I know our rules very well, but if they win, we'll be forcing advanced students into classes we know are too easy for them. This is a matter of their education and I can't sign off on students receiving one that is subpar."

O'Quinn's eyebrow twitched. "You believe the teachers in the F Wing are subpar?"

"For heaven's sake, Julia. That is not what I said."

"It is exactly what you said." O'Quinn pointed at me. "It's been clear from day one that Mr. Manning and Mr. Moon would be better suited to advanced classes, but the administration was happy to let them remain in the F Class. Now, you are saying it is fit for them but not for anyone else?"

Clancy's cat-eye glasses wobbled on her nose as she trembled. "I am looking out for the best interest of my students," she snapped. "Becoming an F would derail their futures."

"It did not derail theirs," O'Quinn was quick to reply. "Mr. Moon has aced every class and rose to the top of the swim team despite his 'subpar' education. Mr. Manning became the president of Future Leaders, led the Archimedean team to victory, and tied for top grade point average. They worked hard to get where they are and if your students become Fs they have the same opportunity to do the same."

She faced Argyle. "The philosophy of this school is that we control our futures. If we want something, only we have the power and responsibility to make it happen. To reject these tournaments would say that we don't believe in what we set out to build and, more than that, we don't believe in our students."

Adam and I shared openmouthed stares. I was blown away. I don't think I could have said any part of that better myself.

As the silence stretched, all eyes fixed on Argyle. "Thank you, Mrs. Clancy and Dr. O'Quinn, for sharing your arguments. I will consider both sides as I make my decision. If I grant in favor of the tournaments, I will do so without your approval if need be, Mrs. Clancy."

Clancy folded her arms. "If that happens, I will resign. I came to this school to nurture young minds. Not to see everything they work for taken away."

Argyle didn't blink. "Whatever you decide to do is your choice."

It didn't sound like a dismissal, but I knew it was one. We left, collecting sneers and hissed insults from Rhys and Zach as they shoved us out of the way. Clancy and O'Quinn pulled ahead, speaking in heated tones as they left us behind.

"Adam?" I asked. "Why are you doing this? You don't have to for me."

He laughed. "Do you imagine I want to be in the F Class without you? You're the only thing that made it bearable."

A smile played at my lips. "Careful. Or I'm going to think I've earned your love."

"Seriously, Zee. I'm not into this 'who is better than who' bullshit and there's nothing wrong with being an F, but we started this together from the day you sat next to me at the opening ceremony. We're going to finish it together."

I didn't reply. I couldn't trust myself not to say something incredibly cheesy and tearful. Instead, I lifted his arm, put it around my shoulder, and burrowed into his side. I'd be lying if I said Adam hadn't made all of this bearable for me too.

The two of us stepped out of the administration building and found a few people waiting for us.

"What happened?" Tanner, Nico, Justin, Cole, Michael, Landon, and Derek asked at the same time.

Adam shook his head. "Argyle is deliberating. Don't know when we'll find out."

"Finals is in two weeks," said Owen, "which means the tournament would have to be next week. You don't have a lot of time to get ready."

"Also, hands off, Moon." Landon plucked Adam's arm off my shoulder and replaced it with his own.

Adam shrugged. "It'll be whatever it is."

Landon pressed his forehead to my temple. "Are you sure about this?"

"It's past time Zach got what was coming to him," I said. "I said I was done getting revenge on you. I never said that about Zach. But that aside, I don't want to lose sleep and run myself into the ground just to get into the library or go to dances. I don't want that for anyone else either. There are things I can do as an Elite. I intend to do them."

"Any chance you'll explain what you mean by that?"

I kissed his jaw. "Eventually, I will, but until then, focus on how much easy access you'll have when I have my own room right down the hall."

He hummed low in his throat and it rumbled through my body. "When you put it like that, I'll get these tournaments approved myself."

Landon didn't have to. Argyle approved the tournaments the following morning and Clancy announced her resignation shortly after. Thus began the most intense week of my life, studying and training harder than I ever had before.

The boys did not let up on me and little things like sleep did not sway them. Derek had me up early practicing basketball. Michael had me up even earlier racing around the track. After school, I wrestled with Landon, played soccer with Tanner, and swam with Adam and Cole. That left the scant amount of time I had at night to devote to studying.

The sophomore Elites had all the same classes as me but everything was advanced. Advanced Chemistry, Advanced World History, Advanced Geometry, and Advanced English. The guys quizzed me on their subjects, and when the first day of the tournament dawned, I was ready.

Whittaker and Argyle stood before us looking more serious than I had ever seen them. We were in the dining room, but it was empty except for them, Dr. O'Quinn, Mrs. Clancy's replacement, me, Adam, Rhys, and Zach.

The four tournament participants sat at the head table under their watchful eyes.

"Here is how it will work," Whittaker announced. "You will be tested on every subject at the Elite level. Four days of academic testing, and on the fifth day you will participate in the physical tests. Your scores will be tabulated over the weekend, and if Mr. Manning and Mr. Moon are the winners, the tournament scores will be considered as their final grades needed to advance to the Elite Class. Do you understand?"

"Yes, sir."

"We'll begin with the English test. After lunch, we'll have the Critical Writing test."

Argyle stepped forward as if on cue and placed four test packets in front of us.

"Pick up your pencils," Whittaker said. "You may begin."

For the next hour and a half, the only sounds in the room were the occasional cough and the scratching of our pencils. Our English topic was an interesting one. It asked us to compare the knowledge gained from books to knowledge gained from experience, and argue why one was better than the other.

I wrote a detailed essay in favor of knowledge gained from experience and referenced my own life learning around the world. When Argyle called time, I placed my pencil down with confidence. Everything was going to be fine.

Students trickled in for lunch but we were shuffled off to our classrooms to eat. This was serious business and they wouldn't risk cheating of any kind.

"How do you think you did?" Adam asked. "It's hard to study for English other than reading books and learning grammar."

"I did well," I said. "I know it."

After lunch, we returned to an empty dining room for the critical writing test. It was another essay that I walked away feeling good about. Day one of the tournament was complete.

Day two, I woke up early and shuffled to the bathroom to shower and get ready. We had geometry and networking today. I had no idea how we were going to be tested in networking, but I stayed up most of the night cramming my least favorite branch of mathematics into my already stuffed head. Planes, angles, proofs, quadrilaterals, and triangles swirled in my brain like the steamy water pooling at my feet. I walked out of the showers pink, fresh, and dripping math.

"A conditional statement is false if the hypothesis is true but the conclusion is false..." My muttering trailed off as I saw something waiting for me in front of my door. A tiny purple box with a blue bow. A smile tugged at my lips as I bent and unwrapped the gift.

Nestled on an ivory pillow was a small pin that glimmered with blue and purple gemstones. The pin was a butterfly of course. I picked it up and noticed a note underneath.

I'd say this was a good luck charm, but you don't need luck. You're going to win, Z, and we'll be together like we should have been from the start.

-Michael

A butterfly was appropriate. The little buggers fluttered in my stomach as I read the note again, and then one more time. I had to keep reminding myself that he must have meant us being together as classmates.

Adam was awake when I walked in.

"You ready to do this?"

My smile vanished. I reached inside my shirt and pinned the butterfly to my bindings, tucking my tiny charm away.

"I'm ready."

Whittaker, Argyle, and our Elite opponents met us in the dining room. Argyle put us in the same seats as the day before. Zach on the far end. Me two seats down. Rhys two seats away from me, and then Adam took up the other end of the table.

"You have two hours for the Advanced Geometry exam," Argyle said as she set them before us. "There will be no talking. You may use the blank sheet of paper and testing calculator to work out problems. We will break in one hour to allow you to go to the bathroom or have a drink of water. Do not ask to leave the testing room at any other time. Understood?"

We all nodded.

"You may begin."

We passed the two hours in almost absolute silence. No one so much as coughed. All I heard were our pencils and the *tap, tap, tap* on the calculators. When Argyle called time, I closed my book with a smile. Of course to get into the Elite Class, we had to prove we could handle the coursework. Advanced geometry wasn't easy and I had to use all of my time to get through the problems, but nothing stumped me. I trusted in the skills my mom taught me and everything I learned from the boys.

I caught movement at the edge of my vision. Zach was looking at me. I turned and gave him the full force of my grin. His lips twisted into such a feral snarl it didn't go unnoticed.

"Mr. Fields?" Argyle said as she collected his test. "Are you alright?"

"I will be, Mrs. Argyle. It's going to be fine."

"I'm glad to hear that," she replied.

The vice principal moved off but our gazes remained locked. In one look, Zach and I said more to each other than we had all year. It wasn't a polite conversation.

THE NEXT FEW DAYS OF the tournament passed in a haze of late-night sessions, bubble answer sheets, and cramped hands. We finished Tuesday with a networking test on what alternatives we considered for our future other than going to college, and how we will or will not be able to achieve our goals if we go down those routes.

Wednesday, we had the World History and Spanish II exams. To say I breezed through those tests sounded cocky, but that's exactly what I did. I finished both with time to spare and Zach shot me a mix of angry, incredulous looks as I sat there twiddling my pencil.

"He's getting scared."

Adam and I were in the classroom, eating our turkey bacon and egg sandwiches while Dr. O'Quinn graded papers at her desk. We had survived to Thursday and the final day of the academic exams.

"You're not sweating it as much as you should be and it bugs him," Adam went on. "I can tell Zach is cracking."

I pressed my fingers to my temple. A late night studying with Cole saw my bedtime moved from ten to two in the morning, and a pounding headache was my gift when I woke that morning. The boy knew his chemistry and he didn't let me go to bed until I knew it too. I appreciated it though. Chemistry was our final academic test and the hardest one for me.

"I'm cracking too," I said. "I know I'm doing well, but Zach is Elite. I doubt he's walking away from the test room with anything less than an A. Getting a tie in the academic tests won't help me if he beats me at the physical ones."

"You've trained harder than anyone this year, Battle Doctor." Adam took my hand. "We're going to win, Zee."

I rested my aching forehead on our hands. "You're going to have to carry the confidence for both of us this time."

He chuckled. "I can do that."

"Alright, boys." O'Quinn put away her grading. "Let's go down to the testing room."

Our morning exam was for debate class. I wasn't sure how they expected to test us on debating in a no-talking zone until Argyle explained the format.

"You and Zachary will be given the same issue and you will write an essay on it," she said to me. "You will make a case for the affirmative while Zachary argues the negative. The resulting score will come down to who makes the most compelling argument for either side. Understand?"

"Yes, Mrs. Argyle," we replied.

When I walked in, I believed that this would be my easiest exam of the day. One look at the question and my confidence took a hit.

Single-sex schools are better for students.

Was I being paranoid or was there an underlying motive for choosing this question? How was I—the girl forced to stuff her breasts in tight wrappings and hide who she truly is—supposed to argue that any of this has been better for us?

I didn't finish early this time. I wrote up to the very last second, trying to form solid arguments to support everything I was raised not to believe.

Argyle collected my paper and then moved down the table. A soft noise to my left drew my attention. Zach laughed—a harsh, mocking noise.

"How did you do on the exam... Zela?"

"Shut up." I snapped my eyes to Argyle but she didn't seem to have heard. "I'm not playing with you."

"Oh, I know that." He rose from his seat. "I'm not playing anymore either."

THE SUN ROSE ON A COOL, crisp morning the next day. The seeking rays made the dewdrops shimmer in the light and I got to see it happen as I sprinted down the track alongside Michael.

I called to him. "Couldn't the argument be made that I shouldn't tire myself out before the race?"

He wasn't too far ahead of me, but that was because he was being nice and not leaving me in the dust.

"Nope," he shouted back. "One more lap and then we'll cool down."

I might have sighed if I wasn't conserving my breath for keeping pace with him.

If we do get together, I'll be signing up for a boyfriend and a taskmaster.

My eyes drifted down to his ass. Michael's track shorts stretched and pulled taut as he moved.

And I will happily complete whatever tasks he gives me.

I bit my lip to hold back a giggle. My change in relationship status with Landon and the subsequent changes to the rules had me thinking of sex all the time. I was approaching ready faster than I thought.

We finished the lap and then went through our cooldown routine. I was a bit tired, but the run felt good.

"How are you feeling about today?" Michael picked my water bottle off the bleachers and handed it to me.

I gulped down a refreshing swig. "I'm not sure. I've trained as hard as I could. I know I can hold my own on the court, mat, and field, but if Zach's better, then he's better. We'll find out today if my best is good enough."

Michael took my towel and dabbed the sweat from my face. I warmed as he slowly moved down my neck and then to my chest.

"It is good enough, Zela," he said. "I know Zach and I know you. Even your worst is better than him."

"I just wish we didn't have to do all five physical tests in one day. We have track first, then swimming, wrestling, soccer, and finally basketball. They're using the girls' side for Adam and Rhys, so I won't be able to cheer him on either."

"But I'll be here to cheer you on."

"Of course you will." I pulled down the collar of my jersey until the little butterfly was exposed.

Michael's smile made my stomach somersault. "And I'll have something else for you when you win."

"Can I get a hint?"

He winked. "Nope."

Michael didn't give me a reason to blush, but I did it anyway as I followed him back inside.

Our seclusion from the student body was over. There wasn't much help my friends could give me on the physical test besides slipping me steroids, so Adam and I were allowed to join everyone for breakfast.

"Where's your food, Zeke?" Justin asked. "You can't go in this on an empty stomach."

I clutched my belly. "I think I'm nervous. I feel a bit queasy. I'm going to stick to water for now and then grab a snack after the race."

"No reason to be nervous. You're going to win, Zee." Derek placed his chocolate scone on my plate and urged me to eat it. I ate a few bites until he was satisfied.

After breakfast, our group tramped out to the track. Classes weren't canceled but Whittaker had shortened the periods from an hour to half an hour so they could watch us. Cole, Michael, Landon, and Derek sat front row to watch me. Melody, Justin, Owen, and the rest went to the other side with Adam.

"Alright, boys. We'll begin shortly," said Coach. He pulled me and Zach to the side as the bleachers filled up. "Do your stretches, warm up, and be ready to race in five minutes. You feeling okay, Manning?"

He squinted at me as I fixed my face into a neutral expression. The scone was a mistake. My stomach was writhing more than ever. "I'm fine, Coach."

"Are you?" asked Zach. "Maybe you should sit this out."

"Nope, I'm fine."

I turned my back on them and found a place on the track to stretch. I bent forward to grab my ankles.

The world turned on its side. I tipped over and my body smacked the turf—hard.

"Manning!"

I struggled upright as Coach ran over to me. "I'm cool," I said quickly. "I just lost my balance."

"Are you sure?"

Forcing a laugh, I spoke in Coach's direction. "I'm ready."

"Okay," he said slowly. "Step up to the line."

I felt his eyes on me as I carefully stood and moved over to my place. My dizzy spell cleared as I got into position.

What is wrong with me?

"Ready?"

Coach blew the first whistle and I braced myself on the block. Second whistle we raised our backsides. On the sounding of the gun, we were off.

I knew instantly that something was wrong. My stomach hurt so much. My breathing labored, expelling ragged, harsh pants as my gut twisted and knotted. Through a fog, I saw Zach pull ahead.

Come on, Zela. You can do this! He is not going to win. Not like this.

The surge of courage gave me a burst of speed. Closing the distance, I drew nearer to Zach until I could reach out and touch his jersey. A proud number one covered his back... or was it a seven?

I stumbled over my feet. Zach was growing fuzzy around the edges. The shouts from the stands and the smacking of our feet against the turf faded.

"Are you okay, little one?"

"N-no."

I whipped my head around. A red sweater made him look presentable and harmless. Just another person enjoying the holiday events. His thin-framed glasses reflected in the light, obscuring his eyes as he bent and grabbed my wrist.

"I'll help you find your daddy."

Pure, naked terror blotted out my mind as my heart shot into my throat. A strangled scream tore from my lips as I ran—harder and faster than I ever had in my life.

"Mom!"

His hand was on my wrist. Tightening. Squeezing. Promising I would never be free.

I screamed. Tears soaked my face and blurred reality as my nightmares swallowed me whole.

A sharp whistle cut through the air.

"Winner! Manning!"

The stands went wild. The thunderous applause ripped me out of the hallucination and I staggered off the track as Michael, Cole, Landon, and Derek ran to me.

"Zee, you fucking did it! That was—"

I shoved Landon out of the way and bolted around the bleachers. The metal and bodies shielded me as I dropped to the ground and vomited.

My stomach viciously contracted, ejecting everything in my system.

"Zee— Shit!"

The boys surrounded me.

"What's wrong?" Michael cried. "Zela?"

"Someone... did something... to me," I gasped. "The water bottle. Something in the water... bottle."

"Fields." Derek said the word like it burned his tongue. A look of hatred twisted his face. He lurched to his feet and I grabbed him.

"No," I rasped. "If you do anything, the coaches will find out and they'll... cancel the matches." I held tight to his legs and tried to stand up. The others were at my side in a flash to help me.

"That must be what he wants," I forced out. "If the tournament is canceled, I'll never be able to challenge him to another one. There will be no winner and his spot as Elite is safe."

"He's not getting away with this!"

I cupped Derek's face in shaky hands. "He's not... because I'm going to beat him. Just get me inside and help me. Please, I need you."

My final sentence cooled the blazing heat in his eyes. "Ugh! Fuck!" He pushed aside the others and put my arm around his shoulder. "Fine. Let's go."

The boys carried me up to Derek's room. I was granted a seventy-minute break to rest and prepare for the next match. I spent the first half of it puking up my guts and then the next half downing painkillers and electrolytes.

The boys flanked me as I headed downstairs.

"Are you sure about this?" Michael asked.

"Yes," I said, a bit hoarsely. "I got whatever was in my system out. I should be okay."

"But you're not a hundred percent," Cole argued. "How do you expect to beat Zach when you're barely walking down these stairs?"

"I'm doing this, Cole. After everything he's done, I'm not stopping until I've seen this through."

The guys waited outside the door while I went in and changed into my swimsuit. The natatorium was packed by the time we arrived. I stepped to Zach's side and didn't miss for a second the smirk as he looked me up and down. I looked like crap and that pleased him like someone who knew why.

"You feeling alright, Manning?" Coach Nelson asked.

I lifted my chin. "Feeling great, Coach."

"Good. Then, let's run through how this will work. This will be much like orientation. Freestyle swim to the other end of the pool. Whoever gets there first is the winner. Take your places."

I stepped onto the platform to cheers and encouragement from my friends. The sound infused my achy limbs with strength.

I can do this. Zach is pathetic and insecure and he knows the only way he can win is to result to dirty, underhanded tactics. I'm not losing to a guy like this.

I lost.

"Yes!" Zach's shout echoed off the beams as he burst out of the water. He was jumping up and down and pumping his fists by the time I touched my pad.

It wasn't too surprising. I never was a strong swimmer and I was still shaking off the effects of what he slipped me. Still, it burned enduring that shit-eating grin.

The boys walked me back to the dorm to change and rest before the wrestling match. Their presence soothed me even though they didn't let up. They gave me tips and advice the whole time while I rested in Derek's bed and fought not to fall asleep.

"It's time, Zela." Landon rubbed my arm. "You got this, baby. You're almost as good a wrestler as me. No way you won't win."

I chuckled as I got myself up. A quick change into my singlet and I was ready to go. We got into the wrestling gym first this time. Coach Franklin beckoned me over.

"You ready for this, boy?"

"I am, Coach."

"You've come far this year. I've never seen a student improve as fast as you." He straightened to his full height, peering at me over the tip of his nose. "Whatever class you're in, it's been a privilege to train you."

I smiled. That was the nicest thing Coach had ever said to me. It was the *only* thing he ever said to me that wasn't barked tips and instructions. "Thank you, Coach."

"Warm up. Clapping push-ups. Now."

And he was back.

Zach came in and began his warm-ups on the other side of the mat. The stands filled up and I noticed Justin, Owen, and Hunter had switched it up and came to watch me. They were not the only ones. Sitting a few rows up was Cameron and Santiago. My mind flashed to the first day of orientation.

"Gentlemen, take your places on the mat."

I looked away from them and focused on Zach. We circled each other like sharks eyeing prey.

My eyes narrowed. "I know what you did," I hissed. "Whatever you put in my drink, it's not enough to take me down."

He bared his teeth. "I have no idea what you're talking about."

Coach blew his whistle and Zach lunged. We grappled as he tried to get a hold of me.

"You're pathetic, Zach." His face was inches from mine. I could count the beads of sweat collecting on his forehead. "You always were pathetic and you always will be. That's the real reason you lost your friends."

"Argh!" Zach twisted and escaped my hold. Getting behind me, he gripped me around the waist and lifted. "Who do you think you're talking to, bitch?" he said before throwing me none-too-gently to the mat.

Coach's whistle cut through the air. "Unnecessary roughness! Point to Manning."

I recovered quickly. Scrambling to my feet, I grabbed his arm and held it fast as I maneuvered the takedown. I made to pin him but he got his arm free and threw it around my neck. I gasped as he squeezed.

The whistle sounded again. "Illegal hold! Point to Manning."

His hold loosened and I yanked free. We scrabbled to opposite sides and faced each other again.

I laughed. "You've given me two points and we just started," I taunted. "You're cracking, Zach. You can't win if you're getting angry." I cocked my head. "But you know you won't win. That's why you're resorting to these little bitch tactics."

Zach flushed bright red. I had a moment to see his face twist and then he ran at me.

It was a sweaty, feverish, heart-pounding match. A battle in the true sense of the word. I wrestled hard, but correctly. No illegal holds or unsportsmanlike conduct. The same couldn't be said for Zach.

I twisted to avoid him getting his arms around me and the next thing I felt was his hand fisting on the back of my singlet. He yanked. I fell back onto him and we collapsed in a heap.

"Grasping clothes!" Coach shouted. "Point to Manning."

I untangled myself and faced him again, breathing hard. Despite being continually called out by Coach, Zach wasn't letting reason in. Every taunt I hissed at him made his blood boil until nothing but fury fueled his mind.

"You never belonged in the Elite Class, Zach." I inched closer. "You know that. If Adam and I had made it to that test, those two spots would have bumped you right out of the top ten. You know it, and you can't stand it."

"Shut up!"

"Fields!" Coach warned.

I didn't let up. "You always wanted to be the handsome, charming, popular one but how could you be when you're standing in Adam's shadow?" I smiled at him. "Don't think of this loss as a bad thing. Think of it like the world going back to the way it was meant—"

"I said shut the fuck up!"

Zach charged me. I couldn't escape before he bowled me over. I flew back, escaping the edges of the mat. My head struck the unprotected gym floor.

Coach's whistle went wild. "That is it! Fields, you're disqualified!"

Looking up at him, I saw his mouth fall open as he was snapped out of his rage. "Wha— What? Coach, no!"

"Out!"

The roar blew him back and Zach practically ran off the mat. I didn't see where he went as the boys raced off the stands and surrounded me. A dozen voices demanded to know if I was okay.

"I'm okay," I replied. I tapped my helmet. "I didn't feel a thing."

Despite my reassurances, everyone fussed over me when we broke for lunch. I didn't feel up for food yet, but that didn't stop Landon from feeding me crackers and juice. I might have fought him more if I didn't find their worrying so cute.

"Fields is fucking dead."

Plus, their death threats. The guys were vibrating with anger at Zach. The rest of my friends felt the same.

"What the hell is he doing? Is he trying to lose?" Owen raged. He stared hard at the Elite table where Zach and Rhys sat with their buddies. "Who is that guy? What happened to my friend?"

"He better not try anything during the soccer match," Adam said.

"If he does," Derek addressed me, "I don't care what you say. I'm kicking his ass."

The whole table nodded.

Maybe Zach knew the threat hanging over his head because he played clean. He didn't elbow me, trip me up, or grab me. What he did instead was play hard. The skills you expect of an Elite came through and Zach scored five points to my three in the first ten minutes.

He messed up flunking the wrestling match. He's not going to risk it again.

I chased after him, straining for an opening to get the ball. I darted forward, foot drawn back to make the kick, and Zach dropped out of frame. I went one way as he and the ball went the other. I spun around in time to see the ball sail into my net.

"*Fweet!*"

Coach called time.

The match was over. Zachary won.

I trudged off the field as Zach and the other Elites celebrated. The last thing I saw before turning was Cameron punch him on the shoulder.

"You're going to win this," Derek stated. He fell in step with me to the main building.

"He won the swimming and soccer match," I said. "Which leaves me the race and the wrestling match by default. Two to two. The basketball game is going to decide it all."

"You're good enough to beat him, Zee."

"I guess we'll find out."

A hand gripped mine. I looked down in surprise as Derek laced our fingers together. "You can do this. You *will* do this. Just remember what we practiced."

"Okay." I rested my head on his shoulder. "I'll do it. I'll win."

Those sentences became my mantra as my break ended and I walked outside for the last time. This was it. The final test. The final battle.

The bleachers were packed with students from both campuses. Classes were over for the day and nothing would stop them from witnessing something that had not happened at Breakbattle in years.

Coach Singh pinned us with a serious look as we stepped up to the center line. "I want a clean game from both of you. Is that understood?"

I stared at Zach as I said, "Yes, Coach."

"You know how this works. Thirty minutes on the clock. The person with the most points wins. Are you ready?"

Coach threw the ball up. I jumped, fingers straining, and Zach soared over my head and knocked it over to his side. The game was on.

A long day of running, swimming, and being tossed around caught up to me quicker due to the weakness that sickness caused. My stomach was sore from the retching. Every labored breath I drew was a sharp reminder of that. I ran slower—reacted sluggishly. Zach used that edge to snatch the ball and put eight points on the board.

"You can do this. You will do this. Remember what we practiced."

The ball swished through the net and I dove for it. Derek's voice in my ear propelled me down the court. I made the shot to applause and boos.

The school was split. My win was a win for all of the lower classes, but a slight to the upper classes who wanted us to stay where we belonged. That thought went through my mind as I caught the ball and threw it again.

I grinned as it fell through the hoop. *How's that for an F?*

Pushing down the fatigue and pain, I played ferociously as Michael, Cole, Landon, and Derek roared from the stands.

"You got this, Zee!" Cole shouted. "You're badass!"

Their spirit kept me going to the final seconds of the game.

Twelve to twelve.

We were tied, but I was running out of steam. My lungs burned like hot pokers in my chest. No matter how much air I sucked in, it wasn't enough.

My feet were lead weights being dragged down the court. I stumbled after Zach and stole the ball mid-dribble. I threw it at the hoop, but it bounced off the rim and came flying back.

Something streaked across my vision. Zach snatched the ball out of the air and took off running. I was right behind him. Hands waving, I covered him as he looked for an opening to shoot.

I darted in front of him just past the center line. Seeing no way around, he went for it. Zach jumped and tossed the ball over my head.

I knocked it out of the air and chased it down the court.

His breath was hot on my neck. My hands closed over the ball and I lifted it above my head. I could see Zach out of the corner of my eye readying to pull the same move I did.

I threw. Zach leaped. It sailed over his fingers and bounced through the hoop to deafening screams.

The buzzer sounded. It was over.

"Shit!" Zach roared. "Fuck, fuck, fuck!"

Furious tears ran down his face. Zach grabbed the ball and flung it as hard as he could. It flew toward the bleachers. A girl screamed as it smashed into her shoulder.

"Fields!" Singh shouted. "My office! Now!"

I almost felt sorry for him as Singh, Whittaker, and Argyle descended on him and dragged him outside.

Then Cole scooped me up and I forgot about Zachary Fields. He punched me in the face, beat me, violated me, and showed not an ounce of remorse afterward. He didn't want my forgiveness, so he didn't need my sympathy.

"I can't believe I did it," I breathed.

"I can." Cole held me tight. "You're amazing, Zela Manning," he whispered in my ear. "I think I've met my match."

Warmth spread through my already overheated body. I lingered too long on the hug until the others got to me and their congratulations broke us apart.

Damn, I thought as Cole slipped through the bodies and got away. *How am I supposed to tell Landon he might have to share me with two somebodies?*

"Incredible, Zeke," Owen said.

"You won the tournament," cried Justin. "There's no way you didn't win. We have to find Adam. He beat Rhys at swimming, track, wrestling, and they tied at soccer. Even if he lost the basketball game, he's in. You're both going to be Elite."

He put his hands up and I smacked them, grinning ear to ear.

"I wouldn't get excited just yet." The voice brought our cheering to an abrupt end. I dropped Owen's hands as Cameron shoved Hunter out of the way. "The academic scores aren't in. You were meant to be an F, Manning. An F is what you'll always be."

Landon launched at him but I threw out my hand, stopping him in his tracks. I didn't need anyone else to step in. This was between me and Cameron.

His lips peeled back as I walked up to him. "You're right. There is still a chance that he beat me on the exams, but it's not likely. I aced those tests. I know I did. Now Zach is going to get a punishment that has been a long time coming. With that done, all I have left"—I rose on tiptoe until we were close enough our lips almost brushed—"is you.

"I told you that day in your room that you had helped me make a decision. I was going to find a way to take what you wanted from you. All year I tried to figure out what and now I know.

"The expansion."

Cameron's sneer twitched. I saw his eyes widen the tiniest fraction. "What?"

"I'm Elite now," I whispered. "I have all the access and all of the privileges. I'm the shining face of the school that Whittaker and Argyle show off as the best this place has to offer. I'm going to use that to sabotage every single attempt to spread this insane system to other schools."

His face hardened. "You can't do that. You're one person."

"You know by now that it's not only me. There are many students against the expansion, and because of the monster you created, they're recognizing For All as someone on their side." I pressed my lips against his ear. "I'm afraid your dad and the leaders of the Network will have to make their millions elsewhere."

"You don't know what you're messing with."

I froze as I pulled back.

"These men are ten times more powerful than a little girl in boys' clothes."

"Someday you're going to learn, Cameron." I stepped away and looked him fully in the eye. "You shouldn't underestimate me."

"No," he replied. Then he flashed me that sweet, charming, heart-stopping smile. "I shouldn't underestimate you." He inclined his head. "Congrats on your win, Manning."

He waved his friends on and the Elites left the gym. I watched him go with conflicting emotions. What was that? Why did he suddenly change his tune?

"Zeke." Owen grasped my shoulder. "Let's find Adam and celebrate."

I looked away from the spot Cameron disappeared from. "I'll be there in a minute. I have to talk to Derek first."

"Okay." My friends gave me their congratulations again as they followed the other students out of the door. The room finally cleared and it was just me and Derek. He rose from the stands and caught me as I threw myself in his arms.

"It was all you," I said as we hugged. "I couldn't have won without you."

"No, Zela. It was you." He set me back on my feet. "You were always Elite and I mean that as more than some stupid class. I've never met anyone as smart, funny, kind, or patient as you."

I laughed. "Thank you, Derek. You really do say the sweetest things to me."

"I mean it." Derek grasped my chin between his fingers. I blinked as he tilted me up to meet his gaze. "There is no one like you and there never will be. I thought I'd never trust anyone again, but then you bulldozed your way into my life. If I'd known some random kid sitting next to me at lunch would bring me here..."

An intensity burned in Derek's eyes that unsettled me. What was going on? Why was he talking like this?

"That night in the hotel I told you that everything is worth it for that one person that drives you insane but you can't see yourself without."

"Derek," I began.

"You're that person for me, Zela."

"Derek, wait—"

He bent and pressed his lips to mine. The kiss was soft and gentle for the second that it lasted.

I tore out of his grasp. "Derek, no!" I stumbled away from him as he blinked dazedly.

Oh no. Oh no. Oh no!

"You— You can't kiss me!" I shrieked.

What the hell did I do!? my mind screamed at me. *How did I not see this?!*

"Why not?" Derek looked so hurt it crushed my heart and pulverized it into dust.

This wasn't supposed to happen. How did I let this happen?

"Is it because of Landon and Michael?" He stepped toward me. "Zela, I don't care about them. All I care about is you. I'll share you if that's what you want."

"Derek, please," I begged as tears stung my eyes. "You have to stop."

"I want to spend all night reading with you. I want to curl up in bed with you while you snore in my arms."

"Derek—"

"I want you and only you." He reached for me. "Zela, I love you—"

"I'm your sister!"

The scream echoed off the walls, reverberating the truth in our ears.

He jerked back, eyes huge. "What are you—?"

"I'm your sister. Your half sister. You can't be in love with me."

"Zela?" His expression morphed from surprised to worried. "We're not related. You know that, right?"

The tears were flowing hot and fast now. This wasn't how I wanted to do this. None of this was right, but there was no turning back now. "We are related, Derek. My mom refused to tell me a single thing about my father except a name: Jeremy Holt. Then we moved back to Chesterfield and while I was unpacking her suitcase, I found a folder with important papers. I found my birth certificate."

A tear flew off my nose as I shook my head. "There never was a Jeremy Holt. He must have been a name my mom made up to stop me asking. A name I never would have been able to track down. Because the name that was written above father was Jonathan Grayson."

"No..." he whispered. "That's not possible. My dad doesn't have any other kids."

"He has me."

"No."

"Yes, Derek."

"No!" He shoved away. A horrible keening noise ripped out of him as he doubled over. "That's not true! It can't be true! Why didn't you tell me?" Derek suddenly turned to me. "Why have you been hanging around me all of this time?!"

"Because you're my brother," I cried. "If it wasn't for them, I would have known you. I would have grown up with you. We would have gone to Switzerland to see our grandparents together. I wouldn't have chased a stranger through the mall looking for the family that was only an hour away from me. You're mine, Derek. The feelings you have are because of the connection we share."

Flinching, he shook his head wildly. "No, I can't— I can't do this."

"I love you too. Just not like that."

Derek backed away from me. His eyes darted in his head like a trapped animal. "Stop it. This isn't happening. This isn't real."

"This is real. You're my brother. I—"

Derek ran.

He shot past me and sped to the door. He threw it open and fled outside before I got the sense to give chase.

"Derek, please!" I screamed. "Listen to me!"

He didn't stop. Derek ran for the main building and I raced after him.

I just have to explain. I've done all of this to get close to him. He'll understand if he just listens. Everything will go back to the way it was.

Our feet thundered on the stairs of the dorm building. He was two floors ahead of me but it didn't matter if he locked himself in his room. I'd stay outside the door all night if that's what it took. I wasn't going to lose my brother again.

I burst through the Elite door. "Derek! Derek, please! I can explain!"

Derek's door was closed. He made it inside.

I stumbled to it as a door across from me opened.

"Isn't this lucky?"

I spun around. Cameron smiled at me as he, Heath, Santiago, and the other Elite boys poured out of the room.

"Nice of you to come to us."

I knew what was coming even before the final boy walked out of the room carrying a black cloth and sack.

"Derek! Hel—"

He shoved the cloth in my mouth. Dozens of hands grabbed me and held me still as my muffled cries reached no one. The last thing I saw before the cloth went over my head was Cameron's smile.

The Judgement

All is not right at Breakbattle Academy.

And it's not just because the Elites discovered my secret.

Cole, Landon, and Michael were never supposed to know. But then, I was also never supposed to forgive them... or fall in love.

I'm losing control. I can't stop now. I can't undo what I've done. I came here for one purpose, but I may lose what is most important in the process.

And if someone has their way, I will lose everything else.

The balance of power is shifting. What began as peaceful protests are spiraling into something more dangerous... even deadly.

The Elite Class can't stop what's coming next, but I've sacrificed everything to be one of them.

What will my boys have to sacrifice for me?

Keep In Touch

Join Ruby's mailing list for news, teasers, and more:
https://www.subscribepage.com/rubyvincentpage
Join Ruby's Facebook Reader Group:
https://bit.ly/3bNuCOq

ABOUT THE AUTHOR

Ruby Vincent is a published author with many novels under her belt but now she's taking a fun foray into contemporary romance. She loves saucy heroines, bold alpha males, and weaving a tale where both get their happy ever after.